# THE THREE BLACK DOTS

# THE
# THREE BLACK DOTS

BY
OTTWELL BINNS

WARD, LOCK & CO., LIMITED
LONDON AND MELBOURNE

MADE IN ENGLAND

Printed in Great Britain by Butler & Tanner Ltd., Frome and London

TO

DOLLY BINNS

WISHING HER MUCH HAPPINESS

# CONTENTS

# THE THREE BLACK DOTS

## CHAPTER I

### THE WEDDING

THE antique church was the pride of a county. It served three hamlets and was remote from all, set amid green pastures and surrounded by moss-grown tombs—a haunt of beauty and stillness. But as Mr. Garfield Standish approached it in his car, he surveyed it with the extreme distaste of a man who had suffered a surfeit of antiquities, and craftily accelerated in the hope that his sister would not insist on an inspection. To his relief, the lady maintained an air of indifference to the glory of Carston Magna, and he was congratulating himself on escaping a boring half-hour, when from the lych-gate a man in cassock and surplice suddenly emerged, and hurrying to the middle of the narrow road, signalled him to stop. The man, as his collar and stole and other regimentals proclaimed, was a clergyman; and since, short of disobeying the priestly signal and running him down, Mr. Standish could do no other, he pulled up, a little wonderingly, and the cleric hurried forward.

" Sir," he began quickly, " you are an instrument of Providence——"

" First I've heard of it," intervened Mr. Standish brusquely.

" Nevertheless it is true," the priest continued hurriedly. " Within the church are a lady and gentleman desiring to be married—and we have no witnesses. The marriage is rather—er—unexpected, being by special licence, and I have had the briefest notice. The verger and his wife would have served, but unfortunately the woman is away from home, and though I sent the verger himself to secure a second witness he has not yet returned, and the time is flying." He broke off and glanced at the clock in the tower. " Seventeen minutes to three ! In a few minutes if Clarkson does not return it will be too late. I—I wonder if you would oblige. You would do the pair within a great favour and relieve my anxiety——"

" Of course," answered Enid Standish quickly, and opened the car door. " Come along, Garfield, I have never been a witness at a wedding, and this has an air of romance."

Garfield Standish frowned and answered grudgingly. " Well, if I must——"

He stepped from the car unhurriedly ; and the clergyman, smiling with relief, led the way under the lych-gate, walking by the lady's side.

" It is very good of you to be so ready," he remarked. Then a twinkle came in his eyes. " You mentioned romance. There really is something of that about this marriage. When the London papers hear of it there will be many paragraphs, and if what is about to take place were known, I should have a crowd of witnesses."

" Like that, is it ? " Mr. Standish's interest visibly quickened. " Who——"

" I think I will not tell you that." The clergyman laughed. " I will leave you to read the names in the register. It will be the more interesting. . . . You, sir, will have the honour to give the bride away."

" The deuce—— I mean I know nothing about the business. What's the drill for it ? "

" It is very simple. When I ask the question : ' Who giveth this woman to be married to this man ? ' you will take her right hand and place it in mine that I may bestow it on her husband. . . . You understand ? "

" Sounds sufficiently easy. If I miss the word of command——"

The clergyman smiled. " I shall repeat it—to your confusion. . . . Er—your hat, sir ! "

They were entering the church, and feeling like a guilty schoolboy, Mr. Standish hastily doffed his hat ; then with swift curiosity glanced towards the chancel steps where the bridal pair stood waiting. After the mellow autumn sunlight outside, the church, with its stained glass, was dark by contrast, and in that first appraising glance, he could make out nothing beyond the fact that the man was tall and burly of figure, and the bride of more than average feminine height and slim as a sapling.

But, as under the priest's directions, he took his place by the man's side, in the light from the chancel window he saw that the bride was young, little more than a girl and very beautiful, with dark, slumbrous eyes, that as he divined might glow to incandescence under great emotion. The man was the elder, by twenty years, he calculated, a clean-shaven, strong-jawed man, with steely eyes, whose hair in the light streaming through the window showed iron-grey. Both were quietly dressed, with the simplicity of perfect and expensive taste ; and on the man's hand, as he stood toying a little nervously with a thin platinum watchguard, a diamond of price scintillated. So much Mr. Standish had time to notice, when the priest, intoning quickly, began the opening exhortation of the wedding office.

" Dearly beloved, we are gathered together here in the sight of God and in the face of this congregation to join together this man and this woman in holy matrimony, which is an honourable estate instituted by God in the time of man's innocency——"

Mr. Standish's eyes, after a sidelong glance at the bride-groom, grew suddenly alert. He had seen that strong, hard face before either in the flesh or in pictorial repre-sentation, yet, for the life of him, he could not recall the occasion.   The idea became a conviction as the ceremony proceeded.   He frowned in the effort of remembrance, cudgelled his brains to recall the circumstances of the previous encounter, and when the priest put the question, ' Wilt thou have this woman ? ' he waited tensely for the answer ; for when the eyes fail a voice will sometimes quicken memory and give the revelation which sight denies.

" I will."

The answer was given in harsh tones, and sounded very like a snappy bark.   Mr. Standish was disappointed. The voice, very individual and noticeable, twanged no chord of memory.   He might have seen the man before, but most certainly he had never heard the man speak.   A moment later his interest was transferred to the bride. He watched her, waiting for her answer with some curiosity, though about her he found nothing in the least reminiscent of the past.

" I will."

The voice was cool and clear, absolutely free from emotion or nervousness, and Mr. Standish's interest grew. He was so absorbed that he forgot the minor part he had to play in the ceremony, and bungled clumsily ; but lost his momentary heat and confusion in listening to the bridegroom's declaration.

" I, Simon, take thee, Cornelia, to be my wedded wife, to have and to hold from this day forward, for better, for worse——"

' Simon !   Cornelia ! '

The names told him nothing.   The only Simon he could remember at the moment was the cocktail-mixer at his own club : whilst Cornelia was strange to his ears.   The elusive identity of the man worried him.   He was of the tribe who tear an idea to tatters, and gnaw at problems as stubbornly as a dog at a bone ; and he was still battling with the thing when the bridegroom began to repeat after the priest :

" With this ring I thee wed, with my body I thee worship——"

" Lord ! " thought Standish, his mind flying off at a tangent. " The girl takes it as cool as ice. This may be a romance, but there isn't much love to wing it through the window. I wonder why she's marrying the fellow."

It was a sufficiently commonplace reflection, and as usual the elucidation of the mystery was not forthcoming. The priest proclaimed the pair man and wife, the benediction was spoken, and the couple moved towards the altar for the homily, leaving the witnesses by the chancel steps. Glancing sideways, Standish saw his sister flash a quick, questioning look.

" Know the man, Enid ? " he whispered quietly.

" I'm not sure, I think——"

" Who—I have the idea I've seen him before. I'd give a hundred dollars to be sure."

The lady smiled. " In five minutes, if the priest is merciful and short-winded, I'll collect them. They'll sign their names in full in the register, and we shall see——"

He nodded, and schooled himself to wait patiently for the moment of revelation, but with curiosity still quick within him as his conviction of previous acquaintance with the bridegroom hardened. The move to the vestry for the signing of the register came at last, just as the belated verger hurried noisily into the church, with a heavy-footed labourer at his heels. Mr. Standish and his sister, conventionally arm-in-arm, followed the bridal pair, and interest grew keener as the bridegroom seated himself and wrote his name with a decision that was clearly characteristic. As he did so, Garfield Standish's eyes chanced to fall on the man's left hand laid to steady the register. It was, he noted, a rather coarse hand, broad and strong, the hand of a man who at some time had been accustomed to manual tasks, and on the back of it was a tattoo mark—three black dots arranged in pyramid form—thus $\therefore$ . Mr. Standish marked them and wondered idly if they had any meaning to the man, whether they were the caste-mark of some society, or just the mark of some boyish folly of years ago that the man had not troubled to rid himself of. He was still wondering when the bridegroom yielded chair and pen to the bride, but forgot all about them in the burning curiosity which surged in him, as his own turn came to sign.

He took the pen, and as he seated himself his eyes went straight to the first of the two names on the wide sheet before him :

" Simon Maxwell."

As he read he came near to shouting in sheer surprise. Then, as he began to write, he glanced at the other name —Cornelia Darracombe. That told him nothing, and even if it had, it could not have matched the surprise he had already experienced. Mechanically he wrote his name, the whilst his mind shouted within itself :

" Maxwell ! . . . Simon Maxwell—the mushroom millionaire broker."

He knew the man by repute. That strong face had been portrayed too often in the New York press for any mistake. That was why it had seemed familiar, though he had never seen it in the flesh before ; and as he yielded the chair and the pen to his sister, he deliberately took a position from which he could look at the man closely.

The hard face showed no sign of the cheerful elation one might expect in a happy bridegroom. It was like a mask, expressionless, and there was no indication of anything but the most cursory interest in the man's steely blue eyes as he stood there, nonchalantly watching Enid Standish sign her name. A moment later Enid rose from the chair. Her eyes, as her brother saw, were dancing with excitement, and he guessed that she had experienced a surprise equal to his own ; but she had a woman's instinct to conceal what she had discovered, and with charming *savoir faire* held out her hand to the bride.

" May I wish you much happiness, Mrs. Maxwell ? "

"Thank you," said the bride with a cold smile.

"And you, Mr. Maxwell——"

"Very good of you, Miss—er——"

"Standish." Enid helped him out with a smile. "This is my brother, Garfield Standish."

"Hey?" The blue eyes flashed a swift glance at the young man. "I knew your father. The likeness to him is in your face plain as a church-door. Well, I guess Cornelia and I are infinitely obliged to you two. You pulled us out of a hole. I'd never thought about witnesses—being new to this business of getting married."

He permitted himself a dry laugh, then set an envelope on the vestry table.

"Yours," he said to the clergyman. "Send the certificate along." Then he addressed the bride, who stood apart cool and aloof. "All over, Cornelia. Time to go."

The lady took his proffered arm, and he turned towards the vestry door.

"We'll take this way," he said over his shoulder to the priest. "I left the car at the back of the church." He nodded to the three as they stood there, his bride bowed slightly, then they moved forward. The door closed behind them and the Standishes and the clergyman were left staring at each other. Mr. Standish's feelings were too strong to be longer repressed.

"Well, I'm d——d!" he ejaculated.

"Sir——" began the clergyman protestingly, but the girl broke in on his expostulation.

"You saw the names, Garry?—Simon Maxwell and Cornelia Darracombe. I shouldn't have missed it for a new hat. But in Heaven's name what is Simon Maxwell doing here on this English country-side?"

"Mr. Maxwell has a place a few miles away," explained the clergyman,—'Farholme Abbey,' which he recently purchased from the Duke of Beaminster——"

"Why, that is the next place to Sir Stephen's, our

host," cried the girl. "I wonder he never mentioned that Simon Maxwell——"

"Didn't strike him, I guess," said Standish with a laugh.

"Mr. Maxwell is not yet—er—*persona grata* with the county," explained the priest.

"No? Well, I'm not surprised. Simon Maxwell is a rough-neck. . . . But you sure gave us a surprise; though I don't know about the romance you were talking of, sir. Neither of those two look like a case of violent love, and I would give a dollar to know what they're doing, marrying on the quiet like this."

The clergyman smiled. "That is their own affair; but curiosity is natural. . . . I myself am intrigued by the lady—who is she and——"

"I can tell you that," laughed Miss Standish. "Cornelia Darracombe is Claire Devereaux—the movie star. If you had been a film-fan you'd have known her on sight, sir."

The priest laughed. "I have heard of the lady. . . . The romantic element grows. To-morrow or the day after, I shall be besieged by reporters, and shall be able to tell them nothing. But there will be photographs of the church——" He broke off. "You would like to inspect it, perhaps? It has unique features, which I shall be glad to point out to you myself, for I really am indebted to you and to your brother——"

"Don't mention it," interrupted Standish. "You've sure given Enid the time of her life. If you'll excuse me a moment, I'll just take a look at that back tyre of mine ——"

He did not wait for an answer, but moved by an earnest desire to avoid adding to his stock of architectural lore, departed precipitately. Once outside in the sunshine he ejaculated to the wide, wide world:

"Simon Maxwell! . . . Married! It beats the band!" He stood there, the back tyre forgotten, staring absently in the rural scene until the drone of an engine high in the air broke on his reflections.

"An airplane !" he said aloud. "In this backwater of the ages. Who'd have thought it ? "

Momentarily dismissing Simon Maxwell from his mind, he lifted his eyes to look for the airman. In a moment he located the machine. It was, he judged, less than a mile away, circling round, as if the pilot were searching for a landing-place. Whilst he watched it began to descend in a long volplane, and finally came to earth in a level pasture a little way from the church. Scarcely had it reached a standstill when one of the two men it held slipped out and began to run towards the gate of the field. Supposing, from his haste, that something was amiss, Mr. Standish hurried to meet him, and reached the gate first with three yards or so to spare.

"Excuse me," cried the runner a little breathlessly, "is that Carston Magna church ? "

"Yes," answered Standish, marking the man's bronzed lean face and the keenness of his eyes.

The new-comer looked towards the church, and as he saw the clock in the tower he started, then jerked up his arm to consult his wristlet watch.

"Jupiter !" he ejaculated. "Is that the time ? "

Mr. Standish glanced at his own timepiece. "The church clock is two minutes behind Greenwich time."

"*Mordieu !*" ejaculated the stranger. "Then I am too late." There was a look of intense chagrin upon his lean face, and Mr. Standish, with a sudden divination of the situation, wagered with himself what the next question would be, and won his wager.

"Pardon me, but do you happen to know if there has been a wedding here this afternoon ? "

Mr. Standish laughed. "I was one of the witnesses."

"The deuce you were ? "

The man's dark eyes grew suddenly keen. They raked the other fore and aft, and Standish would have sworn

B

that his questioner was trying to fathom in what relation
he stood to the bridegroom. Intrigued, and with curiosity
spurring him, he laughed lightly and explained.

" Was requisitioned, you know. Witnesses were missing, and happening to be on the spot I was pressed into
service, and, by request, gave the bride away. Never
done anything of the kind before, and it's a big thing to
start with a millionaire and a cinema star——" He
laughed and then added lightly : " But I hope it will
turn out all right."

" All right ! " There was a cold certainty in the
speaker's tones. " Man, it is like to be damnable."

Abruptly the man turned on his heel and walked back
to the machine, leaving Mr. Standish gasping. With
amazed eyes he watched the man go, saw him start the
propeller and climb quickly to the side of the man at the
controls. A moment later the aeroplane sped across the
field ; then lifted and began to mount in swift whorls,
and finally, when well above the neighbouring wood,
raced eastward.

" Well——"

Complete amazement reduced Mr. Standish to speech-
lessness. He turned towards the church and saw his
sister and the clergyman standing in the porch, watching
him. He moved slowly towards them.

" Who was that, Garry ? " demanded the lady.

" Don't know. But whoever he was I have a fancy
that he had come to declare just cause and impediment
to the wedding we three have just assisted at."

" Garry ! "

" A cold fact ! Arrived too late, of course, and when
he saw the church clock he looked as if he had stepped on
a tack—barefooted. . . . Was mean enough to say that
the wedding was likely to turn out damnable."

" You never say,—Garry ? " cried Miss Standish as her
eyes sought the receding aeroplane.

" But I do, and there are quotation marks to the word."

Enid Standish was more intrigued than her brother. Her eyes danced with excitement and curiosity.

" Oh," she cried, " I would give a hundred dollars to know why——"

She broke off and her brother laughed.

" I would give double. I fancy, however, that neither of us will be out of pocket. That man up there is a mystery. He——"

" What was he like, Garry ? "

" Lean and hard. Puckered about the eyes like a fellow who has lived in a sunny clime, with a look like a dried Californian apricot. And—gee !—I was forgetting ! He swore in French."

" In French ? Then he is——"

" No. English of the English or good old U.S.A. Not a doubt of it. But the French proves that he's accustomed to think that way, and that implies residence in France or some French possession."

Yielding to his appetite for problems, he stood there for a moment lost in thought, following the line of country his mind had struck ; but was recalled from his absorption by his sister, who laughed.

" French or English, we shall never know. But we've news about his neighbour that will make Stephen Langford sit up, I fancy. And there is a question I want to ask him—soon. So if you've finished wool-gathering we'll move along, Garry." She turned to the clergyman.

" Good afternoon, sir. I'm glad you stopped us to make us witnesses. It livens things up to have exclusive news for gossip, and this is some news."

The clergyman laughed. " I expect the world will find it so. . . . To-morrow I think I shall go away from Carston Magna for a couple of days. There will be a procession of news-seekers——"

" Send them on to Garry," laughed the lady. " He knows how to handle them."

Then, with a wave of her hand, she moved down the

path to the lych-gate, followed by her brother, and when they were once more spinning along the road, she gave a little laugh of excitement.

"Step on the gas, Garry. I'm dying to see Stephen's face when he hears the news."

And Garfield Standish, ignoring the speed laws, pressed the accelerator, and swung the car forward at a rattling pace.

## CHAPTER II

### DARKNESS

STEPHEN LANGFORD, as it chanced, was indifferent to the news his guests brought with them, being engrossed in a matter which made Simon Maxwell's wedding a matter of complete indifference.

"Maxwell's own affair!" he said tersely. "And the man's no class anyway—a regular sweep, shoots foxes because they poach his chickens, as if chickens weren't made to be poached by foxes. A cinema-star is his proper fate."

"And the lady's fate?" interrupted Enid Standish with a laugh.

"One worse if anything. Maxwell's a brute. Was prosecuted by the R.S.P.C.A. for lashing a horse unmercifully, so if he turns wife-beater nobody hereabouts will be surprised. The man's outside the pale—rich as Monte Cristo, by all accounts, and a boor. But what matter? There are more important things forward than Maxwell and his cinema lady. My head-keeper has just been along to say that members of a well-known poaching crowd have been seen in the neighbourhood, and he thinks there may be a raid on the copses to-night. Got to make arrangements to counter it. I suppose you won't mind carrying a cudgel in the fray, Standish?"

"Mind? I shall love it."

"And I will carry a hunting-crop," laughed Miss Standish.

" You ! "

Stephen Langford's face expressed his feelings quite as impolitely as the intonation of the word jerked from him by surprise. Then he laughed. " I rose nicely to that."

" It wasn't a fly I threw," said the girl quickly. " I mean it—I want to see——"

" But—but——"

" I'm going," said Miss Standish firmly. " No one shall stop me. Do you think I will be kept out of the fun. Ask Garry—he will tell you."

Garfield Standish smiled ruefully at his host. " You've got it, Langford. When Enid delivers an ultimatum the wise man puts up both hands. It's pure folly, but——"

Sir Stephen laughed. " I shall take no responsibility. But you'll have to stay ' put,' no plunging into the fray, you know. If you'll promise——"

" Oh, anything in reason," laughed the lady, and with a gesture of mock despair their host fled.

Five hours later Enid Standish stood in the place where she had promised to stay ' put,' being already, in her heart, forsworn, having not the least intention of missing what she called the fun. A hunter's moon was just lifting itself above the tree-tops, but the wood was full of shadows, and at the edge of it she waited, still as a statue —alert for any sign of movement. Behind her was a wooden fence, on the further side of which lay a small ditch which bordered the road. The tarred surface of the latter, polished by the passage of many vehicles, gleamed in the moonlight.

There was no wind. The wood was very still, but in the air was a rumbling, grinding sound which told the watcher that some heavy vehicle was coming up the long hill over which the road dipped between the lines of trees. Presently there reached her the sound of stentorian puffs like those of an engine snorting over too-heavy a load, and at the same moment her brother emerged from the woods.

" All's quiet yet, Enid, but——  Oh, confound it !
What's that racket ? "

Miss Standish laughed.   " Road-engine, with a cough,
coming up the hill."

" Confound the owner ! " ejaculated Standish impatiently.   " I wish the fellow's boiler would blow him
sky-high.   He is making enough racket to drown a
barrage."

Almost on the words the snort of the engine ceased
and the pair stood listening, then the lady spoke.

" That is Simon Maxwell's park over there, isn't it ? "
She indicated the trees on the further side of the road as
she spoke, and with a glance in that direction, her brother
answered.

" Yes.   The house lies well on the other side, and——"
A sudden fusillade broke on his words, followed by a
burst of shouting and the clear, sharp note of a whistle.

" That's Langford," cried Standish excitedly.   " He's
up with the gang.   Whistle is a sort of over-the-top
signal.   Better cut home, Enid. . . .   Oh, I know you
won't !   But I must go !   Look after yourself."

He turned and plunged into the wood.   His sister stood
listening, her eyes sparkling with excitement.   For a little
time nothing happened.   The shouting died away, leaving
the night deadly still.   It seemed to her that the poachers
had faded out of existence.   Then while she still waited,
ears alert, the stillness was broken by the sound of a shot,
followed by a sudden sharp scream, which made her shiver
and prickled her skin to goose-flesh.   The shot differed in
quality from those of the fusillade which had taken her
brother headlong into the wood.   It was sharper, more
clearly defined—a pistol shot, as familiarity with firearms
told her, and with that following scream it was of ominous
significance.   She shivered again, and as she did so a
thought struck her.   The sounds had not come from the
wood in front of her.   They had come from behind, from
across the road, where lay Simon Maxwell's park.   Turn-

ing, she stared earnestly in that direction. What did that shot and the ominous scream indicate? Was the prophecy to which the stranger airman had given utterance already reaching fulfilment? With the question in her mind, and beset by dim forebodings, she stood there quite still, listening, every nerve tense, her ears straining.

The park in front of her remained dumb as the grave. Quite a long time passed and no sound came from the moonlit stillness, then the snorting puffs of the road-engine began anew. She made a gesture of impatience, and glanced down the highway. The engine, the coming of which was so noisily heralded, had just topped the hill, and was beginning to rumble along the level with a string of three wagons behind it. Whilst she watched, it drew level, a noisy, hideous thing, which filled the night with its clank and snorts. In the moonlight she made out some foot-long letters painted on the first yellow wagon—" Carey's Tropical Menagerie."

Then several things happened in swift succession. Something went wrong with the engine, which bumped and lurched sideways, dragging its tail of wagons across the road, almost blocking it. In the same second a man vaulted over the rails across the road, stared at the engine for a second, and after a brief pause raced down the road in the direction of the hill. A great fan of light lifted itself above the latter, outlining the hurrying man in blackest silhouette, and the drone of a high-powered car travelling swiftly up the hill reached her ears. She saw the running man leap for the hedge, and in the same instant the car came into view. It was travelling at a great speed, and reached the blocking engine and wagons of Carey's Menagerie in the twinkling of an eye. Its Klaxon sounded furiously, then it swerved for the narrow width of road that lay open to it, taking what was a desperate chance. With two wheels on the grass and at the very edge of the ditch it cleared the engine, and as it did so, to her horror, Enid Standish saw a second running man in the road, right in the path of the swerving car, and apparently making for the wood at the edge of which she stood.

For the briefest fraction of time he seemed to halt uncertainly, possibly bewildered by the glare of the headlights. Miss Standish cried out in sharp fear, thinking he must be struck and shattered. Then she saw the man leap convulsively. As he did so he was struck by the car and flung out of the straight line, landing in the ditch not five yards away from her.

The car droned on for a moment, and with the thought that, indifferent to the condition of the man who had been knocked down, the occupants meant to pass on, a wave of indignation surged within her. Then the car slackened speed, and came to a standstill with screeching brakes. Miss Standish looked down the line of the ditch and saw something moving in its shadow. An instant later the man whom she had thought might be dead crawled up the bank, reached the rails and slipped through the bars. Once on the further side, the man straightened himself, looked swiftly round at the car, which was now running back in reverse gear, then turning he ran stumblingly towards the shadow of the woods.

That he was a fugitive seemed evident, and that he wished to avoid acquaintance with the occupants of the car was equally clear. She wondered what was the meaning of it all, and whilst she did so, the car—a well-lighted saloon—drew up a few yards away. Two men leaped out and running to the ditch stared into its shadows. Then one of them spoke.

"Nothing here, Wilkinson, you must have been mistaken."

"I am sure I am not mistaken, sir. I saw the man clearly and felt the car hit him. . . . I thought he fell in the ditch."

The first speaker walked a few yards up and down the ditch, and whilst he was so engaged the driver of Carey's

Tropical Menagerie, who had been staring open-mouthed at the two men, made a jocular inquiry:

"Looking for Christmas, mate?"

"We're looking for a man with whom we collided, as we passed you. Seen anything of one?"

"No, I ain't seen so much as a rabbit——" The engineer broke off abruptly. The glare of the head-lights revealed a look of almost comic amazement on his face, and then he shouted, "Glory! There's a girl at the top of the bank there!"

It was too late for Enid Standish to move. Three pairs of wondering eyes focussed themselves upon her. All three men seemed utterly dumbfounded; then the one whom she guessed to be the owner of the car, broke out abruptly:

"Pardon me, miss. Have you seen anything of a man who was knocked down by my car as we passed this contraption?"

He indicated the engine with a jerk of his thumb as he spoke, and Miss Standish answered quietly:

"He crawled from the ditch a minute or two ago and ran into the wood—there!"

"Um!" commented the man. "He wasn't killed, then." A moment later he added wonderingly: "A deuced queer thing that he should run away. . . . He's a rare bird in my experience. They usually demand stiff compensation—mental, moral and material damages, and more of all rather than less. Must be wanting to avoid observation. A burglar . . . or possibly a poacher."

"There are poachers in the wood here," broke in Miss Standish with a wave of her whip to indicate the wood she meant. "I am on the look out for them."

The stranger was amused by her words. He laughed as he replied:

"Well, you have seen one of them, I fancy. And it's sheer luck we didn't make dead mutton of him. There's nothing to worry over, Wilkinson. A poacher more or less is of small account, and since the corpse we were looking for has run away, we will move on. Thank you, young lady, for setting our minds at rest. . . . Come along, Wilkinson ; we have done what we could."

The pair took their way back to the saloon, and in a very short time a receding fan of light marked the going of the rapidly vanishing vehicle. The driver of Carey's Menagerie managed to start his engine again, and clanked and rumbled slowly up the road, and presently the night grew still once more. By the fence Enid Standish still waited, her eyes fixed on the park across the road, her mind busy with the two men whom she had seen, and with the sounds that had preceded their advent. What had happened in Farholme Park ? Who were the pair who had been in such a hurry—one of whom had raced down the road, whilst the other, anxious to avoid observation, had taken to the woods ? She was still wondering when there reached her the sound of someone crashing a noisy way through the undergrowth behind her. Almost instantly she found an explanation.

" Poacher ! " she whispered. " In a tearing hurry."

A moment later the last words had confirmation. From the shadows came a sound of impact made by two bodies colliding heavily. A groaning exclamation followed, then a voice growled ferociously.

" Damnation ! Stop that row, or——"

There was the ' plunk ' of a blow, a grunting cry, the thud of someone falling on soft earth, then heavily the feet crunched forward again. Almost before she was aware of his coming, the running man reached her, recoiled, then cried in a startled voice :

" Perdition ! A girl ! "

He thrust a brutal face forward, stared at her in wonder for a moment, and laughed understandingly.

" Yo'r sweetheart's in the bushes back along. Better fetch him out. . . . These blasted copses are crawling with keepers."

Before she could reply or move, the man ran on, and as he went Enid Standish gave a little laugh of amusement.

" My sweetheart ! . . . I wonder who he is ? "

More intrigued than ever, she went forward in the direction the poacher had indicated. Within two minutes from a cluster of bushes and bracken where the moonlight broke through the trees, she heard a voice muttering :

" Now who was that hasty citizen ? Not——"

The accent of the speaker was good, the voice was the voice of culture, and had moreover a reminiscent sound in her ears. She ran forward without fear, and came on a man half sprawling in the bracken—a young man on whose forehead was a recent cut from which the blood still trickled slowly. The man saw her as she stepped into the moonlight, and jerking himself into a sitting posture stared at her with incredulous eyes.

" Sister Enid ! " he ejaculated. " Great Jove, it just can't be. I'm suffering from hallucinations——"

" No, Jeff Warborough," interrupted Miss Standish. " I am real ; as I suppose you are. But . . . what are you doing here ? "

" Meaning that you thought I was far away, Sister ? "

" That . . . and something else. You are the man who was running across the road, and who was struck by that car, just now ? "

" Well——"

The man's voice was cool and non-committal, but there was a tenseness in his face that he could not hide.

" I am wondering why you were in such a mortal hurry ? "

" I'm afraid I cannot tell you that—Sister Enid." Mr. Warborough's voice was grave, and the tenseness of his face was accentuated.

Miss Standish looked away for a second or so, and when her eyes came back to him they were full of troubled light.

" I heard a pistol-shot . . . a scream——" she said hesitatingly.

" So did I," answered the man.    " I am still wondering what they portend."

Relief shone in her eyes and sounded in her voice. " Then you do not know ? . . . You did not fire——"

" No!" The word came sharply.    " I had my hands full without pistol-shooting."

" And you cannot guess what was behind that shot and cry ? "

" Haven't a notion.   The thing is a mystery."

" I think someone was hurt——" began Miss Standish.

" To death, I should say," interrupted Mr. Warborough, with conviction.   " A man doesn't scream twice that way."

Enid Standish shivered a little, partly at the remembrance of the cry and partly at the import of it ; then, a little worried, she asked abruptly :

" You can tell me no more, Jeff ? "

" No-o !"   The word was given a little hesitatingly, as if the man were in some doubt as to the wisdom of making her a confidant ; then he added tersely, " Can't, Sister. You must believe—just that ! But there's a thing I should like to know.   Who was the man who knocked me down just now ? "

" A poacher, I think.   There is a raid on across the wood."

" A   poacher !   Glory !   And   I   thought——"   He broke off with a laugh of relief, and shot a further question. " Those men in the car that hit me ?   Did they—er— see me ? "

" Only indistinctly, I think."   In the moonlight the relief that crept into his face was clearly visible, and Miss Standish knew that he had been afraid what her answer would be.   And because of old they had been friends she elaborated.   " Only the chauffeur saw you at all.   The man whom I take to be the owner of the car was incredulous until I owned to having seen you.   They searched the ditch, and when I said you had gone into the wood, they went their ways, believing you were a poacher."

" Good thing ! It would have been awkward if they had followed me here."

He fell silent, without offering any explanation of why it would have been awkward for him to have been found ; then he spoke crisply :

" Sister Enid, I must get out of this quickly. My leg is hurt—a nasty jar from the wing of that car. I want to get to the junction in time for the night mail. Is there a garage hereabouts where one can hire a car ? "

" Up the road, at the village, a mile or more. The police-sergeant's son has a taxi——"

" Police-sergeant's son ! " the man interjected. " That would be asking for trouble, and I've a trunkful of it now. Think again, Sister Enid—and think hard."

Enid Standish considered him thoughtfully, wondering why he should be anxious to avoid even second-hand contact with the police. Perhaps he read her mind, for he smiled whimsically.

" Haven't got the swag in my hip-pocket, Sister, and —honest Injun—I am still received at the Embassy, when I care to present myself. It is just my retiring nature to avoid the police of this great country, ever since I collected a blue helmet for a souvenir, and——"

Miss Standish laughed, and knowing the man made up her mind suddenly.

" I have an Overland Whippet—in my own right. If you like, I might drive you if it is really urgent."

" Sister Enid," he answered in a voice that was earnest and utterly convincing, " it is as urgent as death."

" Then I will fetch the car," she replied swiftly. " If you will make your way to the fence, I will hoot three times when I return."

She did not wait for thanks. Without another word between them, she turned on her heel and began to hurry from the wood. When she reached the rail she followed it until she found a grassy ' ride ' into which she turned, and hurrying along it came presently to a gate which opened on the park on the further side of which the lights of the house gleamed. Then she broke into a run, and as she ran became aware of the hum of a motor-engine and of a growing light behind her. She looked round. A car was moving up the long approach to the house at what seemed to her a breakneck pace. Whilst she was still on the lawn it reached the terrace in front of the house and drew up at the door. She saw a man fling himself out and rush towards the door. She was less than a dozen yards away when the door opened and the next moment the sound of a frenzied voice reached her.

" Sir Stephen ? I want Sir Stephen, Reynolds. Where is he ? . . . Mr. Maxwell has been murdered ! "

Reynolds, a staid footman, cried out in amazed incredulity, and Enid Standish halted abruptly at the words. For a moment it seemed to her that her heart had ceased to beat. Then she shivered as she had shivered when at the edge of the wood she had heard the sound of the shot and the scream which had followed it. There was a stark look in her eyes as she stared in front of her, seeing not the man who had brought the dread news—but visioning two men, one running like a black shadow in the glare of a car's head-lights, and the other racing recklessly across the road from Farholme Park. The visioned figures displaced each other in turn—now this one, now that, holding her mental vision. She heard the bearer of the dark tidings answer a question, still in the same frenzied voice.

" Shot ? No ! Stuck through the throat. A ghastly thing—and this the man's wedding-night."

Then again before her mental vision leaped the two men, each running as for dear life ; and as she thought of Simon Maxwell lying dead, a single word broke from her lips, embodying the question which seemed to be burning in her brain like a fire.

" Which ? "

## CHAPTER III

### THE VISITING-CARD

SCARCELY had the question leaped from her, when Enid Standish's mind was busy ranging facts. None of them reassured her of the innocence of the man whom she had left in the wood. He had been anxious lest the men in the car had observed him closely—there was his statement that it was a good thing they had not followed him into the copses ; his urgency to leave the neighbourhood ; his most evident desire to avoid contact with the police ; and the last but not least important fact that, when the car had struck him, he had been fleeing from the grounds of Farholme Abbey. All these things, pointed by the news of Simon Maxwell's murder, had an ominous significance.

Then again she saw the other man racing down the road, a black outline in the glare of the head-lights and leaping sharply aside in the darkness. Was he an accomplice ? Had the two together planned——

The thought was not completed. Jeff Warborough, as she knew him, was no man to do a foul thing. Whatever had happened at Farholme, the man whom she had promised to help was above suspicion where so dark a crime as murder was concerned. Of that she was very sure, and having made her promise——

A voice tense with horror and excitement penetrated her absorption, forcing her to listen.

" —swords from a trophy stand in the hall. Mr. Maxwell lies with one in his hand—the other is on the carpet. He must have snatched one to defend himself with, but he wasn't killed with a sword. There's a knife by his side—all bloody, an' seemingly he was struck with that. . . . But I must hurry back. Mrs. Maxwell will be crazed. They haven't told her yet. The maids are scared to death, the housekeeper is in hysterics, and the butler is a chewed rag. . . . You'll find Sir Stephen and let him know ? We need somebody to take charge till the doctor and the police arrive. . . . For God's sake beg him to hurry."

She saw the man turn the car and begin to race down the avenue, then watched whilst Reynolds and another man left the house to find Sir Stephen, but remained where she was for a full three minutes longer, considering the situation. At the end of that time, she nodded to herself and moved quickly across the lawn in the direction of the garage. Sir Stephen's two chauffeurs had been enlisted to assist the keepers, but having her keys with her she was able to enter ; and with a deliberate thoughtfulness she examined the oil well, filled the tank with petrol, and then drove forth into the moonlit night.

She found Warborough seated on the rail waiting for her, and as she gave the signal and pulled up, he slipped down, and limped painfully to the car. She opened the door for him, and as he entered the man glanced sharply at her and in the moonlight saw her face white and troubled. He did not speak, however, until the car was in motion, making for the junction, then he broke the silence, abruptly :

" So, Sister, you've heard the news ? "

" How . . . how did you know ? " stammered the lady.

" It is written in your face. . . . Who told you ? "

" The Farholme chauffeur came for Sir Stephen Langford. He said that his master had been murdered—killed by a knife-thrust in the throat."

" Anything else ? "

" Little that I heard, except that Simon Maxwell had apparently tried to defend himself. He lies with a sword still in his hand."

" Um ! The facts would bear that interpretation ! "

" But you have another explanation ? " she asked in a strained voice.

" Yes. And mine is the right one. But I am not going

to elucidate. Since you are helping me to—er—escape, the less you know about the facts of this bad business the better, I think."

" But *you* did not kill Simon Maxwell ? " she said incredulously.

" No ! " There was a note of grimness in her companion's tone. " But I had meant to——"

The car swerved sharply as the driver started, and Jeff Warborough smiled.

" Steady, Sister ! Your nerves used to be better than that, when the Bosche airmen came over down Vrancourt way."

Enid Standish did not probe the meaning of the words that had so startled her. Instead she cried with sharp conviction :

" It must have been the other man ! "

" What other man ? " he demanded.

" A man whom I saw running down the road just before you appeared."

" Phew ! " Mr. Warborough whistled sharply. Then he ejaculated : " Fellow must have been watching. . . . The window was open and——" He interrupted himself, possibly aware that he was on the verge of indiscreet revelation ; then in a matter-of-fact voice he added : " I dare say you are right. Indeed, I do not question it. . . . The man got clear away ? "

" There was nothing to hinder him. . . . You know him ? "

" Er—slightly. But I do not expect to meet him again after this. What I can't understand is that you saw only one man. There should have been two. I wonder if that shot we heard——"

He did not finish the thought aloud. Glancing at him, by the moonlight, Miss Standish saw that his face had an absorbed look. His eyes under creased brows were staring straight ahead, and quite plainly he was revolving some knotty problem. She did not interrupt his meditation,

C

nor seek to force his confidence; but waited, hoping that he would explain in the fullness of time. The car swept on through the still night, the steady purr of the engine being almost the only sound. They swung by slumbering farms, through two silent villages, and again along stretches of moonlit fields chequered here and there by shadowy woods; but not until they sighted the lights of the junction did her companion's absorption cease. Then he broke silence with a light laugh.

" Sister Enid, Carston Magna and Farholme Abbey will have double headlines in the papers for a week to come——"

" I know that ! " she answered. " It isn't every day that a magnate is murdered on his wedding-night——"

" That isn't all ! " interrupted Warborough. " Daylight will bring forth a second mystery, or I'll eat my hat."

" You mean that shot ? "

" Precisely ! . . . And when you hear the news it means you can set yourself a problem. Who fired it—the man whom you saw running away or Simon Maxwell ? One or——" He interrupted himself. " There's the train coming down the straight. We're just on time. I shall have to hurry to book."

As the car drew up, the train was running into the station. Warborough leaped out and ran limpingly to the ticket window, whilst Miss Standish followed him more leisurely. One of the three men on duty was at the entrance to the platform to examine tickets, and as she made to follow Warborough, barred her way.

" I am just seeing my friend off," she explained.

" Platform ticket required, miss," said the man stubbornly.

She thrust a hand in her pocket and, producing a shilling, said impatiently: " Get me one. Keep the change."

" Thank you, miss ! "

The man stepped aside, and Miss Standish followed the limping Warborough up the platform. She overtook him

as he halted by an empty first-class smoker.  He opened
the door and stood ready to step in.  Except for the
guard at the end of the train and a porter, the pair had
the platform to themselves.

" Jeff," she said, " where are you going ? "

" London, Paris—and then for the hot wastes of Hell,"
he answered with a laugh.

Her curiosity surged up overpoweringly.  " You are
going to tell me nothing more about what happened——"

" Not a blessed word—for your own good.  You
see——"

" The ticket, miss," interrupted a voice behind them,
and, swinging round, Miss Standish saw the porter offering
the platform ticket and staring at Warborough curiously.

" Thank you ! " she said curtly, and then down the
platform came a second porter, crying from force of habit
to the practically empty platform :  " Take your seats !
Take your seats ! "

Warborough laughed and stepping into the train
closed the door.  Then he leaned out.

" I'm awfully obliged."

" I could shake you, Jeff Warborough," she said with
real annoyance.   " To leave me guessing like this——"

The guard's whistle cut in on her words, and the engine
gave a preliminary puff.  The man leaned out of the
window.

" I'll tell you . . . all . . . sometime . . ."

The train began to move, and she ran a little way along
the platform.

" Sometime . . . never ! " she cried.   " You know the
old charm.  Won't you write and explain ? "

The roar of the train drowned his answer.  She saw him
wave a hand, waved back herself, and a second later, a
little chagrined, was staring at the rear-lights of the train
receding in the night.  She watched them for a second or
two, then turned to find the porter who had brought the
ticket to her staring curiously at something on the plat-

form. As she approached him, he glanced up, then pointed downwards.

" Gentleman has been in the wars, seemingly."

She looked at the point he indicated. There were several marks glistening ruddily in the light of the lamp overhead. She recognized them instantly for what they were—spots of blood, and divined that Warborough's injury was more severe than he had owned. The porter she saw was very curious, and in view of the developments the morrow might bring it seemed wise to shake his curiosity.

" He has been in a motor accident," she answered, " and hurt his leg."

" I saw he limped," commented the porter as he moved with her towards the entrance, " an' put him down for a war casualty. Anyone with half an eye could see he was a soldier. Don't need to be a 'tec to tell his sort. It's written——"

The lights on the station were suddenly lowered, and Enid Standish almost blundered into a pillar.

" This way, miss," said the garrulous one.

She made the outlet and almost ran to her car. The man stood watching, and as she stepped into the car, having in mind that he was an observant man, she deliberately turned the switch extinguishing the light over the rear number-plate, and did not turn it on again until she was out of eye-shot of the station. Then, as she drove forward, her mind began to busy itself with the perplexities to which the night had given birth.

What was the meaning of the things within her knowledge ? Some connection there was between them unquestionably. The man whom she had seen running down the road, Simon Maxwell dead by some murderous hand, and the man now speeding in the train were all part of a single problem ; but the inwardness of that problem she could not guess. Then there was the second mystery at which Jeff Warborough had hinted. What was that ?

Was it a thing apart, or was it directly connected with the mystery of Simon Maxwell's end ? Warborough knew or guessed——

Her mind jumped sharply to a new thing. That man whom her brother had seen at Carston Magna—the man from the aeroplane, who apparently had so strongly dis-approved of the wedding which had taken place—who was he ? . . . Was his the hand that had struck down the bridegroom—or was he the man whose scream she had heard—the second man who, according to Jeff War-borough, should have been with the one whom she had seen ? Or yet again was the man from the aeroplane Jeff Warborough himself ? And in that case what had he to do with Simon Maxwell, and how could he have known about a marriage that was to all intents and purposes a secret one ?

She perplexed herself with those questions all the way back, and when she swung into the gates of Langford Priory, in her absorption, almost ran over a man who was hurrying forth. She swerved and pulled up with screeching brakes, then recognized her brother.

" You, Enid ! " cried Mr. Standish. " I've been looking for you everywhere. Where on earth have you been ? "

She answered easily, surprised at her own coolness.

" For a moonlight spin ! . . . Your poachers were not exciting——"

" Poachers ! " he ejaculated, then said tersely, " Enid —a shocking thing has happened. Simon Maxwell has been murdered——"

" Murdered ! " she cried in well-simulated horror.

" Brutally, by all accounts. Langford has gone there and wants you to go with me. There is the wife—widowed on her bridal-night. They haven't told her yet —and another woman ought to be there. . . . You understand ? You have a good nerve and——"

" Of course I'll go, Garry. Stand clear whilst I turn the car."

She turned it expertly. Her brother took the seat by her side, and as they swung down the road explained his views of the crime.

" That fellow from the aeroplane is the man as sure as eggs. He was too late to stop the wedding, and so he wiped out the bridegroom. . . . I wonder if he is in love with Cornelia Maxwell. If so, it is a crime of passion— with jealousy for the motive. . . . I'm glad we're on this. You know how interested I am in criminal problems. And here is the chance of a lifetime. It will be hours before the police arrive, I expect. I shall be able to make notes, to gather data, and work out a theory of——"

His sister shivered a little as he talked. She knew his penchant for criminal investigation—a penchant which, for a time, had led him to serve as crime reporter on a New York paper in which their father had owned a controlling interest. She knew him to be shrewd, was aware of the terrier-like tenacity which characterized him when once his teeth were in a problem, and she had a foreboding of trouble to come as she thought of her own part in the events of the night. If Garry discovered that she had helped a man to the station——

Her thought broke off as she swung the car through the wide gateway of the Abbey. There was a long approach to the house, but the lights in the windows were visible the whole way, and as they flashed into view, and she thought of Cornelia Maxwell, she was aware of a sudden shrinking from the task allotted to herself. How would the bride of a few hours, so terribly widowed, take the dreadful news ? She was of outstanding repute as an actress. She had played great tragical parts—how would she behave under the stress of reality, how react to real tragedy ? She visioned her distraught by the terrible fact, yielding to an emotional temperament and slipping to the verge of madness, and spoke suddenly :

" Garry . . . if—if she doesn't know, I can't tell her. It is too terrible."

" Nonsense, Enid. You've just got to. It's a woman's sympathy she'll need, and I gather there's no woman there except a housekeeper and maids. You've got to go through with it—for her sake, and it isn't the first time you've broken bad news to people I know. Thank Heaven you've had a hospital training."

Miss Standish made no further protest. It seemed that there was nothing for it save to take the part cast for her ; but her discomfort became acute as they approached the house. The ancient, iron-studded double doors stood wide open, and under the lamps of an electrolier glowing in the great hall she made out a little huddle of people, servants as she guessed. Why had not one of them broken the news to——

" My God ! " broke out her brother, hoarsely. " Look, Enid ! Look ! On the stairs ! There she is. Quick ! Or——"

The car was close to the doorway. Everything in the wide hall was visible to both of them, and descending the great staircase was the bride of the afternoon, in charming *négligé*, a look of surprise on her beautiful face. As the car pulled up there was a sudden movement of the women huddled together in the hall. A maid gave a sharp hysterical cry, a second buried her face in her hands and broke into violent weeping, two others shrank backward as if they had seen a ghost, and before Enid Standish had reached the steps, Cornelia Maxwell had passed the last stair.

" What is the matter ? " she asked wonderingly. " Where is Mr. Maxwell ? "

" In there ! " cried the hysterical maid, with index finger outstretched. . . . " God help you, my poor lady."

There was a swift change in the beautiful face. The wonder was still there, but now, as if some secret intuition informed her of the impending stroke, it was shadowed by dreadful anticipation. The colour ebbed swiftly from her cheeks, she stood there wavering like a flame, the slum-

brous eyes suddenly aglow with fear. Her lips opened as
if to speak, but no words came ; then she moved swiftly
towards the door of the room the maid had indicated.
From the threshold, Enid Standish, now running, cried
out imploringly :

"Don't go! Wait! There is something you must hear."

Cornelia Maxwell flashed her a single wondering glance,
but did not so much as pause. She was in the doorway
and pushing at the door which stood ajar, before Enid
Standish was half-way across the hall, then she halted
suddenly. A single broken cry came from her, and in the
same second Miss Standish caught Sir Stephen's voice :

"For God's sake, madame, go back ! "

The lady ignored the urgent request. She stood there
one hand on the door-knob, the other pressed against her
heart, an expression of frozen horror on her face, stony as
if she had looked on some Medusa head. Whilst she so
stood, Enid Standish reached her, and stretched a sym-
pathetic hand.

"Mrs. Maxwell, please come away. For your own sake.
Something terrible has happened——"

She might have addressed a marble image. The actress
did not move. The dark eyes burning in the dead white
face stared at the thing upon the floor, then she spoke in a
tone that wrung Enid Standish's heart :

"What is the matter with Simon ? "

For the moment Miss Standish thought that the stricken
bride was too dazed to comprehend the nature of the
trouble that had befallen ; then looking beyond her into
the room, she realized that such failure was impossible.
The dead man lay no more than a few feet away from
his widowed bride. His eyes were half-closed. The
strong jaw had sagged a little. The face had the pallor
of ivory, and in the throat was a wound from which the
blood had flowed in a stream as if a great artery had been
severed. He lay on his back, one knee drawn up, one
hand clutching a sword as the man who had carried the

news to the Priory had stated, and close beside him on
the carpet gleamed a stiletto-like knife all blood-stained,
whilst nearer the door was a second sword, as if it had
been hurriedly discarded by whomsoever had used it.

Enid Standish took all in with a single flashing glance,
and divined that the question was little more than mech-
anical—the merest conventional inquiry. A second later
her guess was confirmed.

"Who has done this thing?"

There was no tremor in the voice, no throb of revengeful
anger, it was calm as still water and cold as ice. Miss
Standish found it amazing and looked at the speaker in
wonder. Then from the burning eyes, tumultuous with
horrified anger, she learned the truth. This bride,
widowed on her wedding-night, was not so calm and aloof
as she seemed. There was fire within her, a stress and
tumult of feeling beyond words. For a moment no one
replied to her question, then she spoke again, a little
note of impatient peremptoriness in the cool, level tones.

"Answer me! Who has done this thing?"

"Heaven knows, madame," answered Stephen Langford brusquely. "I don't. Maxwell was found as you
see him, half an hour ago. I have telephoned for the
police and a doctor—though the latter can do nothing."

"Simon is dead?"

"Yes. He cannot have lived three minutes after—
er—the death-stroke."

Cornelia Maxwell moved forward a pace or two. But
for the incandescence of the usually slumbrous eyes her
beautiful face was absolutely mask-like, and she might
have been playing a part in one of the dramas that had
brought her fame. Two yards from the dead man she
stopped and looked down at him. Her eyes went to the
sword in his hands and then she looked back to the other
sword lying on the carpet. As she did so, the mask-
like look on her face was broken by a flash of compre-
hension.

"He must have been fighting," she said, still in the passionless voice that to Enid Standish seemed almost dreadful. "A duel, perhaps? That sword there——" She indicated the other weapon with a flash of her eyes, and left the rest unspoken.

"Maybe!" blurted Langford. "It isn't usual here in England. But Maxwell was a naturalized foreigner, wasn't he? It is possible—in any case he wasn't killed by the sword there. It is unsoiled, whilst the knife here is all stained. It was with this that he was slain, I'll take oath."

She looked at the knife curiously, then added sharply, "There is but one knife?"

"But one!" answered Langford. "Why should there be two? One was sufficient for this foulness."

The woman took no notice of his words, but speaking to herself rather than to him, gave him an explanation.

"If the man who did this had that poignard, and Simon had none, it would give the other an unfair advantage."

"That is true," broke in Stephen Langford. "If as you think there was a fight——"

"Those swords!" interrupted the lady. "They shout the fact. Simon had been a soldier abroad. He was a swordsman of parts. I have seen him in the fencing-school. There are few who could excel him. But the man who slew him used the knife. That was murder most foul."

Her voice had still the unemotional stoniness that was so amazing. Her mind it seemed was untouched by any grief, considering the pros and cons of a terrible event with extraordinary calm. It occurred to Miss Standish that the romantic associations of the profession she followed, familiarity with historic and histrionic usage of the sword for the settlement of private quarrels, blinded her to the elements in the situation that others found bizarre and extraordinary. She stood there waiting for an answer to the question, and Langford gave the obvious answer.

" Unquestionably, madame ! Here in England the man will hang—if he is caught."

" Caught ! " The stony calm of her voice was broke at last. The word rang through the chamber, vibrant with passion as the tempest within snapped the bands of restraint. " He shall be caught ! And he shall hang as high as Haman, law or no law. I swear it by all holy things."

Sir Stephen Langford shrugged his shoulders a little at what he conceived a melodramatic outburst, a piece of acting in keeping with the speaker's reputation as a great tragedienne ; but watching her Enid Standish knew that here was no acting. The words rang with earnestness. They were the expression of a resolution suddenly conceived and in a moment hardened to adamant. Glimpsing the truth, she was appalled by it, and watched the now quivering woman with horrified pity. Then there was an unexpected movement behind her. Garfield Standish, thrusting forward, walked towards the fireplace, attracted by a small piece of pasteboard which lay on the hearth, and which none but his questing eyes had noticed. Stooping, he retrieved it—a common visiting-card. In some excitement he looked for a name, then gave an amazed ejaculation :

" My stars ! "

" What——" began Langford, only to be interrupted.

" The key to this mystery, unless I am mistaken," cried Standish, exulting in his discovery.

He thrust the card forward for the other's inspection, but retained his hold on it, jealously. Langford stared at it wonderingly. It was a cheap visiting-card, of the class occasionally sold for emergency use, unprinted. It bore no name, but instead had three black dots arranged in pyramid form, plainly inscribed with a pen, and in the top right-hand corner was a message, carelessly written in French :

" *Nous y voici*," and below a further message, a little huddled : " *Dix heures de du soir au colombier.*"

" *Nous y voici*—Here we are ! . . . But who in Heaven's name does the we stand for ? "

" Don't know," said Standish quickly. " That remains to be discovered. But Simon Maxwell was no stranger to that symbol there. When that card was presented he knew exactly what visitors so enigmatically announced themselves and made an appointment at the dovecot, I'll swear."

" You seem very certain of it, Standish."

" And with reason. Look there ! "

He indicated the dead man's hand as he spoke. It lay palm downwards, and on the back of it, which now had a white bloodless look, the tattoo marks, which Standish had noticed when Maxwell had signed the register a few hours before, showed very clearly. Stephen Langford stared at them with startled eyes. In his amazement he whistled sharply, then asked a question.

" How did you know, Standish ? "

" Noticed the marks this afternoon when he was writing his name in the register," answered Standish, preening himself a little. " Wondered about them at the time, and now, from this piece of pasteboard, it seems clear that Simon Maxwell belonged to some organization or confederacy, which has that symbol for its trade-mark. Probably it is no more than a trio. The number of dots implies that—and it is possible that Maxwell was one of them. Here we are ! The coming of the other two most probably was a great shock to him. Maybe he didn't expect them, but I guess he knew what they wanted, and I'd give a hatful of dollars to know what it was. . . . But anyway there's the thread that leads to the hole in the wall."

" It seems likely——" began Langford thoughtfully, only to be interrupted by Maxwell's widow.

" What is it you are saying ? " she asked in a hard

voice. " You have a clue to the man who killed Simon ? "

" To the man or men," answered Standish triumphantly.

" You think there was more than one ? "

" Two, at least. Those dots, I take it, stand for three people. The message scrawled there is in the plural—implying that there were at least two announced by the card. But there are three dots there and the third——"

" By heaven ! " cried Langford, as the drift of the other's reasoning became clear. " Maxwell himself ! I would wager a cool thousand on it."

" But why——" began the woman, but broke off as from outside there came the purr of a car. There was a little screech of brakes, then the clang of the ancient bell which was in keeping with the house, sounding clamorously in the stillness of the night.

" The doctor—or the police," said Langford, and as voices sounded in the hall turned eagerly towards the door.

## CHAPTER IV

### THE DOVE-TOWER

A MOMENT later, a tall, soldierly-looking man was announced by a trembling maid-servant.

" Inspector Gaddy."

The officer flashed a swift look round, recognized Sir Stephen and saluted, then stepping forward looked down on the dead man.

" Dead ? " he questioned quietly.

" Beyond all doubt," answered Langford.

" Anyone any idea how it happened ? "

" Don't know, but I should imagine not. He was found lying here by the butler awhile back. The servants sent for me as a magistrate and nearest neighbour." He lowered his voice. " His wife had not been told——"

" Wife ! I didn't know he had a wife," the inspector whispered in surprise.

" The tall lady, behind—in *négligé*. He was married this afternoon——"

" Good God ! What a thing to happen ! Wonder if there's any connection between the two events ? "

" Your job to find out, I suppose," answered Langford. The inspector looked carefully around, marked in turn the blood-stained poignard, the sword in the dead man's hand, the second sword lying on the floor, and as he did so a look of amazement came on his face.

" There are queer elements here. These swords——"

" From the hall," broke in Sir Stephen.

" But a man does not snatch two swords with which to defend himself. One is sufficient. It looks as if there had been a fight."

" He wasn't killed with that sword there. This poignard was the weapon the murderer used——"

" Unquestionably ! But——"

The inspector stooped and examined the point of the sword in the dead man's clutch. When he rose there was a gleam in his eyes. Without a word he stepped to the other sword and examined that, then he returned to Langford.

" I think it is certain there was a fight, and that Mr. Maxwell was getting the best of it. There is blood upon his point, but nothing on the other, and it is a moral certainty that the man who killed him suffered a wound. Has anything been found to——"

" This ! " interrupted Garfield Standish, thrusting the visiting-card forward. " I found it in the hearth."

The inspector took the card and examined it carefully.

" Um ! Three black dots : ' *Nous y voici* '—Here we are ! Then if this has anything to do with the crime, on the face of it there was more than one in it. . . . This may be very important."

" Moral certainty, Inspector," said Mr. Standish, who being in the saddle meant to ride. " If you look on

Maxwell's hand you will find there three black dots tattooed in the same formation."

Inspector Gaddy verified the statement, then looked at Langford.

" Does the lady know anything about these dots, Sir Stephen ? "

" Nothing, I should say."

" I shall have to inquire, after I have made a search. This card may be a vital clue. If it was handed in, one of the servants will know, and possibly be able to describe the man or men who brought it. . . . I think I must have the room cleared, Sir Stephen. The quicker I get to work the better, and I shall have much to do and many inquiries to make. You might explain to the ladies, whilst I give orders to the household staff."

" Certainly, Gaddy."

The inspector left the room, and Sir Stephen approached the widow and explained the situation. Without a word Cornelia Maxwell turned and left the room, Enid Standish accompanying her. In the hall she turned. Her face was working painfully, in her eyes there was a very storm of trouble, and it was clear that her self-control was breaking down. She stretched an appealing hand towards Miss Standish and whispered brokenly :

" What can I do ? . . . I have . . . no friends . . . here. And to be alone . . . with this terrible thing——"

" Let me stay with you, Mrs. Maxwell. I came to help you——"

" Oh, if you would."

" I will. Where shall we go ? "

" To the boudoir where I was . . . when . . . when I was waiting for Simon and——"

A dry sob checked her utterance, and with a gesture of impatience at her own weakness she led the way to the wide staircase, fighting back the surging emotion. Garfield Standish watched them until they disappeared, then he turned to Langford, and asked a question :

" Do you think she loved Maxwell ? "

" Lord knows. Women are capable of strange likings. The man is dead and *de mortuis* is a sound rule ; but it is the simple truth that according to decent standards he was a bounder—a naturalized Swede transplanted from New York."

" And a power there," commented Standish. " There'll be big head-lines in the New York papers when the news is flashed across. His death in dramatic circumstances is a first-class mystery."

" Rough on his bride," said Langford reflectively. " I wonder if that airman you saw had anything to do with the crime ? "

" Seems likely," replied Mr. Standish ; then added with a relish, " I'm the only man who saw him, so that inspector won't be able to keep me out of the business entirely."

" Mean to say you want to be in it ? " asked the other in manifest surprise.

" Why not ? " countered Standish. " I have always been interested in this kind of thing, and though I don't want to brag, I used to be counted a decent amateur back home. The thing intrigues me, and I mean to follow it up. So far I've had the amateur's luck. First, I see the airman and hear him express hard views of Maxwell's marriage ; then I find that card and remember the tattoo marks I had noticed on the dead man's hand. That is a fair start, and the clues are promising ; but there is a thing I don't understand at all as yet."

" There is a whole pack of them where I am concerned. Which do you mean ? "

" That message on the card. Not the ' *Nous y voici* ' business, but the other part about the dovecot—which points plainly to a rendezvous." He broke off and jerked a question. " Is there anything special in the way of a dovecot on Maxwell's estate ? "

" By Jove, yes ! A tall tower, sort of monumental thing where the pigeons breed wild, or as good as."

Garfield Standish betrayed a little excitement, and asked quickly, " Where is it ? "

" Across the park in the thick of the trees—quarter of a mile away from here."

" And yet Simon Maxwell was killed in his own house. The first question is, did he keep the appointment the ' Black Dots ' made for him ? If he did, a second arises. Did he bring the man or men who made the appointment back here to the Abbey ; or was he followed on the home-ward way ? "

" Who is to know ? "

" A man might find out if he went to the dovecot——"

" At this hour ? "

" There's a moon, and I've a flashlamp in my pocket," answered Mr. Standish. " I'd like to get ahead of the police if I can ; and the first on the spot picks up the clues, early-bird-and-the-worm-business, you know. Do you think you could show me the way, Langford ? "

" I could—but I'll be shot if I will," replied the other brusquely. " The police can do their own work without our butting in, and Gaddy is quite an efficient officer. Things can be left in his hands."

" Oh, well, if you won't——"

Mr. Standish made a gesture of disappointment and turned away, resigned as it seemed to the inevitable. But his resignation was no more than apparent. He was on the trail of a most intriguing mystery and in no way prepared to forgo the joys of pursuit. The thought of the dovecot drew him like a magnet, and he was resolved at all costs to make a private investigation of the place. He waited until Sir Stephen was called by the inspector for some purpose, then he moved swiftly to the door and slipped out to the moonlit terrace. There he had the luck to encounter the chauffeur who had carried the message of his master's death to the Priory. He addressed the man without ceremony :

" Do you know where the dove-tower is in the park ? "

" Why, to be sure, sir. Everybody knows——"

" I don't. Take me there at once. It is important."

He thrust a hand into his pocket as he spoke and produced a Treasury note. " Here's something for your trouble."

" Well, sir, if you think I ought to go, before that officer has seen me——"

" I've told you that it is important that I should go," said Standish in peremptory tones. " It may help us to catch the man who killed your master. . . . Quick, man ! Every moment that passes is a moment wasted."

Impressed by his manner, the chauffeur made no further demur.

" This way, sir," he said, and moving across the terrace began to cross the wide lawn in front of the house.

Mr. Standish followed him, excited at the prospect of being the first to investigate the rendezvous mentioned on the visiting-card, and hoping for further discoveries. Reaching the edge of the lawn, he glanced back over his shoulder at the lighted house. In the room where the murdered man lay he glimpsed the inspector in conversation with Langford, and smiled triumphantly to himself.

" All right ! " he murmured. " But the secret isn't there, I'll swear."

As he joined the chauffeur and hurried across the lawn he had no compunction about the thing he was doing, and no sense that he was behaving in a way not quite creditable. He was for the moment what he had been in New York—a crimes' reporter, hurrying on a case that was intriguing, and with the old urge to get the solution of it ahead of the police. With that in view he began to talk to the chauffeur about his dead master.

" How long have you been at Farholme ? " he asked.

" Three months, sir, but I'm due to leave on Saturday."

" Is that so ? Under notice, I suppose ? "

" My notice, sir, given a month back. I didn't like the place, and couldn't stand Mr. Maxwell's ways."

" Um ! He wasn't nice to work with, then ? "

" He wasn't the kind of gentleman I've been accustomed to work for, sir. He was—excuse me for being plain, sir —he was like a sergeant-major of the worst sort, never satisfied and for ever bullying a man."

Mr. Standish sympathized. " Some very rich men are like that. I can understand your desire to quit. . . . Did you get many visitors here ? "

" Never a single one, sir, in all the time I've been here, and Mr. Maxwell went nowhere, being seemingly not fond of company."

" Must have been pretty solitary ! " commented Mr. Standish. " What did your master do with himself when he was down here ? "

" Worried the gardeners and the keepers mostly," replied the chauffeur with feeling, " that is when he was taking an off-time from the garage."

Garfield Standish sympathized. " I can understand he must have been pretty trying. I know the kind, having been reared among them. . . . Probably he had enemies who worried him and——"

" I never heard of any, sir."

" And you didn't see the men who called on him to-night."

" Men ? Was there more than one ? . . . But that's likely enough. Mr. Maxwell was a bull of a man, and one man wouldn't have had much chance with him alone. . . . No, sir, I saw no one about the Abbey, but out in the road two or three hours back, something happened which, since I have thought over it, seems to me a bit queer."

" Ah ! What was that ? "

" Well, sir, I was going down to Keeper Thomas's, who lives at the west lodge, when in the dark I met two men coming up the road, whistling a marching tune, and keeping step with it."

" A couple of discharged soldiers, tramping for work, I expect."

" It wasn't an English marching tune, sir. I was in

France during the war and I heard it more than once. It was the march of the Foreign Legion."

Mr. Standish was moved to sudden excitement. " Are you sure ? "

" Dead sure, sir. I don't know the words, being no scholar ; but I have the tune in my head and can whistle it. It runs like this." He began to whistle, and almost unconsciously Standish fitted the words to the melody, humming them aloud.

" *Tiens voila du boudin ! voila du boudin : voila du boudin !*
  *Pour les Alsaciens, les Suisses et les Lorrains,*
  *Pour les Belges il n'y en a point——*"

He broke off sharply. " If that was the air, you're right, chauffeur. It is the march of *les légionaires*. But what were two men who whistled it doing in this God-forsaken district ? "

" Don't know, sir. It's the last thing you'd expect to hear anyone whistling on this quiet country-side. Thinking it over, that's what strikes one as being so mortal queer—that and another thing."

" What other thing ? " asked Standish quickly.

" Well, sir, since I came I've heard the tune whistled once before."

" You have ? "

" Yes, sir. Mr. Maxwell—— "

" Maxwell whistled it ? " Standish was so astonished that he halted sharply to stare at the man. Then he asked incredulously, " Are you sure ? "

" Certain, sir ! 'Tisn't a tune one's likely to mistake something else for."

It wasn't. Garfield Standish owned that to himself and to the chauffeur as he moved on again, his brain busy linking up things which he had heard. Maxwell had died sword in hand, had died not by the sword but by an assassin's dagger—true ; but the assassin had first faced him with the sword ; and it was Maxwell's point that had drawn blood, and not that of his opponent. That fact

implied a certain familiarity on the part of the dead man
with that particular weapon, and on the chauffeur's
testimony he had the manner of a blustering sergeant-
major—of the worst type, whilst he was familiar with and
sometimes whistled the march of the Legion. And those
two men who had passed the chauffeur on the road had
marched to that stirring air—the men who he was morally
certain had sent that odd visiting-card to Maxwell.
Had the latter been in the Legion—a bullying sergeant
of the hopeless and the lost ? It was more than possible,
and as he considered the possibility he saw a suggestive
line of investigation opening before him. If the dead
man had served in that regiment of the lost, if in his
capacity of sergeant he had harried his fierce sheep who
dared not retaliate ; made their lives a burden, possibly
the pair who had marched down the road had come to
Farholme to pay off old scores. Mr. Standish remembered a case that he had read in the newspaper a few years
before—the case of a bullying Irish sergeant, who meeting
a man of his old company in the street, a man on whose
discharge papers the ink was scarcely dry, had been
soundly and deservedly thrashed by him, pounded out of
recognition, whilst the man who had administered the
thrashing had gone joyfully to prison for three months.

If such a thing was possible in an English company,
much more so in a company of the Legion, where men
were often of desperate character, and with everything
already lost, beyond the reach of common restraints.
These men——

He broke off suddenly, and laughed at his own rather
excited anticipations. He was getting ahead of the
band, and that was not altogether wise. It was as well
to march with the hard facts, and not to make deductions
the very reasonableness of which might be misleading.
A second later the man at his side broke on his thoughts.

"There's the dovecot, sir, in front."

Standish looked in the direction indicated, and between

the trees saw a tall tower showing whitely under the moon. Staring closely he saw a number of unglazed windows in the structure, and guessed that they were the means of ingress used by the birds.

" Many doves there ? " he asked.

" Hundreds, sir. They're a regular nuisance in the gardens and in the fields hereabouts."

" Um ! They're housed extravagantly anyway. The man who built that place didn't spare the dollars."

" Must have had more money than sense, sir," agreed the chauffeur, leading the way forward.

In a very few minutes they reached the open place in which the tower was set, and again Garfield Standish considered it curiously. It was a shaft of grey stone, at least sixty feet high, crowned by a vane which gleamed under the moon, and with a narrow door at the foot, little more than a man's height. Green sward ran to its base, and tall trees, set in a circle, stood around it, but well away. The place was utterly still, and as he stood there Standish thought that the tower was like a temple set in a grove—a temple of Astarte to whom the doves flying in and out of those narrow windows were sacred.

As he looked round he thought that whilst this might be the rendezvous appointed by the ' Black Dots,' it promised little enough to an investigator. In the moonlight it was a place of beauty and of almost eerie stillness. In the daytime, with the sun shining upon it, and with the doves cooing and flying and fluttering around or wheeling in flocks above the trees, it would still be beautiful ; but, with the swish and the flutter of wings and the soft cries of the birds, life would be the dominant note, and this eerie quietness would be banished. He listened. No sound came from within the tower, no uneasy movement or disgruntled noise made by some bird overpressed by its fellow. In spite of the hundreds of feathered creatures to whom it was sanctuary, it was like some tower of the dead.

" Nothing here," he muttered to himself with a little stir of disappointment, and even as he did so the chauffeur took a step forward, and picked up something which lay in the shadow of the tower.

He returned with it in his hand, a wondering look upon his face.

" What have you there ? " asked Standish quickly.

" A hat—a man's hat, sir."

In a second Standish's disappointment was swamped by a new surge of hope.

" A hat ! " he cried. " Let me see it."

He took it from the chauffeur and examined it with critical eyes. It was a soft-brimmed hat of felt, even in the moonlight a little garish in colour and of cheap quality—not a hat such as Simon Maxwell was likely to affect. Producing the flashlamp of which he had spoken to Langford, he examined the inside of the hat and there in gold letters on a background found the hat-seller's name, " Jean Lescaut, Rue Lafayette, Marseilles."

" Gee ! " he cried in sharp excitement as he read the name which told that the hat had been purchased in France, whilst the chauffeur, moved by curiosity, asked :

" What is it, sir ? "

" A hat ! As you said," he laughed excitedly. " The hat of one of those men who whistled the March of the Legion. I would wager a thousand dollars on it ! "

" But what is it doing here, sir ? "

That was the question which Standish's mind was already asking silently. What was the hat doing here ? True, the owner of it, as he conceived, had kept an appointment at this place, but why departing should he leave his hat at the rendezvous ? . . . But had he departed ? The question shot into his mind like a lightning flash, and like the stormlight revealed a momentary glimpse of hidden things. Mr. Standish's eyes lifted themselves from the hat to the tower. In the moonlight they fairly danced with excitement, and on his face there was a look which startled the chauffeur.

" What is it, sir ? " he asked, himself looking towards the tower.

" That door ? " asked Mr. Standish tersely. " Is it locked ? "

" I don't know, sir. I've never tried it. It's the under-keeper's duty to look after the birds."

It was easy enough to test the door, and Mr. Standish, carrying the hat in one hand and the flashlight in the other, strode towards it. Before he reached it, however, he came to a sharp halt, as his eyes caught sight of a dark blot on the sward revealed by the flashlight, the beam of which chanced to be directed downwards. He stared at the blot with fascinated gaze. Someone, a workman perhaps, employed about the estate, might have spilled tar there or creosote or—— But he knew in-stinctively that blotch on the sward was made by none of these things. In the glare of the electric lamp, paled though it was by the moonlight, the blotch glistened as though still wet, and it had a ruddy sheen. To make sure, he stooped and gingerly touched the blotch with the tip of his forefinger, then examined the finger in the light of his lamp. There was no doubt left in his mind as he did so. The blotch at his feet was made by spilled blood. The chauffeur, who had been watching him curi-ously, came to a sudden realization of the truth.

" God ! " he whispered hoarsely. " 'Tis blood, sir ! "

" Yes," said Standish, in a tense voice.

" Something's happened here——"

" I am sure of it," agreed Mr. Standish. " Let us look in the tower. It may tell us something more."

" But what in Heaven's name—— " began the man whisperingly.

" That remains to be discovered," interrupted Mr. Standish. " And speculation is foolishness when the facts are waiting to be discovered."

He looked round intently, searching the green sward about the tower with lynx-eyes, directing the ray of his flashlight now here now there, but finding nothing, then stepping over that blot on the grass he moved straight to the door of the tower. When he reached it he directed his lamp on the door, and saw that it had a fancy latch of the kind not uncommon on gateways, and a rather massive keyhole.

" Locked ! " he thought with a pang of disappointment, and without any hope turned the iron handle which lifted the latch, and pressed the door.

To his infinite surprise it yielded with a screeching of unoiled hinges, and instantly from within came the sound of uneasy life disturbed by the noise—the rustling of feathered things and a cooing that seemed to fill the whole tower. He flashed his light to and fro and saw before him a small chamber, from which, blinking sleepily, gleamed a score of pairs of eyes. There was, however, nothing there save the birds roosting on their perches. He looked further and saw the beginnings of a small circular staircase which went up in the inside of the tower. For a moment he considered it thoughtfully, then he set his foot to the first iron step.

" You are going up, sir ? " asked the chauffeur in a scared whisper.

" A little way. The first floor or two," answered Mr. Standish, intent on unmasking the secret which he was convinced the tower held. " You can stop there if——"

" I'll come too," replied the man hurriedly, with a swift glance backward at the stain on the grass. " I would not like to stop here, alone."

Garfield Standish made no reply, but began to ascend the stairs. He reached the first floor, and flashed his searchlight round. There was nothing there but startled doves, and he turned to the staircase again. As he did so, on one of the steps he saw something which reflected the light of his lamp—a wet place, which to his now informed mind told its tale. He said nothing to his companion, but tense with excitement led the way upward. On the next landing he halted, holding his lamp to guide the chauffeur's steps before making his scrutiny. When the man reached his side, he directed the beam of his lamp into the chamber. Unlike those below, it had no roosting birds, which, as he thought to himself, was a strange thing. He was wondering what the reason for their absence was when his companion cried out in a horrified voice :

"God ! . . . There ! in the angle of that broken perch ! "

Swiftly he turned in the direction indicated, and, as he did so, saw the body of a man lying there in a crumpled attitude, feet towards him, and face to the wall. Scarcely had he noted it, when the chauffeur gave a scared gasp, and, swinging round, began to stumble down the dark stairs.

## CHAPTER V

### DISCOVERIES

MR. STANDISH was annoyed at the chauffeur's desertion, and cried after him, a little angrily : "Come back, you fool."

The scared man took no notice. A sound of his hurrying steps on the stairs was the only reply that the other received, and when, presently, the scared man stumbled in earnest and fell with a crash, crying out as he did so, the whole tower became full of the sound of whirring wings and of noises made by frightened birds. Mr. Standish waited listening with straining ears, his eyes on that huddled form in the angle of the chamber. He heard the man below pick himself up and continue his flight ; then the sound of his going ceased, and after a moment or two the whirr of wings in the darkness was hushed, and once more silence settled in the tower.

Mr. Standish's nerves were good, but even so, to him, in the presence of that huddled form across the chamber, the stillness had an eerie quality that it had lacked before. As he stood there he gave a little shiver, then bracing himself walked deliberately across the chamber, and directing his lamp on the man strove to see his face. The position in which the man lay made that well-nigh impossible, and though he knew the wisdom in such a case of leaving things as they were for police inspection, he did not scruple to turn the body over to afford him the view he desired. Then with his lamp focussed on the man he scrutinized him thoroughly. That he was dead the first glance assured him, whilst the second informed him of a thin bearded face with a parchment-like skin— the face of a man of perhaps forty years, and, as he thought, of Latin race. His appraising gaze wandered further, looking for the cause of the man's death, and presently found it in a wound on the right breast, marked by a stain on the light waistcoat, where was a hole that he took for that made by a bullet. Searching more carefully, he found dark marks made by burned powder and nodded to himself.

" Shot through the lung at close range."

Scarcely had he reached that conclusion when the inevitable question flashed into his mind :

" By whom ? "

The answer was not easily forthcoming. The man lying there had made an appointment at this dove-tower with the master of Farholme Abbey, who now lay dead in that long room, sword in hand, and it was a fair presumption that if Maxwell had kept the tryst this man had died at his hands. But there was the second man whose presence was implied in the message on the visiting-card, and who, at a narrow guess, had been seen marching down the road with this one, whistling the song of the Legion ? Where was he ? Had he played any part in his comrade's death—baldly, had he slain his fellow for some private reason, for, say, some traitorous trafficking with Simon Maxwell ? There was that possibility, and it was at least a credible assumption that something of the sort had happened. On the other hand, if Maxwell was responsible, his own death at the hand of the comrade of his victim was a likely thing.

As he stood considering, there flashed into his mind a remembrance of the man who, eager for news of the Maxwell-Darracombe wedding, had descended from the clouds at Carston Magna. This man lying at his feet differed as chalk from cheese from the airman, but villainy, like misfortune, makes strange bedfellows, and however different in type the two might be, there was nothing to preclude the airman from being the one of the whistling pair whom the chauffeur had seen pass up the road. Was *he* the killer——

His question broke off abruptly, as his thoughts swung suddenly in a new direction. Stooping swiftly he lifted the dead man's hand, and, turning it over, directed the flashlight full upon it. As he did so a look of exultation came on his face, for there, in the same place, he saw tattooed triple dots which were the exact replica of those he had seen on Simon Maxwell's hand.

" Knew it ! " he whispered excitedly to himself. " I would have wagered a thousand dollars on it."

He dropped the hand, and, straightening himself, grew absorbed. Here, counting Maxwell for one, was the second of the three ' Black Dots,' but where was the last of the trio—the man who possibly had slain his comrade before going forth to deal with Maxwell ?

" Ranging wide . . . by this time," he muttered. "Unless he's a born fool."

But what was the connection between the three ? To discover that was to discover the motive for the crime, and possibly the killer himself. If Maxwell had been in the Legion, and if the other two had been there also, the secret might well lie in their association in that corps.

He dismissed from his mind now all thought of Maxwell as paying for his former brutality by death at the hands of men whom he had harried. Men standing in such a relation of hostility did not brand themselves with a talismanic mark. Associates, friends, men linked in some secret and common enterprise only did that thing, and whatever hostility had subsequently developed, the first association of these two dead men, similarly tattooed, with that of the third man, must have been of a friendly nature or at least one necessitated by a common interest. Had that ruling interest to do merely with their regimental life, or did it go deeper, and was it rooted in some secret shared by them in which the interest of all three was involved ?

He stopped there, recognizing that he was merely putting posers to himself which for the moment were unanswerable. His eyes turned anew to the dead man, and a hungry light came in them. Perhaps the man had carried on his person the key that would unlock the secret —some letter, a diary perhaps, a note in a pocket-book ? There would be no harm if he were to search—to forestall the police, he told himself, though to be sure the official mind would regard such an action as impertinent and wholly unwarrantable. The hungry light grew more pronounced. He had all the passion of the amateur and the urge of an intense curiosity. If the secret were there, the authorities would keep it to themselves, and so shut him out from a very interesting problem, the *dénouement* of which promised to be tremendously interesting. It was not fair of them to——

His resolve was taken suddenly. For a moment or two he stood listening. The night outside was intensely still, within the tower was no sound save the faint rustling of a restless bird. He would be bound to hear anyone ascending the stairs, and there was no fear of his being surprised whilst he was engaged in the search. His mind made up, he dropped on his knees and began systemati-

cally to go through the dead man's pockets, replacing
things as he found them.

There was some loose money in a trousers pocket,
French and English coins indiscriminately mixed. A
small penknife, a ring with keys in the other side-pocket,
and in the hip-pocket, fully loaded, was a small automatic
pistol of Spanish manufacture. The vest pockets yielded
nothing but a stubby pencil, a petrol-lighter, a sliding
toothpick and a cheap nickel watch ; but in the inside
pocket of the coat he discovered a wallet, one side of
which was stuffed with papers, whilst the other held
paper money, again of two nations.

He began to examine the papers. There were letters—
a hurried glance at which told him they had no bearing
on the crime. There was a folded paper out of which as
he opened it another paper fell out. The larger paper
was an advertisement of a shipping line running to
Morocco, of no importance ; but as he stooped to retrieve
the paper that had fallen to the floor he had an excited
intuition that he was to learn something, for it was plainly
a telegraph message. As he unfolded it and began to
read, his heart leaped. The message was addressed to
Baptiste Caillé at an address in Greek Street, Soho, dated
that day and despatched from the post office of Carston
Magna. The message itself was in French and of a surprising brevity—' *Aujourd'hui à deux heures et demi.*'

" To-day at two-thirty ! " he said, and looked quickly
for the signature. There was none. The sender of the
telegram had not put even an initial, and it was clear
that the receiver of it was assumed to be aware of its
source and of the event to which it referred. But what
was that event ? Scarcely had the question shaped itself
in his mind when the answer was treading on its heels :

" Maxwell's wedding ! "

It must be that, he thought. Secret as the millionaire's
preparations for his nuptials had been, there had been
someone who had been aware of them, and others—say

**this** dead man and his companion—who had waited for news of the marriage. His mind swung sharply to the airman again. Had he been one of the men who had waited for the information? Apparently he had been anxious to prevent the ceremony—had the man laying there dead also shared that desire? There were elements there which Mr. Standish found puzzling.

Granted that Baptiste Caillé and the airman had been in association, why, arriving after the ceremony had taken place, had they delayed so long in seeking an interview, delayed in fact until somewhere near the hour when a man might be supposed to be going to his nuptial chamber? Had their desire been to prevent the consummation of the marriage, they must surely have acted at the earliest moment—hours before the time named for the dovecot rendezvous. And there had been nothing to prevent that. Less than a couple of leagues separated Carston Magna from the Abbey, and even on foot Baptiste Caillé and his friend could have covered that distance in something under two hours. It seemed that some more recondite reason had dictated the delay; but that reason was not clear.

" Blackmail ? "

That was possible. Wealthy men of Maxwell's type were always liable to the attentions of secret terrorizers, and assuming that at some time he had been in the Legion, it was a fair guess that there were things in his life that would make him a target for the shafts of those who exploit human weaknesses and follies. If——

A voice from below broke on his reflections.

" This way, constable. I'll hold the light. It's on the second floor. I expect the gentleman is there still."

Mr. Standish acted quickly. Hurriedly he thrust the letters and the shipping advertisement back into the wallet, hesitated for a second over the telegram, then impulsively thrust it into his own pocket, and restored the wallet to the place whence he had taken it.

A second later he moved towards the stairs to meet those ascending. He knew that he had done an unpardonable thing ; but he was without compunction, his passion for research making him impervious to any prickings of conscience. As a light appeared in the staircase, revealing the chauffeur's white face, he greeted the man easily :

" Ah ! You're back again ? "

" With the constable, sir."

" Good ! I was wondering if you would have the wit to carry the information of this second crime to Inspector Gaddy. . . . Here you are, constable. Another dead man and a second crime to solve. The county police are having work heaped into their hands."

" Yes, sir, where———"

" In the corner there, by that sagging perch."

Mr. Standish obligingly turned the beam of his flashlamp in the direction of the dead man, and the constable moved across the chamber. He stood regarding the body for a moment, then offered comment.

" Dead as a haddock—and shot by the look of it."

" Unquestionably."

" Was he lying like this when you found him, sir ? "

" No, constable. He was face to the wall. I moved him to make sure that life was extinct," replied Mr. Standish easily.

The constable nodded. " Right thing to do, I guess. What's your opinion, sir ? Do you think he was killed here ? "

" No. Outside. There is blood on the grass, and on one stair. I think he was shot outside the tower and that someone carried him up here."

The officer looked at the dead man with an appraising eye.

" One who carried him must have been pretty hefty, I reckon."

" Yes, a man would have to be a strong man to do the thing alone."

" Must have known his way about the place too—to think of bringing his victim here. . . . Well, I can do nothing until the inspector can spare time to come, and as I've to keep guard over the man, though he isn't likely to run away, I reckon I'll do it outside. 'Twill be more cheerful in the moonlight than sitting on the stairs with a corpse at one's shoulder."

" Much more cheerful. I myself am going back to the Abbey."

" Inspector Gaddy's got plenty on there with one mystery, and with another one here I reckon he'll have his barrowful. . . . But as you're going, sir, I'll share the light down those stairs, which in the dark are a bit awkward."

All three of them descended the stairs and moved out of the tower into the moonlit park. The constable closed the door and then looked round.

" A bit lonely here. Just the sort of place for the job that has been done, and I guess the man who did it knew that well enough."

Mr. Standish, aware of the appointment that had been made, but with no knowledge of what had happened beyond that afforded by the dead man, shared the constable's opinion. If Simon Maxwell, responding to the message on the visiting-card, had come to the tower with murder in his heart, he must have rejoiced at the opportunity afforded by the solitude and remoteness of the selected rendezvous ; and apparently he had come armed, which fact, whilst indicative of caution, was also evidence of the possibility of nefarious intention.

His mind was busy with the problem as he made his way to the house, and when he reached it, he had already resolved to keep to himself, for the time being, what he had discovered. English policemen, as he knew, were impatient of amateur interference, and inclined to resent any intrusion on their activities, so he would go his own way, working on such promising data as had already come his way. It would, he thought, be his own fault if he could not keep ahead of the official investigation.

At the Abbey he found Inspector Gaddy still interviewing the household staff, and had the luck to pick up the only piece of information any of them could afford, which was that there had been but one letter in the afternoon postal delivery which was made at about five o'clock.

Inspector Gaddy looked round. An ornate wastepaper basket stood by a desk near one of the windows. He crossed to it and picked up the first crumpled envelope on the top—of thin paper and foreign manufacture. He smoothed it out, glanced at the address, then compared the writing with that on the visiting-card.

" Same hand," he commented to Sir Stephen. " This envelope brought the card, and it was posted in Carston Magna this afternoon. That should help. If they were not natives, someone is bound to have observed them. Villagers are always curiously observant of strangers."

Garfield Standish was tempted to say that strangers had already been noticed in the vicinity, but repressed the temptation. Let the inspector find out for himself. The officer dismissed the man, then looked at Mr. Standish.

" What is this story about a dead man in the dove-tower, Mr. Standish ? " he asked a little coldly.

" A true one. There's a man there who has been shot."

Inspector Gaddy betrayed no excitement at the statement, having already heard the chauffeur's wild account of the finding of the second dead man. His tone was still austere as he asked : " How came you to make the discovery ? "

" Having read that message on the card, I went to the dove-tower out of mere curiosity." Mr. Standish spoke a little hurriedly. " Outside, the chauffeur and I noticed a splotch of blood on the grass and I took it on myself to search the tower."

" Ah ! you took it on yourself——"

" Good thing I did. There's the man there shot through

the lungs, dead, and on his hand there are tattoo marks like those on Simon Maxwell's hand, and like those on that card."

The inspector was a little startled. Face and eyes betrayed the fact, then he recovered himself, and said quietly: "You seem to be observant, Mr. Standish."

The man whom he addressed found the words a compliment.

"I've trained myself for years. But this wasn't a case for observation—but of reasoning. I had the idea the marks would be there when I looked for them, and if you want to catch the murderer of Simon Maxwell you will look for a third man with a similar tattoo mark on his left hand—for a guess, a tall, soldierly-looking man, who speaks English with a very slightly foreign flavour."

"Indeed." The inspector's eyes narrowed. He seemed to be impressed, then he spoke sternly: "Did you learn that at the dove-tower, Mr. Standish?"

Standish laughed at the other's tone, and a little triumphantly explained. "No! I learned it at Carston Magna this afternoon just after I had acted as one of the witnesses at Maxwell's wedding, when an airplane came down in a field near by, bringing the man who had come, as I guess, to stop the wedding—but had arrived too late."

"That is very interesting and tremendously important," said Inspector Gaddy quickly. "Please tell me all that happened."

Mr. Standish, in growing triumph, gave an account of the arrival of the airman, and at the officer's request described the man closely; then the inspector shot another question:

"And you say he had a tattoo mark of three black dots——"

"No. I didn't see his hands. They were gloved. What I did say was that if you want the slayer of Maxwell, you will look for that man, and I'll bet you a thousand dollars you will find the three tattooed dots."

The inspector permitted himself a dry smile. " You over-estimate the wages of a policeman if you think I can wager so large an amount, Mr. Standish."

The officer considered for a moment, and what his thoughts were Mr. Standish could not even guess. Then came a question quietly asked :

" You think that this man from the aeroplane was the one who killed the dead man in the dove-tower ? "

" Lord !  No ! "  Mr. Standish was a little contempt-uous.  " I should say Simon Maxwell knew who did that."

" H'm !  You think that because he had some cause to fear——"

" Well !  He lies there dead, and that's pretty stark evidence of something of the sort."

" Yes ! " agreed the inspector. " Yes ! . . . But mere speculation isn't of much use. I must see the widow, and learn what I can from her. You gentlemen will excuse me, and perhaps, Sir Stephen, you will remain for a little while in case I should need assistance——"

" Of course, Inspector."

The officer withdrew, and Mr. Standish, feeling under no obligation to remain, looked towards the door.

" There's a thing I want to see to——" he said a little hesitatingly.

Stephen Langford's face showed a contemptuous com-prehension. " More Sherlock Holmes' business, hey ? Queer tastes you've got, Standish, to go poking about a thing like this. Better leave Gaddy to do his own job."

" I've helped him so far——" began Mr. Standish, defensively.

Langford shrugged his shoulders.  " Seems so ; but in the end you may mess things up for him."

" Can't—with what is in my mind now."

Sir Stephen forbore further argument, and leaving the house, Standish found his sister's car and within five minutes was on the road moving at a rattling pace. Presently in the moonlight the junction lifted itself into view. As he approached it, with keen disappointment he saw that it was almost in darkness, and had a thought that it must be quite deserted, and that his journey had been in vain. But drawing nearer he glimpsed a cabin in the window of which a light gleamed. The sight of it brought new hope, and as he drew up outside the station and saw the closed door, he sounded his horn vigorously. The summons brought a sleepy porter to the door, who blinked a little wonderingly at the late caller, and then, unasked, volunteered information.

" Last train for the night has gone, sir. An' there isn't another till the newspaper train comes down at——"

" That's all right, my man," interrupted Mr. Standish crisply. " It isn't a train, but information that I want— and information that is so important that I'm willing to pay for it."

The porter wakened up at the words. " I'm your man, sir. Anything I can do——"

" When did the last train go ? "

" Two hours since, sir."

" Were there any passengers from the junction ? "

" One, sir. A gentleman who'd been in a motor accident an' was bleeding like a sheep. Young lady brought him along in a car——"

" The deuce ! "

At the interjection the porter broke off and stared at his questioner wonderingly. There was an amazed look on the other's face, and it was clear to the porter that something had startled him unutterably ; but a moment later Mr. Standish was himself again.

" I wonder if you could describe the gentleman ? "

" Easily, sir. He was one you'd notice. Tall an' straight as a lamp-post, thin-faced, with a cropped moustache, regular army style with officer written all over him."

Mr. Standish, listening, visioned the man who had descended from the aeroplane at Carston Magna and entertained no doubt of his identity with the individual whom the porter was describing. He pondered a moment, then asked another question :

" You say he had been injured in a motor accident ? "

" So the young lady said. And there wasn't any question about the injury. He limped like a lame dog, an' there was blood on the platform where he'd stood talking to the lady. Must have been in a mortal hurry to catch the train not to have stopped for first-aid, sir."

" Apparently. . . . Where did he book for ? "

" London ! "

Mr. Standish pondered again, and was aware that the man was now regarding him with a curiosity that was not altogether desirable in view of a suspicion that he himself entertained. That fact made him shy of pushing his inquiry further, and he ended his inquisition abruptly :

" Thank you. You've given me the information I wanted." He produced a Treasury note and gave it to the man, then started the engine. Just as he did so, he remembered something that in view of what he had heard seemed important, and he risked a further question.

" Did you happen to notice the number of the car ? "

" No, sir ; but come to think of it, 'twas very like the one you're in, an'——"

" It couldn't have been this," interrupted Mr. Standish with a conviction that he did not feel, but which was convincing to the porter.

" No, sir ; but 'twas the image of it—same make, I expect."

" Possibly. . . . It is a popular car. Sorry to have troubled you at this hour——"

" No trouble at all, sir. A pleasure—an' a well-paid one."

" I'm glad you think so," laughed Mr. Standish. " Good night."

He turned the car and drove quickly away ; but when well out of sight of the junction, he drew up at the side of the road, and stepping out struck a match and examined

the mat which covered the floor of the car.   It was fairly
new and clean, and by the flickering light he saw that for
which he was looking—a dark stain, on the side where a
passenger would sit.   As his eyes fell on it, he whistled
sharply :

" Phew ! "

Following that, he nodded his head, then murmured
his conviction.

" So it *was* Enid ! . . .   But, in high Heaven's name,
who was the man ? "

## CHAPTER VI

### A COMPACT

WHEN Mr. Standish met his host at breakfast next
morning, he said nothing of his midnight jaunt
to the junction ; but his ears were alert for what Sir
Stephen had to say about the double crime at Farholme
Abbey.

" Gaddy thinks it a most mysterious affair.   And so it
is, I suppose ; but to my thinking not so surprising where
a man like Simon Maxwell is concerned.   These mushroom
millionaires make enemies as they make money—by the
bushel.   Some confederate whom he cheated tried to
make him disgorge, or some desperate man whom he had
robbed took it out of him this way——"

" And the man in the dove-tower ? " interjected Mr.
Standish.

" A corker, you'd think. . . .   But in a drawer of Maxwell's desk Gaddy found a pistol, recently discharged,
with one shell missing—and there's a search going on in
the park for that missing shell at this moment, I'll wager."

" So the inspector thinks that Maxwell——"

" The rendezvous given in that fancy visiting-card you
picked up is significant.   If Simon Maxwell kept that
appointment——"

" Yes."

" But none will ever know what happened there. Dead men don't yarn, and neither the stranger nor Maxwell will unfold the tale."

" No ! Yet there's a man who knows."

" You mean the man who killed Maxwell. He will be more silent than the dead themselves. A man with the rope loose about his throat won't whisper the word that will tauten it."

" No ! " agreed the other. " That man will not whisper unless he is made."

" But who is to make him ? " countered Sir Stephen. " It is a case of first catch your hare, and by this time the hare is running wide and the scent cold."

Mr. Standish thought of the solitary passenger who had left the junction on the previous night, but kept the thought to himself. Langford had no sympathy with amateur investigators, and besides the discovery he had made was not one to shout abroad. The police would probably hear about that passenger in time ; but until then sleeping dogs might lie. But he had a question to ask his sister, and at the end of the meal he went to the telephone and, ringing up the Abbey, gave her warning of his coming, then he strolled over at his leisure. As he crossed the park he observed a couple of policemen and three other men moving here and there, obviously search-ing for something, and reflected to himself that Langford would have won his bet.

When he reached the house, he found a policeman on guard, but no sign of Inspector Gaddy. He wondered curiously where the latter was, but forbore to ask, and a moment later was ushered into the great drawing-room where his sister awaited him. An appraising glance told him that she had spent a sleepless night ; but he refrained from comment, and greeted her with cheerful dissimu-lation.

" Morning, Enid ! How is your patient ? "

An odd look came in Miss Standish's eyes.

"Garry," she said impulsively, "she puzzles me. She has not slept, but she is outwardly quiet—calm as a lily-pond and intense as fire. I don't believe she cared one bit for Maxwell, yet she has a cold passion to be revenged on the man who killed him. . . . She was making plans in the dead of night—when another woman would have been breaking her heart in horror and grief. At first I thought the shock had deranged her ; but she is as sane as you or me ; outwardly as cold as a statue, with a furnace under the coldness.

"'I will find the jackal,' she said to me in so matter-of-fact a voice that she might have been talking about a lost dog. 'It will cost money—the search ; but that is nothing, and when I have him he shall hang.'

"It made me shiver to listen to her. But she will do it if it is possible."

"And I shall help her."

"You, Garry ? You ? "

There was a note of protest in Miss Standish's voice, but her brother disregarded it.

"Why not ? I find the problem intriguing. Already I have an end or two of the threads that require to be unravelled, whilst there is at least one knot with which you can help."

Garfield Standish spoke with casual insouciance, no hint of eager curiosity in his voice, and his sister never dreamed of the thing in his mind.

"What is that ? " she asked eagerly.

"Tell me whom you drove to the junction last night ? "

A look of consternation came on the lady's face ; for a second there was a gleam of fear in her eyes ; but both passed as she asked in accents of surprise :

"What on earth do you mean, Garry ? "

Mr. Standish smiled, being very sure of his ground.

"I asked a question, Enid. I should like an answer. If you want reasons for my question, here they are.

There was a solitary passenger at the junction for the late train—a man who arrived at the station in a car driven by a lady. You had been out in your car, for a moonlight spin you said, which was rather a thin explanation. It was easy to put two and two together——"

" And make five ! " interjected Miss Standish a little sarcastically.

" No ! Four meets the need of the situation, Enid, and it is no use putting up a bluff. I have the cards. I took your car to the junction and the porter almost identified it with——"

" But how could he, if——"

" Wait. The passenger at the junction had suffered some injury. He left a little pool of blood on the platform. The explanation given was that he had been in a car accident——"

" Well, accidents are quite common."

" They are—unfortunately. But there is a thing you have overlooked. A man who, standing on a platform, left there a splotch of blood by way of a souvenir, was likely to leave similar evidence elsewhere—for example, in the car that carried him to the station."

There was a little note of triumph in his voice, and Enid Standish recognized that it was justified. Her face paled sharply. She ceased to fence.

" Garry," she said in a stammering voice, " you mean . . . that . . . that——"

" It was on the car mat. I found it. When I got back I removed the mat and cleaned it to obviate curious inquiries. . . . Now, Enid, who was the man ? "

His tone stung his sister. Her eyes flashed a little, and there was a touch of temper in her answer.

" Garry, I won't tell you. He didn't do what you are thinking. That I will swear. He . . . he just couldn't."

" ' I have not found so great faith——' " Mr. Standish broke off the quotation and laughed a little harshly. " You haven't heard everything. I got the man's description from the porter—who is an observant fellow. The man you drove was the man who yester-afternoon came to Carston Magna in an aeroplane, at a guess, to stop Simon Maxwell's wedding."

" Oh . . . no ! "

" Haven't a doubt of it. And there's another thing. He left blood on the junction platform and in your Whippet——"

" That accident——"

" With a sword." Mr. Standish almost chuckled. " You are forgetting, Enid. There was blood upon Maxwell's sword-point, which means that he'd pinked the man who killed him."

" But I *saw* the accident. He was hit by a car—knocked into the ditch. It was during the raid, when I was waiting at the edge of the wood. He was running across the road——" She checked herself as she caught the exulting gleam in her brother's eyes, and the man emphasized her admission.

" Across the road ! That is Farholme property. He was coming from the direction of the abbey——"

" Oh ! " broke in his sister indignantly, " you twist everything, Garry. I tell you he couldn't have done so foul a thing. I know him, you don't. Besides, there was another man whom I saw first. He was running down the road——"

" Another ! "

Standish's amazement was almost ludicrous. He stared at his sister incredulously. Then he broke out.

" But there couldn't have been. As I make it there were two men in the business, and one of them—that fellow in the dove-tower—almost certainly died before Simon Maxwell ; whilst the second was the man from the 'plane whom you——" He stopped suddenly, then grasped at an explanation of her statement. " Enid, it won't wash. You want to save that fellow, but a lie——"

" It is the truth. There was another man. I saw him

quite plainly running down the road. He jumped into the hedge out of the way of the car which knocked the other down."

Her simplicity and earnestness were convincing, and realizing that she was speaking the truth, her brother stood for a moment, staring with eyes that indexed astonishment and perplexity. His eyes narrowed, his brow creased in an effort of thought, he gnawed at his underlip, unable to find an explanation of this new complication, then he asked a quick question :

" Did you see or hear anything else—anything unusual, I mean ? "

" Yes ! A long time before I saw either of the two men I heard a shot and a dreadful cry."

Garfield Standish jumped to an explanation immediately. " Shot that killed the man in the dove-tower, I expect, and the cry you heard was his. . . . But if he were innocent I can't fit your man in, and if there were three men in the business my deductions are all abroad—and I'll swear they aren't." He paused a moment, then said tentatively :

" If you would tell me the name of the man who——"

" I shall never do that ! " answered his sister firmly.

Standish was annoyed by her stubbornness, and broke out vehemently : " But, by Heaven, I'll find him if I have to range the world. And I'll get him——"

The opening of a door behind him checked the words. He swung round to see Cornelia Maxwell entering the room. Her wonderful face was very pale, there were rings under her dark eyes, but they were burning.

" Who is it you will find, Mr. Standish ? " she asked quickly.

" The man who killed Simon Maxwell last night," he answered tersely.

The woman was transfigured at his words. Her pale cheeks glowed with sudden colour, and in the dark eyes came a stormy light.

" You will do that ? " she cried.   " You will bring him
to the rope ? "

She spoke in a ringing voice.  There was an almost
fanatical look upon her face.  Her gaze directed at Mr.
Standish seemed to burn him.  For a moment he stood
dumb, appalled at the depth of vengeful passion they
revealed, marvelling at the fierceness of her emotion.  As
he stood without speaking, she stamped her foot, impatient for his answer, and jerked a shapely hand in a
gesture that was well known to the patrons of the picture-
halls, though now it was utterly real, expressing her
tempestuous nature.

" You will do that ? " she demanded tensely.  " You
will do it ? "

" Yes ! " answered the man simply.

" Then we shall work together—for I shall live for it.
The man who struck Simon that foul blow shall pay with
his life.  I swear it now in the daylight, as I swore it in
the night when I thought of him dead."

Enid Standish, watching and hearing her, shivered, and
had a sudden sharp fear for Jeff Warborough.

Standing there, though words and gestures were of the
theatre, Cornelia Maxwell was intensely earnest, and to
Enid appeared as a tragic Nemesis.  She recalled her own
expressed conviction that the actress had not loved Maxwell and now found occasion to revise it.  Such passion as
the woman betrayed could have its spring only in that other
emotion which, beyond even the hate that now swayed
her, was the most powerful in life.  Appalled, she glanced
from the actress to her brother—to be astonished anew.

Garfield Standish stood there regarding the woman with
a strange, intense gaze.  There was a light in his eyes
which his sister had never seen there before, to which her
feminine intuition instantly found an explanation.  The
woman had stirred the deeps in him, set him afire ; in a
single flashing moment bound him to her.  Then the man
spoke.

"Together!" He laughed like a tipsy man, and repeated himself, "Together." Then he added with conviction: "We shall not fail, madame. Already I am a lap or two ahead of the police."

"Police!" The actress shrugged her fine shoulders. "Those men! They have no imagination for an affair like this. They look for finger-prints, for what they call clues, for small links out of which to make a chain. They ask endless questions and probe into empty corners. They search Simon's files for threatening letters—— Fools! As if such a man as Simon would hoard trash. . . . 'Blackmail!' they whisper. But behind Simon's death there is more than that. The man whom he fought with a sword was no common man to escape with his life. An assassin—certainly, but no mere Apache. And the secret lies somewhere in Simon's life, not in the room where he died, nor in the dove-tower where they found that other man. I have thought—God, how I have thought!—in the night. And you and I will find the secret that will lead us to the man who shall be hanged. Presently we will talk——"

"And I shall have something to tell you," broke in Mr. Standish a little exultantly.

"I know. I have heard of the man whom you saw— the man who came to Carston Magna in an aeroplane. The inspector spoke to me of him, asked me if I knew him." She broke off. For a second a slight frown deepened above her wonderful eyes. Then she resumed, a little sharp note in her voice: "You were the one who saw him. . . . You think he came here to prevent my marriage with Simon?"

"I am sure of it," answered Standish with conviction.

The woman made a gesture expressive of puzzled helplessness.

"But I can think of none who could do so with reason."

"The reason may not have lain with you."

"With Simon, you think. . . . That is possible. A

man who climbs to power makes steps of his enemies, and one who has lived hard has had experiences. But "—she checked, hesitated, then a challenging note came in her voice—" But there was no other woman in Simon's life ? "

" I have heard of none," answered Standish suavely.

" Yet that man— And that other one, whom they think Simon shot— Steady, my friend," she said coolly, as Standish made a startled movement. " I also think so. And I have no pity for the man who came here to bait my husband on his wedding-night. Whoever he was, he died as he deserved, as that other unknown one shall die. . . . In two days after the funeral you will come and see me and we will talk. . . . You will come ? "

" I will come."

" Then I have a friend in the world ! "

She made a gesture of farewell, and moving swiftly passed from the room, closing the door behind her. For a brief time neither of the pair whom she had left either moved or spoke, then Enid Standish broke the silence with a quivering whisper.

" Garry . . . you will not do what . . . what she wants ? "

" Why not ? " he demanded harshly.

" Oh—she is distraught with hate. You can see it in her eyes, hear it in her voice."

" Distraught, possibly. But you would not say that I——"

" You also," she whispered. " I saw your eyes just now when you looked at her. Garry, it is madness. You must go away. Leave the thing alone. Let the police do their own work. There can be nothing but trouble in it for you—no happiness. Cornelia Maxwell is not for you——"

" She's for the man who wins her as Maxwell did . . . and just now the way to do that is to serve her, and serve with her," answered Standish quickly. " The man who serves her hate can win her love as I mean to——"

" It is crass folly ! " cried his sister.

" It is the way to the heart of such a woman as Cornelia,"
countered Standish. " She's no puling miss, as I'll wager
Simon Maxwell knew. There's fire in her. Now it is fed
by hate, but when that is burnt out——"

" Garry, you are a besotted fool ! "

" With work to do," he laughed harshly. " I wouldn't
let loose of it for a kingdom. I can understand your
objection. That man whom you helped to get away is
involved. You are afraid of him. You think that he is
in danger——"

" No ! "

" Then tell me his name."

" No ! "

" But I shall learn it. I shall get on his track. I shall
follow him. I know already where to begin to look for
him."

" You know already ? "

Enid Standish was appalled. Not for a moment did
she doubt his statement. The exultation in his voice was
convincing ; and in that moment she would have given
much for knowledge of Jeff Warborough's whereabouts,
that she might send him warning.

" Yes ! I've a whole handful of clues, and in a week I
fancy they'll take me out of England." He laughed a
little triumphantly and added : " So if you're inclined to
travel you had better collect your frocks—light stuff, for
a warm climate, preferably. . . . But now you must excuse me, Enid. There are things I want to see to."

He left her without more ado, and going from the house
met Inspector Gaddy face to face. The officer's manner
was a little stiff and formal. Quite plainly he did not
approve of the amateur, but Standish was genial.

" Good morning, Inspector. You are about early and
busy as the devil in a whirlwind, by all accounts. Have
you learned anything about the man I found in the dove-
tower last night—or is it too soon to hope for news about
him ? "

" Nothing whatever ! " replied the inspector distantly.

Mr. Standish could not resist a temptation to crow. He laughed a little condescendingly.

" Then I can give you news."

" News ! About that man ? "

The inspector's eyes grew keen, but his face expressed his doubts.

" Yes." The other laughed again and whistled a few bars, then asked cheerfully : " Do you know that air, Inspector ? "

The officer shook his head, and Mr. Standish explained.

" It was whistled by two men who marched up the road last night, strangers, I fancy ; and it is the march of the French Foreign Legion. They were keeping step with it, and as you can judge it is an admirable song to help men along the road."

He began to hum it, the whilst he watched the inspector with amused eyes.

" *Tiens voila du boudin ! Voila du boudin ! Voila du boudin !*
*Pour les Alsaciens, les Suisses et les Lorrains——*"

The inspector lost patience. " What on earth are you getting at, Mr. Standish ? "

" Surely it is clear. Two men marched this way last night whistling that crashing march. It is a fair presumption that they were accustomed to move to its lilt, and that they were strangers is something more than a presumption, for I imagine you might comb this countryside without finding a native who had served in the Desert Legion. And that man in the dove-tower to my eyes was of Latin race, he had the parchment look of a man who has lived between burning suns and hot sands——"

" Great Harry," cried the inspector, his reserve forgotten, " this is important. How do you know about those men ? "

" I had the news of them from Maxwell's chauffeur who had heard the march whilst serving in France. It struck

F

him as a little odd that two men should whistle it here in
Dorset——"

" Odd ! It is significant ! But it explains nothing.
What had Simon Maxwell to do with two men who had
served in the Legion ? You do not find millionaires in
that regiment of the damned."

Mr. Standish did not reveal his suspicion that Maxwell
had served there. He had made his little crow, and he
let it remain at that. He shook his head.

" That is true ; and it is hard to answer your conun-
drum, Inspector. But——"

He broke off as he caught sight of a burly policeman
hurrying across the lawn, with another officer and two or
three men tailing out behind him.

" Here is someone who brings you news, or I am mistaken, Inspector Gaddy."

The inspector swung round, and as he did so the leading
constable waved a hand, triumphantly.

" And the news is interesting," commented Standish
with a smile. A moment later he knew that he was right,
for the leading policeman, eager to announce his errand,
cried triumphantly :

" Found it, sir."

Garfield Standish smiled to himself. He did not inquire
what it was the constable had found. There was no need,
for it was easy to guess ; and a moment later, as the
policeman passed a small brass cylinder to the inspector,
he knew that he had guessed right.

" Where did you find it, Wilson ? "

" In some rhododendron bushes half-way between the
dove-tower and the abbey."

" Good ! " The inspector considered the thing in his
hand, then nodded his head. " It should clear up one
mystery, at any rate. . . . Excuse me, Mr. Standish,
I must go into the house."

He turned abruptly and walked towards the steps,
leaving the other alone with the constable.

" A lucky find, officer," said Mr. Standish genially.
" If that and the pistol mate——"

" There's no doubt of that, I reckon," interrupted the
officer, " an' it don't need no Solomon to put two an' two
together. If Mr. Simon Maxwell wasn't already dead,
he'd have to scrape the skin off him to get by the gallows."

Garfield Standish agreed with him, but forbore direct
comment.

" A rum go, but it's no business of mine ! " Then
carelessly he shot a question. " Anything been heard of
the second man, who it is supposed was with that man
in the tower, and who no doubt killed Mr. Maxwell ? "

" Nothing, sir. And nothing ever will be. Unless the
man's a born fool he's hopping it for a foreign strand as
fast as he can, I reckon."

Mr. Standish thought that was extremely likely and
said so, and the constable expanded a little more.

" It's a queer affair. Seems some fellow dropped out
of the skies at Carston yesterday, to stop the wedding, and
nobody knows how he got wind of it at all, for it was meant
to be secret."

" Yes, that is a little mysterious. I am the man who
saw the airman and reported the fact to Inspector Gaddy."

" I know that, sir." The constable ruminated for a
moment, then he spoke again. " There's an idea that a
French maid who'd been doing temporary duty passed the
word, madame's own maid having been ill. She may have
got hold of it—and she left for London yesterday morning."

" That is possible," agreed Mr. Standish, the mild
interest he betrayed masking one that was intense and
vivid. Here was the explanation of the filched telegram
in his letter-case. And the French maid had gone to
London, no doubt to that address in Greek Street, where
her telegram had found the unfortunate Baptiste Caillé.
That thought gave him something of a jolt ; and when
he moved on, his mind was absorbed with it. He named
himself for a dolt for not having thought of that end of

the stick.   In Soho he might possibly come in touch with
the dead man's associates—perhaps face to face with the
man of the aeroplane, for whom somehow he had a feeling
that almost amounted to hatred, and for which in no way
could he account.

As he walked on, he made a sudden resolve to go to
Town.   There, if the birds had not already flown, there
might be a swift *dénouement* of the mysterious affair at
Farholme Abbey ; and in any case he would once more
be ahead of Inspector Gaddy, who apparently had not yet
learned anything of the telegram which the French maid
had almost certainly despatched.   Arrived at his host's
house he consulted a time-table, wrote a couple of notes,
one for his host and one for Cornelia Maxwell, giving instructions that the last was to be sent by hand, and then
drove to the junction, catching a connecting train with
some minutes to spare.   It was not, however, until he was
in the express hurrying to Town that a thought occurred
to him which caused him to reflect that perhaps he had
been a little precipitate in making the journey.   The
maid had left Farholme yesterday morning.   Suppose the
telegram to Baptiste Caillé had been no more than a mere
announcement of her return and the hour given the time
of her arrival in London ?   It was most natural that she
should send such a telegram, and the message might be
the most innocent in the world.

That consideration troubled him considerably during
the journey to Town, but presently he found other con-
siderations which outweighed it utterly.   First the message
had been sent to a man who, almost certainly, had died
at the hands of Simon Maxwell, which, given that the
maid was the sender of the telegram, proved that Caillé
and she were in close association.   That might be no more
than a coincidence—but the circumstances were heavily
against that.   Further, whilst the hour mentioned might
be the mere announcement of the time of the sender's
arrival, it was most certainly the time fixed for the Max-

well-Darracombe wedding. Again mere coincidence might
be the explanation, and again the circumstances were
weighted against the possibility.

"No!" he told himself with conviction. "It just can't
be the pre-journey message. The other thing is behind
it as sure as a gun."

And when, on arrival, he walked down the taxi-rank
and, securing his cab, gave instructions to the man to
take him to Soho, his heart was beating with excitement,
and his blood running like that of a hunter in the heat
of the chase with the kill already in sight.

## CHAPTER VII

### IN GREEK STREET

SET down according to instructions at the corner of
Greek Street, Mr. Standish strolled slowly down the
side-walk, considering each restaurant in turn, until he
came to the address he wanted. Like its neighbours it
proved to be an eating-house, though as there was a
tariff of rooms, it was, it seemed, also a private hotel,
probably of the discreet order not unknown in the district. It displayed a framed menu on one of the door-
posts, and putting on his horn-rimmed goggles, Mr.
Standish read the list of dishes available with an air
that might have been that of a gourmet, or again that
of a man who desires full value for his money.

Whilst he so stood a client passed out, affording him a
brief glimpse of the interior. It looked harmless enough
—the usual scattering of small tables and chairs, with a
couple of waiters at their ease for the moment, and perhaps half a dozen customers. He waited a moment or
two longer, then pushing open the swing door he passed
inside. As he did so one of the waiters, galvanized into
action, hurried forward and relieved him of hat and coat,
and a second later put a menu in his hands.

It was long past the usual hour, but Mr. Standish, having had the misfortune to travel by a train that had no restaurant car, was still without lunch, and proceeded to order a fairly lengthy one to match his appetite, and to give himself ample time to take his bearings and examine such people as were in sight.

The waiters, as he saw at a glance, were Italians. Four people sitting at a table half-way up the room were English of the English, a pair at another were of Jewish race and obviously lovers; whilst the woman seated near the window, watching the street through the curtain, might have been Spanish, but from the chic way she wore her clothes and held herself, was as likely to be French as not.

To Mr. Standish she was the only interesting person in the room. The others were most certainly what they seemed, but this woman with her eyes on the street might be one of those whom he sought—the sender of the telegram which had taken Baptiste Caillé to his death. There was a coffee-pot and cup and saucer on the table before her, and a lighted cigarette was between the first fingers of the left hand which rested upon the table; but neither the coffee nor the cigarette seemed to interest her. She kept her eyes steadily on the street, which at that hour afforded little to arrest attention; and it was easy to guess that she expected someone and was on the look out. As the time passed, a little frown deepened above her eyes; and once or twice she made nervous movements as if she were losing patience. The lovers departed; five minutes later the English group also left; but still the woman watched the street with manifest anxiety.

Mr. Standish's lunch came to an end. He ordered coffee and lit a cigarette, continuing to watch the woman whilst he revolved plans of procedure. Having arrived at this place, he could not sit there for ever alert, watchful, merely waiting for something to turn up; and finally

he decided to approach the waiter.   He wrote a name on
the back of the menu, took a ten-shilling note from his
wallet, and set it beside the card, then signalled to the
waiter, who hurried to him, his eyes on the Treasury note.

Mr. Standish indicated the name he had written, and
spoke in low tones :

" Tell me if that gentleman is here still, waiter."

Since the name he had written was that of Baptiste
Caillé, who lay dead at Farholme, he could have had little
doubt of the answer, yet waited it with some interest,
realizing that the answer might reveal whether the identity
of the dead man in the dove-tower had been discovered
by the police.

He watched the man closely whilst he read the name,
but was able to detect no sign of unusual interest.

" No, m'sieur.   He left yesterday, but was hoping
shortly to return."

Mr. Standish's face registered disappointment—for the
waiter's eyes, then he spoke quickly as one who has yet a
hope left him.

" But his friend is here—perhaps ? "

The waiter shook his head.   " M'sieur Steinmann accompanied the other."

Again the questioner's face indicated his disappointment, but he shrugged his shoulders.

" One has no luck," he said, and pushed the note
towards the waiter, who gathered it up greedily, and
presently left the room, his place being taken by
another man, who walked about flicking the flies with the
napkin he carried.

Mr. Standish gave himself to reflection again.   He had
learned a name that might be useful or not, but it seemed
more than a little doubtful if he would learn anything else.
If M. Steinmann were the second man who had been at
Farholme, as seemed likely, it was possible that he would
not return to Greek Street at all, in which case to linger
in Town was to waste time.   His eyes went again to the

waiting woman.   She was still watching the street and
there was a strained look upon her face.   Was Steinmann
the one whose coming she awaited, or was she merely
watching for some laggard lover who——

" Ah ! "

The woman had moved suddenly, and almost simultane-
ously a taxi drew up in the street.   A second later a look
of relief came on the woman's face, and Mr. Standish
knew that the one for whom she had waited so long had
arrived.   Lighting a fresh cigarette, he picked up a newspaper, hastily unfolded it, and over the top watched the
swing door.   It opened sharply, admitting a burly-
figured man, on whose face were the sabre scars which
were the hall-marks of one who in his youth had studied
at some German university—a man of forty, with close-
cropped hair, a moustache which aped that of William of
Prussia, and keen eyes, much puckered at the corners.

Mr. Standish suffered a sharp disappointment.   He had
expected the man from the airplane, but here was one
who was a complete stranger.   Then he remembered his
sister's statement about the second man whom she had
seen, and watched carefully.

Was he Steinmann ?   He could not guess.   To the waiter
at any rate he was a stranger, for as he handed the menu
to the new-comer he gave him no sort of greeting.   On his
part the customer dropped the card without looking at it.

" Café," he snapped, and stared round the room.

For one moment his keen eyes rested on Mr. Standish
appraisingly, then he looked away, leaned back in his
chair, produced a cheroot and lit it.   The woman at his
side, clearly in a twitter of impatience, asked a question,
whisperingly.   Mr. Standish could not catch the words,
but the answer was like a miniature explosion.

" Mort ! "

The woman gave a little cry of dismay and stared at
her companion incredulously.   Then apparently she asked
a further question to which the man replied briefly, but

in a whisper so low that Mr. Standish's straining ears were baffled, though he would have given worlds to hear what the man was saying. His eyes, however, informed him of the woman's growing consternation, and whilst there followed a rapid whispered interchange of question and answer, he watched the woman's face, and asked himself who it was that was dead. Baptiste Caillé ? That was likely, but it was not a fact on which he could presume. He cast about for some way of finding the truth, but drew a blank ; and, in his absorption, unaware of the fact, sat in a strained, listening attitude, hoping for some word that would be like the flash of revelation.

The word, however, was not granted him. There was an abrupt cessation of the whispering, and he realized suddenly that the man was staring at him with fixed gaze. Their eyes met, and Mr. Standish hastily averted his, and as coolly as he could lit a fresh cigarette, uncomfortably aware that the man was still staring at him with a fixed gaze that amounted to rudeness. Did the fellow suspect him of listening ? Had he seen him last night at Farholme and recognized him now ? Or if he were the second man whom Enid had seen, and aware of what had befallen Baptiste, was he merely suspicious, seeing in every stranger a policeman ?

He could not guess, but he was conscious of relief when the man turned his eyes elsewhere. His relief, however, was but short-lived, for he heard the man give a sharp exclamation :

" *Tiens !* "

Mr. Standish shot a furtive glance in the direction of the speaker. The man had the menu card in his hands and was staring at it with blazing eyes. He looked down quickly. The card which had been on his own table had gone, doubtless removed by the waiter after answering his question. In a flash he understood what was interesting the man. By some mischance that particular menu card had been presented to him, and he had seen the name written upon it. The watcher had not the least doubt of it ; and as he continued his furtive observation, he saw the man point to something on the card, directing the woman's attention to it, and then most obviously he asked a question.

" *Non !* " answered the woman with a shake of her head. Still holding the card, her companion summoned the waiter.

" *Garçon !* "

The waiter hurried to him and Mr. Standish caught the question, asked though it was in a low voice, and in French.

" Who wrote that name ? "

The waiter shook his head. " I do not know, m'sieur."

The man shot a suspicious glance at Standish, then rose abruptly, and addressed his companion.

" Come. It is time to go."

Mr. Standish surmised that the man was afraid, and was proposing flight. The unexpected sight of the dead Caillé's name written in a strange hand had stirred apprehensions. Plainly he suspected the reason for that name on the card, and divined that already inquiries were afoot. His haste was evidence of a guilty conscience, and Mr. Standish was hurriedly trying to evolve a plan of action, when he himself suffered a little shock which froze him into temporary immobility. The man had stretched a hand to help the lady to arise. The back of that hand was in a direct line with Mr. Standish's eyes, and plain as the pips on a card he saw three black dots.

He had not been looking for anything of the kind, but the sight of them was convincing. Here beyond question was one who had been in association with Baptiste Caillé and who possibly had been with him at Farholme last night. And the woman almost certainly was the French maid who——

The pair were already moving towards the door. They reached it and were passing through before Mr. Standish quite grasped the fact that they were in full flight. In his haste to follow them he upset the table at which he had been seated, smashing the coffee cups and saucers to smithereens, and before he reached the door he found himself confronted by a vociferous waiter. Hurriedly he searched his pocket, found a couple of florins and thrusting them in the waiter's hand continued his pursuit. He reached the street to find the man and woman standing at the kerb, a little way off, with a taxi-cab just pulling in. He fairly ran towards them. The woman had entered the cab and the man was giving the driver directions when Mr. Standish reached the place.

"Say," he began breathlessly, "if you want to know anything about Baptiste Caillé——"

Apparently the man did not. He swung round sharply on the speaker. His eyes were blazing with fear, and there was an almost demoniacal look upon his face. Without a word he lifted a clenched hand and smote the other a brutal blow. It caught Mr. Standish squarely between the eyes, knocking him clean off his feet. His head hit the kerb with a stunning crash. A myriad stars flashed before his eyes, dazzling him with their phantom brightness, then darkness utter and profound descended upon him.

From that darkness he emerged to find himself lying on the floor of the restaurant he had so recently quitted. There was the sting of cognac in his mouth, and an unusual heaviness about his eyes, with a nasty soreness at the back of his head. He heard a voice as he opened his eyes :

"Coming to, *garçon*. He will be all right in a jiffy. No need to 'phone the doctor ; and it is possible the gentleman may not desire the police."

The voice twanged a chord in Mr. Standish's memory, which however responded only feebly, and he stared upward in an endeavour to locate the speaker. A great bump spreading from the top of the nose half-way over each eyebrow obscured his vision, and it was not until the man spoke again that he caught sight of him.

"Steady, my friend. You've suffered a knock-out,

though why and for what cause Heaven knows. Better lie still a minute or two longer. That fellow who hit you was a scientist and——"

Mr. Standish disregarded the advice. The sight of the speaker was like a shock that fairly galvanized him. He sat up in a single jerking movement, and struggled for words.

" You ? " he began, and broke off, choked by sheer excitement.

" No one else ! " laughed the man. " Seems as if you knew me, but I'll own the advantage is yours."

Mr. Standish felt his head reeling. He was still muddled by the blow, and at the same time a little incredulous of his stupendous luck. Under his rapidly swelling brows his eyes blinked as they focussed themselves upon the tall, lean-faced man who was regarding him a little quizzically. then he blurted in jerks :

" You are the man . . . of the airplane . . . at Carston Magna——"

" Dieu ! "

The word seemed wrenched from the stranger by sheer surprise. He stood looking at Mr. Standish as if trying to recall his face, then he laughed shortly as the recognition came to him.

" Ah ! " he said. " The impromptu witness at the wedding. Well, I expect you know just how damnable——"

" You . . . came back ! " broke in Mr. Standish.

There was a swift change in the other's manner. His lightness of demeanour dropped from him like a garment. Just the faintest gleam of apprehension came in his eyes ; then he asked sharply :

" Now how the deuce do you know that ? "

Mr. Standish at the moment was conscious of a new dizziness and a feeling of nausea, but he fought both back, and answered discreetly.

" I had your description from a porter at the junction."

" The devil ! "

As he made the ejaculation the stranger looked round and addressed the waiter : " *Garçon*, more brandy ! "

The waiter hurried away, then the man spoke again. " So you had my description, hey ? And you recognized me from it ? That was clever, I will own ; but if the porter gave the description, you I guess must have asked for it. . . . I wonder why ? "

" Because . . . Simon Maxwell was found murdered last night and you . . . and you——"

Mr. Standish faltered over the accusation. It was not easy to charge this lean-faced man with murder, with his keen eyes focussed in a fierce gaze. The man shrugged his shoulders, and spoke dryly :

" I understand what you would say, my friend. You think I killed Simon Maxwell. But for unforeseen circumstances you might have been further out. As it is, I assure you that you are under a misapprehension. You must look elsewhere for——"

" If you think you can bluff me like that——"

" S-s-s-h-h ! Here's the waiter."

The man turned to meet the waiter, and taking the brandy from him, gave a curt order :

" Call a taxi for the gentleman."

Mr. Standish heard the order, and as the stranger approached him with the brandy, staggered to his feet. The action brought again the dizzy feeling that he had experienced and forced him to clutch at a table for support, but he managed to stutter :

" If you imagine you're going to get rid of me so easily ——"

" I don't," the other interrupted with a laugh. " Drink this brandy, man ; it will brace you. Don't worry about me. I want a little talk with you. . . . Drink it all up. You seem to need it."

Mr. Standish took the brandy, and following the other's sage counsel drained the glass. Just as he finished the waiter returned.

" Taxi at the door, sir."

" Thank you."

The tall man turned to the still shaking Standish, and spoke quickly.

" Are you ready ?  Can I give you a shoulder or an arm ? "

Mr. Standish, still clinging to the table and almost sick with dizziness, was yet able to think.  If this man chose to take his departure he was in no condition to prevent him, and in the circumstances it was not likely that the waiter, if called upon, would intervene.  It would be as well to keep in touch with the man until he himself was in a condition to act ; but it would not be wise to commit himself entirely to the other's hands.

" You want to talk. . . . So do I.  But I choose the place——"

" Of course," the man laughed.

" Then we'll go to the Savoy.  I've a room reserved there."

" The Savoy !  Capital ! . . . Take my arm.  Waiter, give the gentleman an arm on the other side."

The waiter hurried to help, and between the two Mr. Standish was conducted to the taxi, the driver of which scarcely suppressed a grin at the sight of him.  He was helped into a corner, the stranger tipped the waiter, and with the door of the taxi open ready for his entrance, proceeded to give the driver directions.

" The Savoy," he said loudly, and then slid a Treasury note into the driver's hand ; adding, " He's drunk as an owl.  Don't stop, if he bangs the glass.  Keep going."

" Yessir ! "

The driver gave a grin of complete understanding, and the stranger moved to the door.  Mr. Standish at that precise moment was overcome by a wave of dizziness and closed his eyes.

" Right you are ! "

The stranger gave the signal, and the door closed with

a snap. The taxi was moving when Mr. Standish opened his eyes again, to find himself alone. He had a brief glimpse of the stranger with smiling face and hand raised in a mocking salute—a glimpse and no more, for the taxi quickly gathered speed. He dragged himself out of the seat to the window. It was closed and it stuck in some way so that he could not open it. Desperately he tapped upon the glass to attract the driver's attention ; but, faithful to his instructions, that worthy kept right on. He caught sight of a speaking tube, and bawled down it angrily, but his Jehu was apparently deaf and sat at his wheel stolid as a rock. The taxi sped along, and in desperation its passenger loosed the catch and opened the door a foot or so, but he was in no condition for a flying leap, and his nerve failed him. He closed the door and tapped the glass behind the driver's back, anew ; all vainly. His taxi had luck. It was not held up at a single crossing, and in a remarkable short time it reached the Savoy. Mindful of the condition of his passenger, the taxi-driver opened the door, and prepared to assist him to alight. He was met by such fuming abuse that he fell back a little, and Mr. Standish descended unaided.

" Five shillings, sir ! " The driver held out his hand. Mr. Standish stormed. " You infernal fool ! Why didn't you stop when I signalled ? I'll see you in perdition before I——"

A little crowd was gathering, attracted by the passenger's eloquence. A policeman thrust his way through.

" Here, what's this ? " he demanded.

" Gentleman's drunk an' refuses to pay the fare," explained the driver tersely.

The officer turned his attention to Mr. Standish, whose appearance certainly warranted the driver's description of his condition. There was a stern look in his eye, albeit his tact was to the fore.

" It's a pound fine an' costs for a drunk an' disorderly or seven days, an' that's dearer than a five-shilling fare, besides there's the publicity an' the nasty remarks of the magistrate. Better pay an' be done with it, sir."

Mr. Standish had visions of himself in the dock and was suddenly aware of the weakness of his position. To explain all that was behind his misadventure would be impossible, and a truncated version of events would be little more than a confirmation of his guilt. He shuddered at the visioned possibilities, and taking the easiest way paid with a ten-shilling note and did not wait for the change. Yearning for refuge from laughing eyes, he moved towards the door of the hotel. A uniformed porter barred his way, considering him superciliously, but recognized the doubtful visitor in time.

" Mr. Standish ! " he cried.

" It's all right, Henry," said Mr. Standish, fearful of another scene. " I've been assaulted by a low ruffian, and want to rest. Call another taxi and keep it waiting. I shall be out in a few minutes."

And boiling with wrath and. chagrin he passed the portals of the great caravanserai and sought his reserved room to repair damages as best he could.

## CHAPTER VIII

### GRANDPÈRE JACQUES

EXACTLY forty minutes later, Mr. Standish's second taxi drew up outside the restaurant in Greek Street, and without delay but with little hope to sustain him, he passed inside. But for the solitary waiter laying tables apparently for the evening meal, the place was empty. A look of surprise came on the man's face as he recognized the visitor, but following the instincts of his tribe, he indicated a table and began to pull out a chair.

" Dolt ! " thought Mr. Standish, and made no move towards the chair.

" I want to ask you something, waiter."

" Yes, sir ! "

" That man who was here just now—the tall man, I mean who was helping me when I was senseless—is he here still ? "

" No, sir ! He did not come back after seeing you away."

Mr. Standish was disappointed but not surprised, and asked his next question :

" You know him possibly ? Perhaps he is a regular client here ? "

The waiter shook his head. " Not a regular one, sir, or I should know it. He is not one to be overlooked or to go unnoticed. May have been here before, but I was not on duty when he came."

Recognizing that from the waiter there was nothing to be learned about the stranger who had befriended and evaded him so coolly, Mr. Standish stood considering for a moment or two, then asked tentatively :

" You saw the man who struck me—the man who was with that woman, I mean ? "

" Yes, sir."

" Do you know him ? "

" Only by name, which is Steinmann. He's been here once or twice lately to see a French gentleman who is staying here."

" Monsieur Caillé, I suppose ? "

" Yes, sir."

" And the woman. Is she a stranger ? "

" I've never seen her before," replied the man ; then his curiosity got the upper hand. " Is there something crooked about them, sir ? That Caillé struck me as being a queer sort of fish."

" If you are a diligent student of the newspapers, you will probably read something quite startling about Caillé in the next few days," answered Mr. Standish, and turning on his heel, went out to his waiting taxi, and gave instructions for the man to take him to Waterloo.

G

He had almost two hours to wait for a train, and that time and part of the journey down he spent in reading the various evening newspaper accounts of the double tragedy at Farholme and in carefully comparing them. Not one of them mentioned the name of the man found in the dove-tower, from which he deduced that so far the police had not discovered it ; and whilst the accounts were lurid and speculated rather wildly about the two-fold mystery, there was nothing in them that any way added to his knowledge.

Assured of that he turned from the news-sheets, and began to consider the events of the day. One thing, and one thing only, he had discovered, and that was the name of the associate of Baptiste Caillé, who was another of the three black dots fraternity. Was the tall airman also of the confederacy ? He did not know, but he had a strong suspicion that he was ; and found an explanation of the man's helpful action in succouring him in the fellow's desire to discover how much he knew. He remembered the way in which the man had evaded him, his ironical salute at parting, and hated him more than ever. It was a little puzzling to fit the man in with Steinmann and the dead Caillé, but he entertained no doubt that he had played a part in the tragedy at Farholme. The facts, as they appeared to him, were too conclusive for any other suppositions.

" If only Enid would tell what she knows," he thought. But his sister would not tell. When he approached her again on the matter, she was as secret as an oyster. She would tell him nothing about the tall stranger ; and as Inspector Gaddy could learn nothing about the airman, both of them were up against a blank wall. But much reflection pointed to another line of investigation, to which presently his mind turned steadily.

Cornelia Maxwell had declared in her passion that the secret of the tragedy lay not at Farholme, but in something in her husband's past life, and as he reflected he

shared her conviction, and finally, four days after Maxwell's funeral, he sought out the window.  She wore no
trappings of mourning.  Her face was still pale, and the
evidence of care was written there and in the circles
under her eyes, but the eyes themselves kindled at the
sight of him.

"My friend, you have brought me news ? "

"No.  I have come for information.  Tell me, do you
know if Maxwell ever served in the Foreign Legion ? "

The actress's eyes glowed with eager light at the
question.

"Ah ! " she cried.  "Now I know you are in the way,
for Simon was in the Legion as a sergeant.  We found
his discharge papers in his old name with his medals in
his safe yesterday.  How did you discover the fact ? "

"I had no knowledge.  It was a long shot," answered
Mr. Standish, and forthwith detailed the various things
which had led him to the idea.  When he had finished
the lady spoke again with tense conviction :

"It is there, in the past, that the explanation lies.  In
Algiers—not at Farholme."

"So I think. . . . I shall leave the police to their
investigations here, and I shall go to Algiers."

"And I also ! " answered the woman resolutely.  "As
soon as I can leave this place, which already I hate.  But,
alas ! that may be some time yet.  The lawyers and the
police both set demands on me."

"But I can go at once to serve you," answered Mr.
Standish with the air of a knight-errant.  "In five days,
at the most, I can be in Africa, and in six I may have my
hand on the secret."

"Go," said the lady impetuously.  "I shall be ever in
your debt for what you do.  Telegraph your address.
When these lawyers have finished, I will take the air like
a bird and join you."

There was a flame of eagerness in the slumbrous eyes,
and noting it, Garfield Standish found in her promise a

good augury.   On the morrow, without so much as a hint
to his sister, he took his way south, and five days later,
at Oran he entered a train for Sidi-bel-Abbès, the headquarters of the Legion, and after a crawl of eighty miles
was decanted at his destination, more than a little weary.
He engaged a room at the Hôtel d'Oran, and having dined
strolled forth to the boulevard and found a café on the
Place Sadi Carnot, where the electric lights round the
bandstand of the Foreign Legion glared a tawdry challenge to the lustrous stars.   The band was playing, and,
listening indifferently to the music, he watched the variegated crowd move to and fro.   Half the tribes of Africa
and most of the nations of Europe seemed to have fore-
gathered there ; and the talk was that of Babel after the
tongues of men had been stricken with confusion.   Black
and white, full-blooded negroes, Arabs of the town and
fierce-eyed men of the desert, Algerian Jews, Armenian
and Greek traders, Spanish and French civilians and their
women folk, with a scattering of curious tourists, moved to
and fro, a motley of races, compelling interest and stirring
curiosity.

But Mr. Standish's interest in these was of the slightest.
The soldiers who thronged the place held his eyes—Spahis,
Zouaves, Chasseurs d'Afrique and les légionnaires.   Par-
ticularly he was interested in these last, wondering if any
one of them had the secret that he sought ; and how
he might acquaint himself with it.   As he watched them,
he was assailed by a feeling of hopelessness.   Hundreds
strolled by him, and it seemed to him that to pick out of
them the one man he wanted was the three-card trick with
the odds against ' finding the lady ' enormously multiplied.

Also he remembered an omission which increased the
difficulty of his task greatly.   He had forgotten to ask
the date on Maxwell's discharge papers ; and so was without any indication of the time that had elapsed since he
had strolled in this Place with his fellow légionnaires.
His mind was busy with this when a young soldier of

the first regiment strolled by, with a longing glance at the bottle by the civilian's elbow.    Mr. Standish marked the glance, remembered that the magnificent pay of a legionary was one sou a day, which does not go very far towards gratifying the palate even where wine is cheap, and on a sudden impulse he signalled to the man.

The latter halted as smartly as if his officer had given the order ; then, as the signal was repeated, marched quickly to the table.    Mr. Standish indicated a chair.

"You will perhaps share the bottle with me ? " he said affably in French.

" It will be an honour, m'sieur," replied the soldier.

Mr. Standish called for a glass, and himself poured out the wine ; then offered his guest a cigar, and whilst the other was lighting it thought rapidly.    It must have been at least several years since Simon Maxwell had taken his discharge.    The man on the other side of the table was young.    He had been in the Legion perhaps a couple of years, and he could not have known Maxwell personally, but he might know someone who had.

" You are new to the Legion ? " he asked with genial curiosity.

" One year's service, m'sieur."

Mr. Standish smiled.    " One guessed so much.    But there are men who have been many years in the regiment of the desert, are there not ? "

The soldier laughed.    " Most of them are dead, m'sieur. The sands get the old ones in the end.    But one or two survive as punishment for their sins.    There is Grandpère Jacques, of the first regiment, who has been with it more years than men remember——"

" An interesting man, no doubt, with stories to tell, I'll warrant.    Where is he to be found ? "

The legionary laughed again.    " At this hour he is at the Café Voison, drinking. Always he consumes the sour wine and sits watching like a spider for one who

will pay for yet another bottle, for which he will lie till
the cows come home."

"A veteran, with memories of old Touareg days, hey?
I should like to stand him a bottle."

"There will be no difficulty," the young soldier grinned,
"and if m'sieur makes it two bottles the talks will be
fantastic, for Grandpère Jacques has the imagination—a
true romantic!"

Mr. Standish laughed and pushed the bottle across the
table.

"Drink up the wine, my friend, and you shall
take me to the Café Voison, and to Grandpère Jacques."

The soldier emptied the bottle with avidity; then, in
his capacity as guide, led Mr. Standish down the great
boulevard, and presently into a narrow street, which it
seemed was the way to the true romance. The street
was dark and odorous, but by no means a deserted
thoroughfare. Though the stars blazed whitely in the
dark blue sky overhead, the stalls on either side still
offered strange wares for sale, and customers chaffered
for the wares. Many foot-passengers drifted up and down,
veiled women of the East, women of the Occident who
had reached the ultimate deep; tourists going a night-
round of sights, légionnaires on the prowl for loot or gifts
that could be turned to liquor, tall Arabs and coal-black
negroes jostled each other, and at a turn in the street
from the minaret of a mosque a muezzin voiced musically
the ancient faith:

"Allah Akbar! La Allah il Allah—"

Another turn and they swung into a narrow alley with
blind buildings either side, and awakening misgivings in
Mr. Standish, who saw to it that his guard marched in
front, whilst he himself trod almost on the heels of the
other's brodquins. At the end of this narrow gut a
light appeared, and they turned the corners into a wider
thoroughfare, which in fact was a bazaar, and a little

way down it, the guide indicated a café with an awning, from which streamed a murky light.

" We arrive, m'sieur.  Behold—the Café Voison."

It had, thought Mr. Standish, on a nearer view, nothing to recommend it.  There was the usual array of iron or marble-topped tables, some tawdry Moorish lamps, a few fly-blown mirrors and at the far end what was neither more nor less than a common bar.  At one table sat two or three soldiers, at another a Spahi talked with a woman of negro race, and near the open front, with a bottle and an empty glass before him, lolled a grey-headed legionary, with fierce moustaches.  His lean face was the texture and colour of parchment, with the scar of an old wound like a white seam down his left cheek.  His grey eyebrows were as fierce as the moustache, but underneath the dark eyes had a twinkle as if the owner of them found the world a humorous place.

" Grandpère Jacques," said the guide, and indicated with a jerk the ancient warrior ; then steered Mr. Standish towards the table where he was seated.

" Grandpère," he said, " I bring you one to listen to your stories of the Legion.  He will pay for wine."

Grandpère Jacques' face wrinkled in a welcoming grin. He clapped his hands and cried : " *Garçon !* "

A coloured waiter came at the run, and received the order, holding out a hand for the money.  Mr. Standish put a ten-franc note in the unclean palm, and when the waiter returned left the change with him by way of *pourboire*.  Then he looked at his guide.

" I will talk to Grandpère Jacques alone, but you will order wine, and wait to guide me back to the boulevard. You comprehend ?  Here is money to pay for the wine and a packet of cigarettes."

The young soldier withdrew, nothing loath ; probably he knew Grandpère's tales of derring do by heart ; and in any case he was willing to oblige one so generous. His benefactor lit a cigarette, and calling the *garçon* anew ordered coffee as likely to be the most innocuous drink the place provided, at which Jacques looked at him in surprise.

" M'sieur has the money for wine and drinks café—which here is poison ? "

" A matter of taste," laughed Mr. Standish.

" As m'sieur says, a matter of taste, and the wine of the country has a trick of lying sour on the stomach that is unaccustomed to it.    But in the Legion one grows hardened to many things, as m'sieur will know when he has heard the stories I shall tell him."

" It is not stories that I wish to hear, Grandpère Jacques.    I seek information and come to you because you are old in the Legion."

Grandpère's eyes narrowed, and a covetous gleam came in them.

" *Tiens !*   You seek information—of a long-lost brother perhaps ; or maybe of a father——"

" Of neither !   But of others, for news of whom I shall be willing to pay."

" Good !   There is none who could serve you better, m'sieur.   If you will speak the names ? "

" One name, first, Grandpère Jacques.   Do you remember one Alex Steffanson, a sergeant of——"

He got no further, his question being broken by a wrathful bellow.

" *Cet diable !* "

The legionary's face was twisted with hate, there was a glare of rage in his eyes, and he half started from his chair.

Standish's heart leaped at the transformation, but his voice was cool as he inquired :

" So you remember."

" Remember, m'sieur.   Shall I forget a man for whom I would face the firing-squad this very night."

" Neither to-night nor any other night," said the other.

" He is dead ! "

" Dead !   Then may God curse his black soul !   When died he ? "

"He was murdered—a matter of ten or eleven days ago."

"Murdered! That is good news! How was he slain?"

"In his fine house in England, by someone who fought with a sword but stuck him in the throat with a knife. He was slain on his wedding-night."

"Then a woman was saved from sorrow. Is it known who slew him?"

"No! But on the night he died two men walked down the road by his house whistling the march of the Legion."

"*Tiens!* Then some men revenged a regiment——"

"The name of one of them was Baptiste Caillé, that of the other Steinmann——"

"*Mordieu!*" cried Grandpère Jacques. "Those two slew him at the last."

"One of them—with another man, I think. Caillé was shot by Steffanson who called himself Simon Maxwell."

"That I know, m'sieur. There were rumours that he had gathered great wealth——"

"He was very rich!"

"And that pair of hawks who had once hunted with him tried to pluck his liver, *hein?*"

"I do not know. I think it is likely. Tell me what you remember about the trio."

"M'sieur, I remember nothing good. They were in my company, and inseparable, and were known among us as the three black dots, because each was so tattooed on the left hand——"

"Why?"

"That was known to them alone, m'sieur; but I think it was like a masonic sign between them. M'sieur understands they were like triplets joined together, even when Steffanson became a sergeant, for whom it is not etiquette to fraternize with the men whom he commands. They were still *les points noir*, and they went to France to fight the Bosches together, but Steffanson did not return with the others, and there were rumours that he deserted to the Allemands, which is possible if he were paid."

" No, you are wrong there, he had an honourable discharge. You do not know why those others sought his life ? "

" I can only conjecture that somehow he cheated them, and they sought him out to make him pay."

" That is possible, Grandpère. . . . But listen ! On the night that Maxwell died, there was a third man who may have been with that pair of hawks—a tall man, lean of face, dark-eyed, a soldier, I am certain, and of the officer class, though to be sure, if he were of the Legion, he may have been no more than was Maxwell himself. But he used an airplane and he was English or American——"

" An officer, you say, m'sieur ? "

" For a guess, yes ! "

Grandpère Jacques did not hurry to reply. For one second a crafty look came on his face, and a second later gave place to one of curiosity, and he inquired blandly :

" What is m'sieur's interest in this man ? Is m'sieur of the police ? "

" No ! " snapped Mr. Standish. " But I want to get that man."

" Ah ! M'sieur is a private agent ! I comprehend." The legionary's face took a wooden expression, and a hint of reserve crept in his manner. Then he shook his head. "Non, m'sieur, I do not know the man of whom you ask."

Garfield Standish did not believe him. He was sure the man was lying, that he had recognized the man whom he had described and for some reason was disinclined to own it.

" That is to be regretted," he commented. " For news of that man I would pay five hundred francs ! "

Grandpère Jacques was moved by the greatness of the sum.

"*Mordieu!*" he whispered covetously. "It is a fortune—for a legionary. . . . And I cannot earn it. Fate is a cruel jade."

"The sum might be doubled if I were brought face to face with the man," remarked Mr. Standish carelessly, and was a little surprised by the answer his words provoked.

"M'sieur would bribe me—Grandpère Jacques of the Legion. He has yet something to learn. A man will do much for wine—which is the elixir of life and more precious than the love of women, but he will not betray a friend for it. *Non!* . . . Perhaps m'sieur will call for the second bottle and hear the story of how my company crossed the desert to Bir-el-Ghiramo and there fought the Touaregs for the wells?"

Standish paid for the second bottle in the hope that the heady wine would loosen a guarded tongue, but generosity was unavailing. He heard the story of the fight at the wells of Bir-el-Ghiramo; and two other stories, lurid and grim enough to be true—in themselves a complete evening's entertainment; but not even a third bottle would make Grandpère open-out on the subject of the other's heart. A leading question failed.

"There can be few American or English officers in the Legion, Grandpère."

"*Non!* m'sieur!" answered Jacques promptly. "They are all in the ranks."

"But I am sure that man was not of the ranks. You hinted he was a friend——"

"And m'sieur must respect the hint. . . . But I have another story of how Corporal André loved a veiled Moorish maiden—a droll story that the great Balzac should have told——"

Mr. Standish recognized defeat, and wasted no more time. He rose from his seat and signalled to his guide. Then he addressed a last persuasion to the old soldier.

"Grandpère Jacques, you are unwise. You know the man whom I seek——"

"I have not said so, and always one may be mistaken."

"For a scruple you refuse a thousand francs——"

"A whole thousand. *Mon Dieu!* The fool I am," groaned the soldier as if he were in pain.

"It is indeed folly on your part, for if the man is here I cannot but find him."

Grandpère Jacques laughed suddenly. "I will wager you a bottle that you do not, m'sieur."

In the legionary's voice was the note of one who bets on a certainty. The other marked it and was annoyed by it. With a brusque "*Bon soir!*" he took his way to the street, whilst Grandpère Jacques stared after him a little wonderingly.

"A private agent, *hein!* And if *le capitaine* should be the man who killed Alex Steffanson? That would perhaps be nothing of a miracle. But——"

His meditation broke off. He chuckled and commented to himself. "He may find the needle in the hay, or the grain of sand in the desert, but he will not find *mon capitaine!* If he should—I will slit his throat before he can speak. . . . Yes, his throat, for that makes a man very silent."

He lifted the bottle, drained the heel-taps and then, struck by a sudden thought, lurched out into the street.

"It will be well to know!" he muttered, as getting control of his legs he began to hurry. At the point where the narrower street led to the main boulevard he saw Mr. Standish and his guide, and moderating his pace, he stalked the pair to the Hôtel d'Oran, and when the stranger disappeared through its portals, Grandpère nodded cheerfully.

"*Oui!* It is well to know where one can find the throat in case of need."

## CHAPTER IX

### ENCOUNTERS

THE uniformed official of the Messageries Maritimes was a ladies' man, with the excessive politeness of his race, and Cornelia Maxwell was one to take an appreciative eye. He lifted his peaked cap, smiled as on one he loved, and spoke ingratiatingly.

" Mademoiselle is for the steamer——"

" Madame, sir ! "

" *Tiens !* And so young. It is confounding ! " The man laughed. " But what matter ? I am at madame's service. This way. The baggage will follow. And madame's friend—she also is for Oran ? Good ! . . . If she will follow in our steps——"

Madame's friend, who chanced to be Enid Standish, followed, mounted the gangway, and five seconds later found herself face to face with one the sight of whom gave her a shock.

" Jeff Warborough. . . . You ? . . . here ? "

" In the flesh, but breathless," laughed Warborough, " and with no thought but an echo. . . . ' You ? . . . Here ? ' "

Miss Standish looked swiftly round, then spoke with almost distressing urgency :

" Jeff, you must be careful. She is here——"

" She ? " he interrupted. " The not impossible she—is who ? "

" Cornelia Maxwell—Simon Maxwell's widow. She is half-crazed to find the man who killed her husband."

" Ah ! " Warborough looked quickly round. " So that is what brings you to the packet for Oran, hey ? Where is the lady ? "

" There ! . . . You must not meet—oh ! She has stopped. She has seen us. She comes this way. Unless you run I must introduce you. . . ."

" Run, from a lady, Sister Enid. I am not so un-gallant."

" But——" She checked, and added swiftly in a whisper, " There is no help for it now. . . . Be careful, Jeff."

A moment later Jeff Warborough had clicked heels and was bowing to the lady for whose marriage he had arrived too late. As he straightened himself, for the first time he looked straight into Cornelia Maxwell's face, and was conscious of dark eyes kindling with curiosity, of a face imperiously lovely, of a scarlet mouth that was made for love. The picture disconcerted him a little, and for the moment he was dumb and awkward. But the actress did not appear to notice his gaucherie. With perfect self-possession she held out a hand.

" If you are Enid's friend, then you must be mine also, Mr. Warborough."

He found his tongue at that. " I shall be greatly honoured, madame. All men know the fame of Claire Devereaux."

A light kindled in her eyes at the words. It was clear to him that she had the vanity of the artiste, and was not insensible to praise. But a second later the light died and the beautiful face had a clouded look.

" Possibly. But just now they are more interested in the sorrow of Mrs. Simon Maxwell."

" Sorrow ? " he stammered. " Ah, I remember. . . . I heard something——" He broke off, conscious of the look on Enid Standish's face ; whilst a little light of wonder kindled in the actress's eyes.

" You heard something ? " she said in a voice that betrayed surprise. " You do not read the newspapers closely, then ? "

" Not the English," answered Warborough quickly. " The French only—and not those minutely."

Cornelia flashed an appraising look at the soldierly figure and the clean-cut face.

" But you are not French ? " she challenged.

" A stepson of the Republic," he laughed, " serving in her army."

The woman's dark eyes grew suddenly very keen. An odd questioning look came on her face.

" Then you are a soldier of the Legion ? "

" A captain—without a company," he laughed, amused at the look of amazement in Enid Standish's eyes.

The questioning look on the actress's face grew more pronounced, and the dark eyes burned with a hard light.

" A captain. . . . You have served long then ? " she asked in a voice that was near a challenge.

Her tone brought a look of apprehension to Miss Standish's face, but the man whom she addressed seemed unconscious of anything unusual in it. He shrugged his shoulders, and replied nonchalantly :

" Since half-way through the war. My own country at that time was sitting on the fence or coining dollars in the munition shops, so I joined the Legion as did others to serve France, and at the end of the war I remained."

" You remained ? " she echoed, her dark eyes fixed on him in a steady scrutiny. " I wonder why ? "

" I like soldiering—real soldiering, and the Legion offers that, always."

" But you are without a company, you said ? "

" For the present ; but believe me I am not without adventure."

Her brows knitted at the words. " You are not without adventure. I wonder where you find it."

Warborough laughed easily. " Africa is the native land of adventure, and just now the North is fruitful that way."

" I wonder——" the lady began, and then stopped short.

" Yes ? " he asked encouragingly. " You were about to ask a question ? "

" I was wondering if you found adventures only in Africa ? "

Enid Standish, scenting a reference to the affair at

Farholme Abbey, betrayed some apprehension, and her
eyes shot a silent warning to the man.    Jeff Warborough,
however, gave no sign of any understanding of the hidden
allusion in the actress's question.    His lean face was
guileless, and his light laughter unforced as he replied :

" One finds adventure where he seeks it—everywhere."

" Yes," she nodded.    " Yes—if one is an adventurer,
I suppose, it is all the same.    Africa, France or England
——"

" London or Timbuktu," answered Warborough with
another laugh.

" Timbuktu ?    You have been there ? "

" Twice."

" How very interesting," commented the lady.    " One
does not meet one who has been to that sentinel of the
Southern Sahara."    She paused, there was the faintest
flicker of the dark eyes, then came a question that brought
a tense look to Miss Standish's face.    " And London ?
You mentioned London as a place of adventure.    You
know London well ?    England ? "

" Passably.    I am newly come from there."

" Indeed ! "    The word came sharply—then the lady
laughed softly as if amused at her own question.    " And
you found it a place of adventure, Captain Warborough ? "

" No," answered Warborough easily, without any sign
that he understood the bearing of the catechism to which
he was being subjected.    " I found it dull.    But then I
was but a bird of passage, going and coming, with no
time for adventure to seek one out."

" So ? . . .    But you will have better luck next time
perhaps."    The actress shrugged her shoulders and half-
turned.    " We are keeping this gentleman waiting, Miss
Standish," she said, indicating the official of the shipping
company.    " And he will be impatient."

" At your leisure," protested the officer with a bow.
" Time is not when one serves madame."

The actress ignored the compliment.    " Doubtless we

shall see you again, Captain Warborough, that is if you are for Oran."

"For Oran and beyond to Sidi-bel-Abbès," replied the soldier.

"Our own journey," the lady nodded, and passed on with the official dancing like a marionette on one side of her, and with Enid Standish on the other.

Jeff Warborough watched their going with speculative eyes, and as they disappeared down the companion way, nodded thoughtfully.

"A blind shot, or——"

He left the thought unfinished as a man in uniform came hurrying up the gangway with a telegram in his hand. He watched the soldier as one might watch a messenger of fate, with an intuition that the man was seeking him. The intuition proved to be right. The soldier-messenger spoke to one of the ship's officers, and Warborough caught his own name, and saw the officer look round and point to him. The messenger hurried forward, clicked heels and saluted.

"Captain Warborough?" he asked.

"Yes," answered Warborough, and held out his hand for the telegram.

He read it carefully, twice, then tore it into small pieces, which he dropped over the ship's side.

"There is no answer," he said, and the man dismissed saluted again and departed.

When he had gone, Warborough stood for some time lost in thought. The telegram had told him that Sidi-bel-Abbès was not after all to be his destination, and Cornelia Maxwell would have to make its acquaintance without him acting as guide. After a few minutes he went to his cabin and remained there until the steamer was well at sea, then went on deck once more. Scarcely had he reached it when he was pounced upon by Miss Standish, who, as it appeared, had been waiting for him.

H

" Jeff Warborough," she began hurriedly, " why did you come on this ship ? "

" Because it goes to Oran," he answered laughingly. There was no answering laughter from Enid Standish.

" Of course I know that ; but for you and Cornelia to meet like this is dangerous. You heard her questions. You must have guessed the drift of them——"

" I had an inkling," he owned.

" If she discovers that you are the man who arrived at Carston Magna in an aeroplane——" Observing the expression on his face she broke off sharply, then asked abruptly : " What is it ? "

" How did you know that I did anything of the kind ? "

" The man to whom you spoke when you landed was my brother."

" Phew ! "

" He will be waiting for us at Oran. He has taken up this business of Simon Maxwell's death—having a penchant for crime investigation."

" And he has gone to Oran looking for me ? "

" To Sidi-bel-Abbès—the headquarters of the Legion, to learn what he can of Simon Maxwell's past and——"

" He's got the end of the string, right enough."

" He is to meet us. If he recognizes you——"

" He has done so once, in London."

" Well, you can see, can't you ? With Cornelia already suspicious it will be well to avoid association with us."

" And slip ashore at Oran like a stowaway, hey ? Sister Enid, it can't be done and—well, I just won't do it. A man must take his risks, and if Cornelia Maxwell is one of mine, I shall face that particular one cheerfully."

" Oh ! " cried Miss Standish, " you are very wilful."

" I was a spoiled child," he owned with a laugh, and then gave a little jerk with his head. " Hush ! The lady comes. To please you I will practise the art of making myself scarce. Au revoir, Sister."

He turned and strolled nonchalantly away, and a

minute later, looking backward, saw Cornelia and Miss Standish talking together, and made a guess that he was the subject of conversation. As it chanced, his guess was the right one, for the actress was much interested in the legionary-officer, and had questioned the other about her acquaintance with him.

"We are old friends," Miss Standish was explaining.

"Friends?" There was a note in the actress's voice which brought the warm blood to her companion's face.

"Platonic—strictly. And it dates back to a night when German aeroplanes crossed the lines and bombed a hospital where I was Sister. I was knocked senseless, and when I came to the place was burning, but I was lying on the grass a hundred yards away, with a man in hospital pyjamas at my side. It was Jeff Warborough. I thought he was dead, and as a matter of fact he almost was, and it was not until a week later I learned that rising from a bed, lame with shrapnel and a sick man, he had somehow carried me away from the flames and had then collapsed."

"A brave man," said the actress. "And the story should have a romantic end."

"It never will have that kind of end. Jeff and I are just good friends."

"Then I myself must slip into the comradely fellowship," declared Cornelia. "I must cultivate his acquaintance, and by the time we reach Oran we shall be friends."

Enid Standish devoutly hoped that they would not be; but found her hope denied. That same night after dinner the actress annexed Jeff Warborough, and walked with him on the deck. Under the soft moonlight her beauty was alluring, and so the man found it, whilst they talked, the woman exceedingly gracious, and at some pains to charm. She encouraged him to talk of his life in the Legion, which he did willingly enough, alert against any leading question that she might put. But presently his guard was down. Her beauty in the soft moonlight stirred him deeply. He found her presence an exhilaration, her interest a flattery not to be resisted, and he was more than gratified when she whispered : " Oh, but you live a man's life ! "

" But yours," he answered, " is one of triumph."

" A triumph in a mimic world, with no reality anywhere."

" But you are the idol of thousands."

" Who worship a shadow—mine !—in the pictures."

" They would be on their knees to the living woman," he answered with laughing fervour.

" You think so ? " she asked musingly.

" I am sure of it. You have power. You move a man to babble about himself, you make him want to confess his sins to you, which is man's uttermost flattery of a woman."

" Oh, but you have no sins ! "

" On the contrary—a host dogs me."

" But none that keeps you awake at nights ? "

Warborough laughed outright, then replied cheerfully. " That at least is true. I can honestly say it."

The actress faced him swiftly. In the light of the ship's lamps he saw her eyes. They were burning in the intensity of their gaze. Then the flame died out.

" You are happy to be able to claim that," she said lightly, and moved up the moonlit deck a little way. Jeff Warborough moved with her, starting with a little limp due to the stiffness of his injured leg. The actress noticed it, and asked a question.

" You are lame," she said. " An old wound perhaps ? "

" On the contrary, a very recent one." He laughed. " I had a little accident whilst I was in England. A car hit me."

" Oh ! "

There was again an abrupt change in the woman's manner. Her eyes measured him again appraisingly, then she said in an odd voice, " But that was not in London ? You said you did not find any adventure there ? "

Warborough laughed. " No, it was not in London."

" In the country, perhaps ? " she persisted.

" Yes," he answered easily, but with his guard up again, " in the country. In these days English lanes are not so safe to stroll along at nights as the Sahara."

" I can well believe that," answered the woman, and desisted from questioning, staring thoughtfully across the moonlit sea.

Warborough refrained from breaking on her thoughts. Thrusting a hand into an inner pocket, he felt for his cigarette-case. It was a long one and having slipped cross-wise had wedged in the pocket and was a little difficult to dislodge. It came out at last with a jerk, bringing with it a little sheaf of letters and papers which were scattered on the deck.

" Confound it," he laughed, and stooped to gather up his possessions.

Cornelia Maxwell condescended to help, and in spite of a protestation from him persisted, chasing a light sheet caught by the night wind down the deck. She caught it, and as she picked it up a little piece of pasteboard fell out of it. That also she retrieved, and as she did so looked at it a little curiously, for it was an unused railway ticket. She was in a circle of light cast by a lamp, and was able to see clearly. A name on the ticket leaped out at her and for a moment she was frozen to immobility. Then she looked hastily along the deck. Warborough was still busy gathering his papers. In a second she thrust the ticket in the bosom of her dress, and then, moving forward, held out to him the paper she had saved.

"Here's a love letter saved from the sea," she said merrily.

" No love letter, I assure you," he laughed back.

" La ! la ! " she mocked sceptically. " You will not own it. That is the way with men."

Warborough scarcely glanced at the paper. He was assailed by an unreasoning desire to convince her.

" Prove the truth for yourself," he laughed. " You have my permission to read."

Rather to his surprise she availed herself of the per-

mission accorded, standing full under the deck light to
read. Then she laughed, a little oddly as it seemed, and
let the paper flutter from her in the wind.

" An old hotel bill, only. . . . ' Truth teller was our
English Alfred's name,' " she quoted, and laughed again.
Then gave a little shiver. " This night breeze is chilly.
I must find a wrap."

Without more ado she moved away. He waited hoping
that she would return, but was disappointed and presently retired to his cabin. At breakfast time next
morning he looked for her in vain. Neither she nor Enid
Standish put in an appearance and an inquiry elicited
from a steward that one of the ladies was not well.

Not until the packet had made the harbour at Oran did
he see them again. The boat was making the quay, and
they were plainly eager for shore. Remembering that
Miss Standish's brother was to meet them, and having in
mind her warning, he approached the ladies to make his
adieus before landing. It was the actress who was indis-
posed, but at the sight of him she threw off the incubus
of sickness, and forced a smile as she noted that he was
now in uniform.

" So, Captain Warborough, you are the soldier again."

" Yes ! " he laughed. " Duty calls when one touches
the quay."

" Then you will be too busy to be a squire of dames."

" Alas ! The privilege will be denied me ! "

" But at Sidi-bel-Abbès, perhaps, we shall renew
acquaintance." She laughed with pleasant raillery.
" When you can spare time from adventures, you will
perhaps dine with us at the Hôtel d'Oran."

Not for a second did Warborough hesitate. He knew
that Sidi-bel-Abbès was not to see him that tide, but the
secret was not his own, and he did not betray it. He
laughed back, easily.

" To-morrow, if circumstances allow."

" And the day after if they do not ? "

"The day after," he agreed, and as the boat made the quayside took the lady's offered hand, and over her shoulder saw Enid Standish's eyes flash a warning glance towards the quay. He followed its direction and among the spectators and idlers caught sight of a tall civilian whom he recognized instantly for the man of whom he had so neatly rid himself in Greek Street. As he shook hands with her in turn, his eyes assured Miss Standish that he understood the warning, then he moved away, and whilst the gangway was made fast looked along the quay again for a man who should be awaiting him. The man was not to the fore ; but just as the sailors finished their task he found the soldier he sought at the very edge of the idling crowd watching the vessel. The man caught his eyes and made a warning signal, then moved a little further away.

"The deuce," he thought. "What is nipping the good Jacques to-day ? "

He did not hurry to land. That warning, whatever was behind it, was unmistakable, and he searched the quayside with keen eyes for any possible reason. The only one he found was the man whom he now knew was Miss Standish's brother. And he it seemed was engrossed with the two ladies, and with the man who was handling their baggage.

Standish's back was towards him as he crossed the gangway, and he smiled to himself as the soldier hurried to him.

"Quick, *mon capitaine*, there is need."

"What flea is biting you, Grandpère ? " he asked genially.

"No flea, *mon capitaine*, but a devil of an American on the quay here who offered a thousand francs for news of you. And not even an American pays so much for nothing."

"That to be sure is true. But——"

"He looks this way, m'sieur. One of the ladies directs his gaze. Quick, I have a *voiture* waiting to take us where we must go."

Warborough did not look round, but as he moved

towards the *voiture* he was aware of sounds of hurrying steps on the quay, and as he climbed into the conveyance the footsteps drew nearer.

"Quick, *cocher*!" cried Jacques. "Drive like the devil who was your sire."

The cocher laughed and cracked his whip. The *voiture* began to move. A voice behind cried a little frantically:

"Hallo, there! Stop!"

Warborough turned round. The voice was the voice of Mr. Standish, who, red in the face, was in hot pursuit, and gaining on the horse. He drew level and Warborough, moved by some imp of mischief, encouraged him.

"Run, my friend," he cried between gusts of laughter. "Run! Last time you were in the coach . . . now it is my turn."

Mr. Standish had no appreciation of the jest. He cried out something that Warborough did not catch. Then the horse got into its stride and began to leave the man behind. Recognizing the hopelessness of the chase, the pursuer gave up.

Grandpère Jacques laughed.

"A troublesome citizen that, *mon capitaine*. What he wants the devil knows, but he wants it badly. One might think you had run off with his wife."

Then again he looked back. The man who had tried to bribe him was standing in the road, watching the receding vehicle, and Grandpère Jacques, lawless by nature, and outside the Legion no respecter of persons, put his fingers to his nose in a gesture of contempt.


## CHAPTER X

### A NIGHT'S ADVENTURE

THREE nights later Cornelia Maxwell looked across the table set for dinner, and with a touch of hardness in her tones said to her companion:

" Again he has not come."

Enid Standish did not inquire the name of the laggard, and the actress continued musingly.

" For two nights we have waited with a cover laid. If he were in Sidi-bel-Abbès I should say that Captain Warborough was lacking in courtesy. But as he is not——"

" Ah ! You have learned that, Cornelia ? "

" An hour ago." Cornelia shrugged her shoulders. " These soldiers are not difficult. That hatchet-faced Colonel of Spahies who recognized me yesterday, and sent the bouquet, was eager to serve me. He gathered the information for me. Captain Warborough is not in bel-Abbès, indeed he has not been here for a month. Your brother was right in his conjecture that when he left the steamer he did not take the train to Oran. Apparently he had no intention of doing so. He misled us—deliberately. Why ? "

Again Miss Standish let the question go unanswered, but looked swiftly round at the sound of her brother's voice.

" Here is Garry," she said, with an air of relief.

" And he has news," commented the actress. " It is shining in his eyes. His journey to Oran has not been in vain."

She was right. Mr. Standish had news, and it burst from him explosively as he took his seat.

" He has gone to Fez ! "

" To Fez ! " echoed Cornelia.

" The very day he landed at Oran. It was easy to learn, for he is well known at the port, and by the railway people."

" There was no secret about his going ? "

Garfield Standish laughed. " If there was a secret I bought it cheap—for two bottles of Algerian wine."

" You learned more ? "

" Not much ! Warborough is of the Legion, as you know——"

" But he is detached for special service. My Colonel told me that."

"So ! A political officer, perhaps."

"That is likely. His comings and goings are something of a mystery, I gather. And he has gone to Fez ? "

"Unquestionably." Mr. Standish looked at the cover laid for the absent Warborough, and laughed lugubriously. "He has cheated us. He never meant to eat a dinner with you."

Cornelia was stung to anger and chagrin by the thought.

"But," she said in a quivering voice, " he cannot cheat us all the time. We also can go to Fez."

"I was about to suggest that," said Standish. "We can follow like hounds on a trail."

"The trail of the wild-goose," commented his sister. "Do you think if he wished to evade you it would be difficult in this country, where he is at home ? "

"He shall not evade us," said the actress, with anger in her voice. "If need be, we will follow him to the desert's heart."

Enid Standish was infinitely perturbed at Cornelia's attitude. There was, she knew, an iron resolution behind the words ; but she sought a way to thwart it.

"But I shall not go to Fez," she said with a thought that the other woman would not go with Garry alone. But social convenances it seemed were nothing to Cornelia.

"Then Garry and I will go alone."

"But you can't ! " said Miss Standish.

"Why not ? " demanded her brother. "Mrs. Grundy has no address in Morocco, if that is in your mind." He laughed noisily at his own jest, and turned to Cornelia. "We will go together. We will find him and bring him to book."

"Yes ! Yes . . . That he should run from you is more than suspicious. And there were things he let slip upon the boat that taken with this flight and the things you have told me are convincing. We will go to Fez. We will find him. We will see him taken and bring him to the rope."

Looking at her, Enid Standish argued no more. There was a flame of revengeful passion in the woman's dark eyes, a frozen look of resolution on her face. Dissuasion would have been a waste of breath. She turned to her brother. His eyes were exultant and the sight stung her to anger.

"Oh," she cried, "you are crazy! Both of you," and rising suddenly she fled the room.

A sleepless night brought with it no change of counsel. In the early cold of the morning, with the bugles of the Legion in her ears, she looked from her window, with her mind made up.

"I will not be dragged at the heels of a pair of lunatics. They must go their own way. Jeff Warborough is well able to guard himself."

Her brother heard her considered decision without tears; indeed he had, she saw, some difficulty in hiding his pleasure at the announcement.

"I will look out the train," he said coolly. "We can travel to Oran together, and I will see you on to the steamer."

He did both, and with Cornelia at his side waved to her from the quay. As they turned away his companion shot a question:

"She loves that man Warborough? That is why she goes angry away?"

"Good Lord, no! By the time we get back to England I expect to be asked to give her away in church to Stephen Langford."

"But, in that case, why is she so contrary?"

"Warborough and she are old friends. Some plucky thing he did for her during the war. She cherishes the idea that he saved her life."

The woman nodded, understanding.

"And out of gratitude she would have served him by turning me aside. There is some strain of good in the man somewhere, I suppose, but for me he is utterly corrupt."

"A murderous scoundrel," agreed the man heartily.

The next day they started for Fez, but at Taza were told that for two days the train would go no further. An indignant inquiry by Mr. Standish elicited the fact that the line was under repair owing to sabotage.

"Great heavens, man!" cried Mr. Standish, "but there's no rail-workers' union in this country, surely?"

"There are tribesmen who are worse," answered the official tersely. "If monsieur's business at Fez is not urgent, I should advise a return to Oran. One is safe there."

"Safe!" Mr. Standish laughed. "Trying to put the wind up, hey? But madame's business in Fez is urgent, and we got forward at once. We shall no doubt be able to hire an automobile in the town?"

"I think not. But there are mules to be purchased."

They purchased mules—hired a couple of Arabs, and three days later drew near the Bab Guissa—the northerly gate of Fez. It was the hour of the Third Prayer, near sunset, and from the minaret above the old walls sounded the muzzein's cry.

Mr. Standish looked about him with interest, and there was much to take his eyes. The workmen of the quarter, released from labour, were come to rest themselves in sight of the declining sun, and at one point were gathered around a story-teller—a tall, lean, black-bearded man, with flashing eyes, who with poetic frenzy was singing in a high chant and reciting passages from the romantic Arabic tale of El-Antar. Beside him seated cross-legged was a man of great age, who thumped a tambourine by way of accompaniment to his fellow's classic tale. Among the crowd moved a water-seller with his goat-skin bottle slung at his loins, selling to the thirsty, but now and again pausing, business forgotten, absorbed by some dramatic episode of the story that holds the Mahomedan mind from Tangier to Cairo, and from Cairo to distant Bagdad. A little further away, a snake-charmer, with twisted reptiles about his neck, was doing wild things with his sinuous pets to the beating of a drum, and quite close a sweetmeat-seller plied his trade, and at times mocked the performer by some comic pantomime of his deadly improvisations.

It was not new to Mr. Standish, and Cornelia, who in one of her pictures had figured as the white bride of a desert sheik, had seen the like before ; but both found it interesting, and looked not without wonder on the motley throng. A string of camels moved towards the gate, a drove of small donkeys heavily ladened forced its way through the crowd. Soft-footed men and veiled women drifted by. A trio of dark-faced Chasseurs d'Afrique in their brilliant uniforms stood watching, cheek by jowl with desert Arabs clad in white burnouses, whilst blue-eyed Berbers brushed shoulders with coal-black Africans —the true sons of Ham. A Jew of the lost tribes, a merchant and, from his richly-caparisoned mule, a man of wealth, grunted a curse at a camel-driver, the head of whose ungainly mount was bobbing at his shoulder, as he made the gate, and in and out played children, fair-skinned, chocolate-coloured, coal-black, teasing the beggars, worrying the sweetmeat-seller or dodging impishly under the bellies of the donkeys.

Mr. Standish nodded at it all, and laughed to his companion. " Here's the haystack where we shall find our needle."

They moved towards the gate. Above the old walls rose a minaret luminous in the light of evening. Standish considered it with some interest. From that tower of prayer less than fourteen years before, Chardonnet had been shot with half his men, whilst he held the gate when the men of Fez had risen in bloody revolt against the newly-proclaimed French protectorate. Thirteen years, he reflected, was not a very long time in this land so impervious to change, and what had been might well be again. There came to his mind the warning of the official at Taza, then he laughed at the idea. The French had learned their lesson ; they were not likely to be caught napping again, and, besides, Fez to-day had cinemas and banks and hotels and all the other amenities which Western culture and business was imposing on Old Morocco, and it was nonsense to associate such things with fanatical action. To be sure, there was that pirate Abdul-el-Krim up in the Spanish zone——

His reflections broke off sharply as he caught sight of four blind beggars seated almost in the shadow of the gate, appealing vociferously to the passers-by. As he saw them he met the stony gaze of one of them in level glance. The man's eyes were wide open as were those of a companion who sat near by ; but as Standish was quick to note there was a wide difference in their gaze. The second man's chin was lifted, his unseeing stare directed to the sky, a habit of those who denied the light yet yearn for the sun ; but as he would have sworn the eyes into which he stared were aware of the encounter, and in the instant of their meeting they grew bright and wide with amazed incredulity. Mr. Standish was an observant man. That amazement was evidence that the beggar was aware of him and of Cornelia, for the eyes of the blind so far as the expression of emotion is concerned are the eyes of the dead. He laughed silently.

" A fraud ! " he thought. " A most palpable fraud, or how the devil could he know that I was watching him ? "

He kept his eyes on the man, taking stock of him, and noted that whilst he did so the man kept his face averted. Deliberately he looked away, and after an interval turned swiftly in the man's direction again. He was in time to surprise the beggar staring at Cornelia with undisguised amazement. The lids dropped swiftly, hiding the eyes ; but Mr. Standish had seen, and a wild suspicion occurred to him that not only had he found the haystack but the needle sticking out of it. Under a sudden impulse he pushed his mule forward, and halted before the beggar, who, unlike his companion, was silent, and still as a statue. But as Standish advanced the man seemed to remember, and began to rock himself to and fro, crying clamorously, " Allah Beh ! Allah Beh ! "

Mr. Standish looked at him critically. The face, with a flowing beard, was lifted towards him, with the eyelids closed. It told him but one thing, and that was that the fraudulent beggar was not the man whom he sought. But he had seen wonder and as he thought recognition in the man's eyes, and he desired to make sure. He wanted to see those eyes again. His desire was met almost immediately, for the lids lifted and he looked down into the pupils. He was disappointed. They had a dull look : they were as devoid of expression as those of a dead fish, and so far as being seen of them the observer might have been a thousand miles away. But Mr. Standish was not satisfied. He was sure that the man could see as well as himself, and he was decided that he would try a little experiment. His hand went to his pocket and silently produced a franc. There was no movement on the part of the beggar, and the eyes remained absolutely devoid of expression. Again Mr. Standish experienced disappointment, but tried again. He knew no Arabic or Moghrebbin, and it was not likely that a blind beggar in that roaring square would have any acquaintance with the English tongue if he were what he seemed, but it was worth trying, so in a tone of insulting contempt, he spoke :

" You're a holy fraud, my fine fellow."

The only sign the beggar gave was to rock himself to and fro more quickly on his heels, whilst as if suddenly aware of a possible benefactor he grew more vociferous.

" Allah Beh ! Allah Beh ! "

The man's eyes had not so much as a flicker in them. They had still the dead stony look of one who sees not the sun, but stares through unending darkness to the Eternal. Once or twice they blinked quickly as the eyes of the blind will, but no light of perception shone in them, and but for that movement they might have belonged to a stone image.   Mr. Standish began to think he must have been mistaken in supposing the man could see and had been interested in Cornelia and himself.

Some trick of light, a reflection from those glassy eyeballs might account for what he had seen, and as the beggar rocked on and continued his unending whine, he decided that it must be so.   He laughed at his own suspicions, and as the beggar, hearing his laughter, extended a grimy palm and cried more urgently, he dropped the franc he held into it, and led the way to the gate.   At the very entrance they were held up for a moment by an obstreperous camel, and in the pause Standish looked back.   The beggar who had received his largess had risen, and with one hand on a stout staff, with the other was brushing the dust from his clothing.   He smiled at the sight.

" A careful man," he thought, and as the refractory camel was dragged away, with Cornelia by his side moved through the gate, quite unconscious of the fact that the man who had occasioned the smile was now almost at his heels, the stony look gone, his eyes now aflame with eagerness.

They found a lodging-place in an hotel in the square adjoining the Ghetto, where were the banks and cinemas and cafés, the thought of which had been so reassuring. In the interval before the evening meal, standing with Cornelia Mr. Standish looked from a balcony into the roaring square.   It was Babel, strident and tumultuous, seething with diverse humanity, and was the embodiment of that modern progress, imposed on a people that had been static for hundreds of years.   But, he wondered, was the change more than skin-deep ?   The flare of the electric sign of the cinema-house across the square was a strident sign against the quiet stars set in the indigo vault above ; but the unobtrusive stars were unfading, symbolical perhaps of those ancient lights which guided the soul of a mysterious people.   Was it possible to root up the old ideals of a people whose faith was publicly voiced from a score of minarets, hoary with history and great tradition?

Whilst he stood there a tall man in a burnous halted full in the light of the cinema, and standing sideways stared up at the sign. Standish could see him quite clearly—hawk-faced, eagle-eyed, keen as a steel blade, beyond question a man of the desert with the predatory instincts of his race, and the immemorial masterfulness of a warrior clan. Was he the type to be changed by the gaudy things in that square, by a tawdry civilization which sought to school the desert lords, to rob them of their immemorial rights, but which the desert itself defied? As he asked himself the question, words spoken by a guttural voice from behind him supplied the answer.

"But that Abdul-el-Krim is Satan's son."

He turned to look at the speaker, a pock-marked, elderly Jew, who was with another of his race, and as he did so he caught the reply.

"He is the cloud, a little while ago no bigger than a man's hand, but now covering the land from Tangier to Marrakesh. Before him the Spaniards are dogs. Another victory or two and he will be emperor of Morocco, and master of all from the sea to the desert, for the infection of victory spread like a fever. Have you thought, Yacoub, what might befall here—in Fez?"

The man addressed as Yacoub nodded. "I was here in the Ghetto when the great revolt broke out and the French fought for their lives. It may well be so again, and if it should be——"

"Yacoub, this very day a Talib of the Madusa spat at my feet in the street and cursed me for a dog of a Jew. And when the priests bark their jackals will harry and rend."

Again Yacoub nodded. "There are whispers in the cafés, rumours everywhere. Rifles are plentiful as dates on the palms, and there are machine-guns and artillery in concealed places, with officers from Germany——"

At that moment Cornelia entered the room and joined

I

him at the window, so that the rest of the conversation was lost to him. Her face had a little flush, her dark eyes were afire, she was keyed up with excitement, and more radiant than he had ever seen her. At the sight of her he was shaken by a sudden wind of passion.

" By heaven, Cornelia, you're rarely beautiful to-night."

Cornelia gave a little laugh of gratification. She recognized the accent of sincerity and accepted the praise without offence. She laid a hand lightly on his arm and looked out to the square.

" I am afire with expectation," she said. " Somewhere in this city is the man we seek—perhaps down there in the crowd, maybe here in this hotel. . . . We must find him soon, my friend. To-morrow——"

" No, to-night I must begin. There are places where I can ask openly for this Warborough——"

" I cannot check your zeal," said Cornelia with an approving smile ; then added softly, " I shall have to think how I may best reward it."

The blood surged to Mr. Standish's head, for a moment his face was suffused, and he whispered hoarsely, stammeringly : " There is . . . a way——"

" Do you think I do not know that, my friend ? " The hand on his arm exerted a gentle pressure. " But it is early . . . for that . . . yet. There is but one thought in my mind—an Aaron's rod that eats up all other thoughts."

Standish did not press the matter of reward further. There was he felt no need. In the fullness of time the thing would come. He stood there staring down into the noisy square with an absent look in his eyes. In the kaleidoscopic crowd under the lights there were many things to interest, but for the moment he saw none of them. The woman's hint had gone to his head like wine. He visioned a rosy future when—— But whilst he stared absently real things thrust themselves through his absorption. The garish life of the square broke through the romantic vision, and he found himself watching a man, but a little way from the hotel, leaning upon a staff, and apparently staring up at the balcony where he and Cornelia stood. Something familiar in the man's aspect quickened his interest. He stared intently, then suddenly he exclaimed :

" Now there is a strange thing."

" What ? " asked Cornelia quickly.

" This afternoon as we rode to the gate I gave a franc to a blind beggar——"

" Yes, yes ! I remember the man."

" When first I spoke to him I thought he was a fraud."

Cornelia gave a shrug. " That is the truth of most beggars. One need not question it."

" But I had a reason for the thought. When my eyes met his which should have been blind, I thought I saw amazement—recognition in them."

" A beggar at the northern gate whom you had never seen before ! " Cornelia laughed. " My friend, you have an imagination."

" No ! " answered Mr. Standish stubbornly. " The man was not blind. I am sure of that now ; and equally sure that he recognized me or you."

" Why so sure ? "

" Because he is down there in the square at this moment watching us—and a blind man could never have followed ——"

" Ah ! You think he may be the man we seek."

" No ! I know he is not. I had that thought this afternoon whilst we waited at the gate. I examined him minutely. He was not Warborough."

" Then who——"

" That is what I am asking myself."

The woman pondered for a moment, then she offered an explanation. " There is no one to know us here—but one man. That man may be a spy of his, or what is more likely he is hoping for another franc from you."

Mr. Standish laughed. " Upon my word, Cornelia, I believe you have hit the nail. See, the fellow is going."

" But no doubt he will return presently," she laughed back. " He will not desert a generous patron."

. . . An hour and a half later, having sought information from the manager of the hotel, Garfield Standish departed on his quest.

" The Café de Paris is the place for you." The manager had counselled him. " There you will find many officers, and if you seek a friend someone will know him."

The directions he had received were of the fullest, nevertheless he missed his way, and found himself wandering down a narrow lane. Through open door came the soft light of lamps and once through the wide-open doors of a mosque he glimpsed rows on rows of white-robed people, in the attitude of prayer, whilst all about were soft-footed pedestrians moving this way or that in the lane, the sides of which were tall houses that made the lane almost a canyon. It was very dark, and knowing himself astray, he had a thought to turn back, when round a dark corner came three or four mules with the man in charge beating them with a stick. He had no time to avoid them, except by springing into a doorway. By an unfortunate chance the doorway gave on to steps down which he rolled so heavily, that for a little time he lay at the bottom, too shaken to move.

A voice came to him out of the darkness, a woman with a lamp appeared. She held the lamp high, and the light, striking upward, showed him at the head of the steps, a dusky face with dark eyes staring down into the well where he lay. That cursed muleteer, he thought, and as the face vanished he picked himself up, and too shaken to remember that she would not understand in English offered an explanation.

" I fell down your steps."

The woman stared at him curiously. Perhaps she understood what had happened, but she gave no sign, and he took his way up the steps, to the darkness of the cobbled street again. He was in something of a whirl as he turned in his tracks to find his way back. The houses on either hand, so close that with arms outstretched he could touch both sides, worried him a good deal. He had a fear that he might step into another well of darkness and maybe break his neck. The silent pedestrians who brushed him as they passed softly shod, seemed to rise out of the night like ghosts, and for aught he knew they might be bandits or murderers. He regretted not having engaged a guide, and stumbled on over the cobbles looking for the lighted mosque into which he had glimpsed as he passed it. That should be on his right, and presently when it did not appear he stopped to consider. Had he in the confusion occasioned by his fall turned the corner round which the mules had so unexpectedly appeared ? It was more than possible, in which case with every step he took he was going further from his objective, deeper into the native city, where there was the risk that he might be immured for the night if the gates that divided the quarters were closed for the night as they often were. He began to be seriously alarmed. Out of the darkness came a sound of running water—one of the streams of the city—which he did not remember to have heard on his way down. Also the chasm-like alley where he stood had grown suddenly silent and deserted. There was no traffic, no shadowy pedestrian looming unexpectedly in front of him and passing by with a tread soft as a cat's.

A little way from where he stood a dim radiance broke from an open doorway. He determined to go to that house and seek a guide, sure that he could somehow make a shift to explain his needs. But as he started to move forward, the light disappeared, obliterated by the closing of a door. In the same second also he caught a sound of movement near at hand, behind him as he thought. The street, it seemed, was not so deserted as appeared. There was someone who perhaps for a franc would conduct him back to the square by the Ghetto. He peered into the darkness but could see no one, and the sound of movement had ceased. That seemed to him an ominous thing. It brought his heart to his mouth, and sent his hand to his hip-pocket for the small automatic which he carried. He could see nothing, but he was sure that someone waited there, furtive and baleful—someone who had seen him enter this gut of darkness and proposed to turn his disturbing situation to personal advantage. He recalled the man who had peered down the steps. Perhaps, after all, he had not been the muleteer. Possibly he had been the man whose presence he sensed so close to him, a bandit who had dogged his steps in order to rob him. Well! The secret one would have the shock of his life. With the pistol he was more than a match for——

He got no further. The thing happened with the swiftness of light. There was a soft footfall almost at his side. He glimpsed a shadow-like form, with arm uplifted to strike.

" Keep off, you dog——"

The lifted arm fell just as his pistol spat a stream of flame, and he crashed to the ground, sandbagged with a neatness that a Paris Apache could not have surpassed, and as he dropped the dark street faded from his consciousness, lost in a sevenfold blackness.

## CHAPTER XI

### A MISSING LADY

WHEN Mr. Standish came to himself, his eyes blinked in the light of a lantern and for a minute he lay quite still, listening to two men who were exchanging comments in French.

" This citizen has got his gruel. He must be a fool to wander in the Tala alone at night."

" But he has not been robbed. No. There is his watch and the ring on his hand."

" Then there is a woman somewhere. These Moors
are jealous dogs, and——"

" François, he opens his eyes. He lives, after all."

Mr. Standish gave proof of the fact by sitting upright.
The lantern seemed to his eyes to be dancing a jig, and the
faces of the two men appeared to come and go ; but with
a great effort of will he steadied his reeling senses, and
after a moment, as the lantern ceased its phantom gyra-
tions and the faces of the pair became clear to his vision,
he asked a question.

" What has happened ? "

" *Mon Dieu !* How should we know ? We are at the
corner in the darkness of the gate, François and I, when
we hear a cry and a shot, and we run and fall over you, as
you lie in the street."

" There was no one about ? "

" Monsieur, the street was like a grave. Every door
was fast shut, and there was no light anywhere. But
that is what may be expected. A shot in the Tala at
night means trouble, and in Fez men avoid that trouble
which is not their own, monsieur." He looked down the
alley-way, then made a grimace. " I will wager that
every door is locked and with the wooden bars in the slots.
We had much trouble to get even this lantern."

Standish himself looked down the street. It was quite
empty so far as he could see in the darkness, and, save
for a sound of murmuring water, silent as a vault. He
remembered something that one of the men had said, and
put an exploring hand to his pockets. He felt the bulge
of his pocket-book, there was a jingle of loose coin in
another pocket, his watch was safe, and the ring on his
hand gleamed in the light of the lantern. One of the men
asked a question and answered it himself.

" Monsieur has not been robbed ? No ! Then it was a
woman monsieur sought, and a jealous man who struck
him down. Monsieur is a stranger, no doubt, and does
not know how perilous it is to follow——"

Mr. Standish could not allow himself to remain under a doubtful aspersion.

" There was no woman," he said sharply. " I do not know why I was attacked. I was seeking the Café de Paris and lost my way, that is all."

" *Diable!* Then it was robbery, and François and I have saved monsieur's valuables, as perhaps monsieur will remember, for soldiers are poor men."

" I shall not forget, if you will help me back to my hotel in the square by the Ghetto."

" Willingly, monsieur."

The soldier-Samaritans helped him to his feet. One of them at his request found his automatic, and that done, ran back with the lantern to its owner and then, one of the men on either side of him, Standish started on the backward way. As they moved down the cobbled street there was a creaking of doors cautiously opened, here and there a little beam of light appeared, and Standish had a sense of watching eyes, and turning quickly saw a seamed old face at one of the doorways. It seemed that this narrow gut in the Tala had awakened again, and he guessed that behind the iron-studded doors men had been waiting, listening to learn the meaning of the shot which had shattered the silence of the night.

Marching with his escort, by inquiry, he learned that they belonged to a regiment of Tirailleurs, and had been in Fez and its neighbourhood for a year or more. The knowledge of that fact moved him to question them further.

" Do you know Captain Warborough of the first regiment of the Legion ? "

The pair, however, had never heard of the man he sought, and he walked on in silence, wondering why he had been attacked. Had robbery been the motive and had the unexpected appearance of the soldiers saved his valuables ? It seemed the only explanation, and whilst his head was sore, he rejoiced that the thief had been baulked of his prize. But having taken out his wallet and dismissed the Tirailleurs with a substantial *pourboire*, he made the discovery that after all he had lost something. His passport was missing. He habitually carried it in the pocket next to his wallet ; and it was not there now.

The discovery sent him rather hurriedly to his room to make sure. On entering the city he had changed his suit, and it was possible that he had failed to make the transfer from one pocket to the other, though hardly likely ; for he was sure that he had done so. The passport was not in the pocket where he had looked for it. He searched his room, turned over all his possessions without finding it, then stood whistling thoughtfully to himself. There was no question that in that narrow street whilst he lay unconscious the passport had been stolen. But who on earth had taken it ? No Moor, surely. And for what reason had it been stolen ? Some European who had lost his own passport or who had never possessed one perhaps desired to leave Morocco, and had taken this way of securing for himself the necessary ' papers.' To be sure there was a photograph upon the passport, but a photograph could be changed, and a man with a different face might pass out of Morocco under his name. If that were all, it was a nuisance. The French, he remembered, were rather crazy about papers, and he foresaw trouble ahead. But was it all ? Was there something more sinister behind it ?

A few minutes later he was driven to the conclusion that there was, for going to look for Cornelia he failed to find her. She was not in her own room, nor in any of the public-rooms, and an inquiry at the office revealed the fact that she had left the hotel in company with a stranger who had called for her. The hotel clerk did not know the caller, but he was unquestionably European—German, the clerk thought ; and he had sent a message to the lady, in which monsieur's name had occurred. Madame, on receiving the message, had seen the gentleman, had conversed with him a little time, and then, after slipping on a hat and cloak, had gone forth with him.

That was all he could learn. The clerk had taken little notice of the caller, except to mark that he was smartly dressed, and that his accent suggested the Fatherland as the country of his birth. Considering the little information available, he was filled with apprehension. Who was this man who had mentioned his name, no doubt to induce Cornelia to accompany him, and for what purpose had he taken her forth into this city where all things evil were possible? Had the stranger had anything to do with the attack upon himself? He could think of only one man in all Fez who would know his name, and it was unlikely that the man knew of his presence in the city. A question put to the clerk disposed of all possibility of Warborough being the man who had called.

"No, monsieur," answered the clerk after hearing Standish's description. "That was not the gentleman, I am sure. That one who called was fair, and heavy of face."

Standish turned away. There was nothing for it but to wait with what patience he could muster for Cornelia's return. To go forth into the city to look for her amid its teeming life and its mazes of narrow streets would be a mere waste of time; and besides he had suffered a surfeit of exploration for one night. He seated himself in the lounge to wait. His head ached intolerably from the blow that he had suffered; but in spite of its cruel throbbing his brain was busy trying to solve the mystery of Cornelia's going forth and of his lost passport. Was there a connection between the two? He saw one dim possibility of that. If the man with whom Cornelia had left the hotel had been connected with that attack in the dark street, he might have stolen the passport merely to discover his name. It seemed a thin explanation, but he could think of no other and he sat there consumed with anxiety, impatient for Cornelia's return.

A long time passed without the lady appearing; then

through his apprehensions and absorption in the problem of her going forth a certain buzz of excitement among the people in the lounge forced itself upon his attention. He heard a man shout excitedly :

" The news is that they have attacked the Beni Zeroual."

" Then next it will be our outposts."

" And Taza and Fez, unless the administration gets busy. Abdul-el-Krim conceives himself as a new Mahdi and proposes to rally all Islam to his banners. Having dished the Spaniards, he sets out to roast the French."

The excitement remained unabated, and in spite of his anxiety he was moved to inquire the reason for it. It was a Jew from Casablanca who gave him a succinct explanation.

" It is that devil El-Krim. He is ravaging on the French frontiers. It may be a mere piratical raid or it may be war. If it is war, then God help us in Fez. There will be trouble here, as there was in 1912—insurrection and wholesale murder as like as not. The Moors are a fanatical lot and Abdul-el-Krim is the new star of Islam. The Maréchal will have his work cut out to meet him."

The Jew drifted away to join a group who were heatedly discussing the news, leaving Garfield Standish to his reflections. They were not pleasant ones. If this news were true Fez would be in turmoil, and the purpose which had brought him there would be impossible to accomplish. Who would care two cents about a murder in England, with a hostile army on the frontiers and a fanatical populace at the door waiting for the signal to rise and slay as it had risen and slain in that week only thirteen years ago ? But there was Cornelia—— If the trouble came she would be driven to him, and that was no bad prospect. Abdul-el-Krim might raid all Morocco for him, if only Cornelia were his——

But Cornelia did not return. An hour passed and his anxiety mounted to fever-pitch. He walked to the balcony and stared forth on to the garish square. There was a crowd there—an excited crowd, the sight of which told him that the news he had heard in the lounge was known in the city. But there was no sign of the woman for whom he watched. He waited another half-hour, then in a fever of apprehension he consulted the manager of the hotel, a Frenchman from Pau. The manager was not helpful. He smiled and shrugged his shoulders.

" Who can tell what the ladies will do, monsieur ? Their whims are many ! . . . No doubt it was a friend of madame's who called, and she has gone forth to see the night life of the city, which is interesting to the sex."

Mr. Standish could have bashed that cynical, smiling face, and only with an effort refrained from cursing the man. He went back to the balcony, and resumed his vigil. He watched quite a long time with vultures of anxiety at his heart. Across the square in the light of the Cinema an European woman with a French officer hove into sight. Was it——? No ! Still he waited and watched, helpless, torn with apprehension. The motley tide of life in the square began to ebb. Lights were extinguished. The noise died down ; but in Mr. Standish's heart was a very tumult of fear. There was no doubt now that something evil had befallen Cornelia. She had been lured away to some den in this barbaric city. He looked at his watch. It was almost midnight, and as he marked the fact his control was broken. He could wait no longer. It was time to act. Already he had waited too long, and now he might be a century too late. Raving with anxiety, he ran from the balcony and sought the smiling manager, demanding wildly that he should be taken to the Sûreté, to the Commandant, to any authority who could help him in the catastrophe that had befallen. . . .

As it chanced there was a substantial ground for Mr. Standish's anxiety, and the facts, had he known them, must have driven him insane with apprehension, for half an hour after his return to the hotel, Cornelia stood in an apartment in the very heart of the native city facing the man who had brought her there, and asking crisply :

" Where is Mr. Standish ? "

The man of whom she made the demand laughed harshly.

" That fool ! God knows ! When last I saw him he was lying stunned on the cobbles in the dark. By this time no doubt he has been stripped and dropped into the river."

Cornelia's face blanched at the news. " Then it was a lie you told me when you said that he wanted me. That I was to come to him at once."

The man laughed again. " You are a pretty bird," he said, " and easily limed."

Cornelia was aghast at this confirmation of the fear which had suddenly surged within her, and for a moment stood there dumb with terror, looking dazedly round the apartment, which was furnished in the Moorish fashion. Then, whilst she so stood, the man chuckled and spoke again :

" A pretty bird. . . . No wonder you took Simon Maxwell's eye."

At the words utter terror gripped her. She stared wildly at the man and cried :

" Who are you ? "

The man did not immediately reply. Perhaps he understood the effect of suspense, and was desirous of letting the terror now visible in her eyes complete its work. Very deliberately he took from his pocket a silver tobacco-box and a roll of papers and began to make a cigarette. Mechanically the woman watched the stubby fingers rolling the tobacco in the paper. Then an utterly amazed light came in the dark eyes and a startled gasp broke from her. At the sound the man looked up sharply from his half-made cigarette.

" What——"

He caught the direction of her gaze and laughed harshly. " So you understand ? "

Cornelia still stared with fascinated gaze at the fellow's

left hand, where was the replica of the three black dots which Simon Maxwell had worn.

" You are one of them ? " she cried.

" Of the Three Black Dots ? " he asked, with a laugh. " Why, of course.   You knew that when you came to Fez to seek me."

" No," replied Cornelia quickly.   " And I did not come here seeking you."

" You didn't ? "   The man was plainly surprised and more than a little sceptical.   " You tell me that ? "

" It is the truth ! " she cried.

" But that fool who was with you ?   You do not speak for him.   But he knew, and that is why he came.   He followed me——"

" I assure you——"

The man broke in with a snort of unbelief.   " It is no use, my pretty one.   A woman can lie better than Ananias. Thunder !   Yes.   And when I saw you and that fool ride up to the Bab Guissa this afternoon——"

" You were at the gate ? "

" A blind beggar-man to whom your escort charitably gave a franc."

" You . . . the blind beggar ! "

The fellow laughed.   " It is a profitable calling, and a blind man can watch without being suspected if he is careful."

" But you were not watching for me ! " cried Cornelia.

" *Gott im Himmel !*   No !   No man in Morocco was more surprised than I when you appeared.   I was watching for a tiger and I caught a butterfly. . . .   But do not feel hurt, madame.   You were more welcome even than the tiger—though unexpected.   So welcome, that, as you know, I have been at some pains to ensure our meeting."

" But why—why ? "

" That you shall hear presently, madame.   First you shall tell me why you came to Fez."

Cornelia began to recover from her first unbridled terror

and spoke plainly and with sincerity which was convincing.

" I came to find the slayer of Simon Maxwell—my husband."

" And you think that I——"

" I was looking for another than you," interrupted Cornelia quickly.

" Ah ! my tiger ! You know then that Captain Warborough slew your husband."

" I suspected him, but——"

She checked herself. It was no use telling this man that she associated him with the crime. She was in his hands in this strange house, and anything might happen if he were spurred by fear.

" And you came to Fez to look for him ? "

" Yes ! He is here somewhere."

At her words the man betrayed an unaccountable excitement.

" He is here ? You are sure he is here, madame ? "

" We had word that he had come here. That is all I know."

The man nodded his head, and spoke to himself rather than to her.

" It is likely. He would come straight here if he knew what was to happen. I must have missed him." He was silent for a moment or two lost in thought, then he asked abruptly :

" And when you found the dear Warborough, what meant you to do with him ? "

" Bring him to justice, and have him hanged," answered the woman quickly.

Her interlocutor laughed. " You would pluck Captain Warborough out of Morocco just now ? You do not know the task you have set yourself. You could easier lift a Touareg out of the desert or that eagle El-Krim out of his eyrie."

" Yet I shall find him. I shall do it."

A flash of admiration came in the man's eyes.

" You would try," he said, " but you would fail. . . . If I thought you would succeed, I might let you free of the cage, my pretty bird." Then he shook his head. " But no ! It is impossible."

At his words and the purpose implied in them Cornelia's mind was switched back to the realities of her position, and stark fear gripped her afresh.

" What do you mean ? " she cried. " That you mean to keep me here ? "

" Here or elsewhere ! " the man answered brusquely.

" But why ? What——"

" The widow of Simon Maxwell must be a rich woman. It is not unknown in Morocco for a prisoner to be held to ransom."

The man laughed brutally as he made the statement, and even in the midst of her fear that laughter stung the woman to retort.

" Then you are a common bandit ! "

Her captor shrugged his shoulders. " A name is nothing to me. And there are peculiar elements in this case. Anything that you pay will be no more than the liquidation of a debt owed by Maxwell."

" But there are lawyers who——"

" The debt would not be recoverable in law. Maxwell was a rogue and a thief who cheated his partners and left them without legal redress. As it is, you must pay."

" Not a shilling," said Cornelia stoutly.

The man laughed.

" You are brave. Yes, but you are ignorant of Morocco. You do not know what can happen to a woman here. If you did, you would write the cheque for a hundred thousand pounds——"

" Preposterous ! Do you think such a cheque would be honoured by my husband's executors without inquiry ? "

" You would make the cheque payable to yourself, and

arrange to have the money transferred to Tangier or Casablanca."

" But that would take time ? "

" Time ! Oh yes ! And in that time you, madame, would remain with me. It is quite simple, and one would be privileged with the companionship of a beautiful woman."

" If you think——"

" I am convinced that you will agree, madame."

" I will not ! And if you think you can force me, you are mistaken. Do you think that I shall not be missed ? that my friend——"

" Who is by this time stripped and in the river, as I suggested just now."

" But there are others. I am known. There will be a search——"

" Madame does not know this quarter. It is a rabbit-warren. Also the Moors are jealous of their women, and at this time the authorities will be chary of arousing their fanatical ire. Madame has not heard the news that has come in to-night—the news that El-Krim has moved against the French outposts in the North. But Fez has heard and is wondering what it will do—whetting its knives, and taking out its carbines from secret places ready for the uprising. In such a situation madame is a straw in the wind ; none will trouble about so small a thing as a woman when a kingdom is at stake. So you will write the order——"

He broke off at the sound of a crashing door, and went swiftly to the entrance of the apartment. To Cornelia it was clear that he expected someone to enter, and a moment later she caught the slip-slap of slippered feet. The man watched the door intently and in turn Cornelia used the opportunity to examine him as he sat there with his face now full in the light of the swinging lamp. She caught sight of scars running down either cheek, and remembered something that Garfield Standish had told her about the man whom he had encountered in Greek Street, and the remembrance brought with it a name.

" Steinmann ! "

In the excitement of the moment she cried the name aloud, and the man half-turned and inclined his head mockingly :

" Your servant, madame."

A second later his eyes were on the door again, as a man reached the threshold—a Moor, richly attired in serwal, chamir, faragra and haik. At the sight of Cornelia the new-comer halted swiftly and a look of wonder and admiration leaped in his dark eyes. Steinmann signalled him forward and spoke to him in the Moghrebbin dialect.

The Moor answered quickly and at length. The actress had not the remotest idea what he was saying ; but the tense, nervous note in his voice told her that he brought important news, which was confirmed by Steinmann's demeanour as the other continued to speak. Then her captor began to ask questions, tersely, with the unconscious brusqueness of a man eager for news and confronted by something that troubled him. For a little time the catechism went on, then Steinmann began to speak whilst the Moor listened. To the listening woman, ignorant as she was of the language spoken, it seemed clear that he was giving the Moor instructions ; and after a little time, she divined that those instructions had to do with herself ; for again and again the Moor's eyes turned to her, and once or twice he smiled as a graven image might have smiled and nodded his head. Then he withdrew, flashing a glance at her as he went, which brought the blood to her face and set a chill in her heart.

For what seemed quite a long time Steinmann did not speak, and Cornelia stood there listening to the flip-flap of the retreating feet, and waiting for the crashing of the door. She waited in vain. The expected sound did not come. The Moor, it seemed, had not left the house, but had merely gone to some other apartment. Then Steinmann broke on her thoughts.

" A great man, that, madame, and obviously an admirer of yours."

Cornelia shivered a little at the words and at the significant note in them, and the man continued :

" He has brought me news of import. You were right about Captain Warborough having come to Fez. He was at the Bab Guissa this afternoon, and whilst I was watching for the tiger—the tiger was watching for me. It is possible that he saw madame and her so generous friend. . . . But he did not speak. *Nein !* He has his reasons for silence as madame knows, and he is clever that one, for I never suspected the teller of tales and that old fool with the tambourine."

Cornelia remembered the story-teller at the gate and cried out in surprise :

" That was Captain Warborough ? "

Steinmann made a laughing grimace. " The devil in disguise. He is a man of many incarnations, and the fact that he was there by the Bab Guissa is significant. He may have been watching me ; so there will be one blind beggar the less at the gate to-morrow ; for I must leave Fez to-night in spite of the closed gates."

Cornelia's heart leaped at the words.

" Then I am to go free ? "

Steinmann laughed. " When you have paid the debt I mentioned. And that is a matter of time, as you insisted a little while ago. I cannot take you with me, but to-morrow Si Mohammed Amaati—our friend whom you saw just now—will bring you after me——"

" I shall not go," cried Cornelia vehemently.

The man laughed, then he spoke softly in a purring voice:

" You will not go ? As I have told you—you do not know Morocco. But you have heard stories of men found mutilated on the battlefields ; of soldiers who in a losing game keep a last shot for themselves ; of men who neg-

lecting that precaution have been tortured in ways that
the polite do not speak of. . . .   You have heard, yes ?
But you do not know that the torturers are women—
always women, and it is Si Mohammed's women who will
make you glad to follow me, and make you crave for my
company."

He laughed at some thought which came to him, then
he added lightly : " Women the wide world over are
creatures of jealousy.   It is possible that Si Mohammed's
women may mistake the nature of their lord's interest in
you, madame.   They will not be too scrupulous as to the
means they will use to compel your obedience ; and it is
likely that they will welcome recalcitration on the part of
so pretty a bird as an excuse for their jealous activities."
He laughed again as he saw her shiver.   " You will go—
yes—at the word, I think."

He rose.   " I leave you now.   But we shall meet again
very soon, madame.   In the meantime it were well for
you to rest.   That divan there offers comfort, and you
will find the road on mule-back a little tiring, I fear. . . .
Adieu, madame ! "

He clicked his heels, bowed in a stiff German fashion,
then swinging round, marched from the room.   She stood
listening to the sounds of his heels, now sharp upon a
marble floor, now deadened by a rug.   They grew fainter
and she guessed he was descending the stairs.   Presently
they were lost altogether in the creak and crash of a heavy
door opened and closed.   Assured that he had left the
house, she awoke to the necessity for action.   She glanced
at the curtained archway through which he had gone,
but knowing that it would be guarded, she turned aside
and running lightly to some other hangings across the
room dragged them aside to find a balcony before her.
She stepped on to it and found herself looking down on
the lighted roof of a house twenty feet below where some
women sat chattering.   Further away were other roofs,
from one of which came the melancholy note of a pipe

mingling with the sound of running water ascending from a depth of darkness which her eyes could not penetrate.

She realized instantly that there was no escape for her that way. The one way out was the way that Steinmann had taken—the great door which opened on the street. Perhaps if she were quick she might slip past any watcher of the stairs, and once in the street she could get away. She turned to leave the balcony, and as she did so caught a burst of cackling laughter, and in the chamber saw two unveiled Moorish women, one of whom seemed wizened with age, but whose still keen eyes twinkled with evil mirth.

## CHAPTER XII

### IN PURSUIT

" *MON DIEU!* But who am I to find a lady who has fled her escort with a lover ? It is the way of ladies——"

The harassed official whom Mr. Standish had dragged from his couch, shrugged his shoulders as an indication that what was disturbing his visitor was really no affair of his. Mr. Standish, however, was not so easily dismissed. He was an American citizen and very insistent on his rights to be heard, and all the administration must be at his call to save Cornelia Maxwell from heaven knew what fate. The official with a thought for his bed took the line of least resistance.

" Very well, monsieur, if you insist." He seated himself at a table, drew paper towards him, and pen in hand spoke again. " If you will give me a description of the lady—— Name, please ? "

" Cornelia Maxwell—better known as Claire Devereaux. You must have heard of her. She is the star cinema-actress."

Apparently the fame of the lady had not penetrated to Fez. The official lifted his shoulders again.

" Ah ! An actress ! " he said dryly, his tone and

manner asking as plain as words, " My dear monsieur, what can you expect ? "

" Age, monsieur ? "

Mr. Standish made a guess, and later, on request, gave a glowing description of the lady's charms. French though he was, the official was not moved by it. He reduced the description to official terms, asked another question or two which Mr. Standish considered were impertinently personal, then he demanded brusquely :

" And the gentleman who lured the lady away ? You have his description."

" Yes ! He was a heavy-faced European, a German the clerk thought——"

" A German ? " The official's eyes grew suddenly keen, and his demeanour became alert. " Is monsieur sure of that ? "

" That was the clerk's judgment, and——" Mr. Standish broke off, sharply assailed by a startling thought. Then he spoke with quick apprehension : " My God ! If it should be ! "

The official marked both Mr. Standish's words and startled manner, and said smoothly :

" Monsieur has remembered something ? He knows the man ? "

" I'm not sure, it was just an idea that came to me— too wild to be true. But if by a stretch it could be, then I know the scoundrel's name."

" Monsieur, in this land most wild stories, however incredible, are usually true. It would be helpful to hear the abductor's name."

" Well, it's only a guess, and one that came to me suddenly just now, but the name is possibly Steinmann."

" Le diable ! "

A bomb might have been dropped on the table from the way the official jumped to his feet. And a second later he was crying excitedly : " You know the man ? You have seen him here ? "

" Not here. . . . In London."

" But you think that this man who took your lady away is Steinmann ? "

" The fellow who called at the hotel was German. As it chanced, Steinmann is the only German I've any acquaintance with, and he laid me out in a London street. He was mixed up with a murder in Dorsetshire, England, with a fellow called Caillé——"

" That man also ! "

" No need to worry about him, monsieur. He is dead as a door-nail. But the more I think of it, the more Steinmann seems to be the likely man, though what he is doing here in——"

" Excuse me, monsieur," broke in the official. " This is most important. There is a man who may help you——"

He hurried from the room, leaving his visitor pacing to and fro in great agitation. He was absent quite a considerable time, so long indeed that Mr. Standish lost patience and was in the act of opening the door with the intention of calling for him, when the man returned. The official was in no way put out by his caller's impatience. He rubbed his hands and spoke cheerfully.

" We have the luck, monsieur. The man who is able to help you is in Fez. He will be here within a very few minutes. Please be seated. These cigarettes are worth trying, and coffee will be served almost immediately."

Mr. Standish took a cigarette, a black servant appeared with coffee, and when he had withdrawn and closed the door, the host asked a question :

" You said just now that Baptiste Caillé was dead. That is certain, I presume."

" A coroner's jury found it so. He was shot by the husband of the lady for whom I am seeking—Simon Maxwell—the millionaire."

" Ah ! I have read of him. He was murdered in his own house and on his wedding-night, was he not ? "

" Yes."

" And you think that this Steinmann who has taken
madame from your care was the man who slew——"

" No. I don't. He had a finger in the pie, but the
killer was another man."

" You are sure, monsieur ?  His name is known ? "

" Dead sure, and I have his name ; but for the present
I keep it secret.  But he is in Morocco, and in Fez, which
accounts for madame and myself being here."

The official smiled.  " You may keep your secret,
monsieur, if you think it wise.  But can you explain why
this man Steinmann should abduct madame ? "

" I haven't an inkling, unless it is that she is enormously
rich and a very beautiful woman."

" A sufficient reason, either of them, to tempt a bandit
to a bold stroke.  I know——"

The official stopped.  His caller was not listening and
his eyes were fixed tensely on the door.

" Excuse me, monsieur," whispered Mr. Standish.
" There is someone outside the door."

He neither sought nor waited for his host's permission.
With cat-like tread he moved to the door and opened it
sharply.  A man in native attire stood outside.  Quite
obviously he had been listening to the conversation within
the room, and the realization of the fact annoyed Mr.
Standish.

" Here's a confounded eavesdropper——" he began
testily, and then broke off as he realized there was something familiar about the man.  Then, as the remembrance
came to him, he cried out in surprise : " The tale-teller
of the northern gate."

" And the man for whom we were waiting, monsieur.
There is no need for alarm.  Be seated again, I beg you."

Mr. Standish did not immediately resume his chair.
He backed a yard or so into the room, and stared at the
tall man who entered, his slipper heels flopping, his rather
grimy djellaba sweeping the floor.  Dark eyes met his
own without flinching ; the man apparently was in no

way abashed by the fact that he had been surprised with ear at the keyhole, and Mr. Standish had an instinctive dislike to the fellow. But it was no time to indulge one's fancies, as he recognized ; and it was clear that the new-comer was not to be lightly treated.

" Monsieur Standish, you will please report to this man all that you have told me—in French, if possible. Though he is of Arab race, he will understand you. He is the only man in Morocco who can help you in this dilemma."

Mr. Standish looked at the tale-teller and almost grunted. Things, he thought, were come to a pretty pass if only this play-acting fellow could help him. But he waited no time and having told his story once, made a better and a briefer business of it at the second telling. The tale-teller listened imperturbably, and did not speak until the very end of the story. Then he asked a question in Arabic which the official translated to Mr. Standish.

" The woman left no message ? "

" None ! There was no need. She was coming to me, as she thought."

" And this Steinmann was a stranger to her ? "

" She'd never seen him to her knowledge."

The official conferred with the tale-teller, then addressed Mr. Standish again.

" Monsieur, the man will do what he can—but Fez is Fez and its bolt-holes and secret places are many. I think, however, you may leave the matter in his hands. Steinmann is wanted by the Administration for greater crimes than the abduction of your lady. My counsel is that you return to your hotel, and as soon as anything is known I will communicate with you, and——"

" But, good heavens, man, am I to twiddle my thumbs ? "

The official was a little nettled by Mr. Standish's tone, and replied curtly :

" It will be as useful as anything else you can do to-night, monsieur."

" But——"

" Already you have learned what may happen to a man who wanders in dark streets without protection, Monsieur Standish. You have the luck to be alive still, and if you reflect you will see how little a stranger to the city and its ways can do in this situation. In the morning as soon as there is news you shall hear from me. Be assured that every stone shall be turned, for the Administration is more anxious to find Steinmann than you are to find madame. . . . Monsieur will excuse me now. There is much that I must do before morning, and, also, one must sleep."

Mr. Standish found himself bowed out, and in the street silently cursed the Administration and all its works. That man could talk of sleep with Cornelia Maxwell in the power of a man no better than a murderer, held in some hole in this stinking city ! He walked to his hotel fuming, and made a hopeless inquiry of the sleepy attendant.

" No, madame had not returned. . . . Has monsieur seen the officer at the Sûreté ? "

He had, and said so with a vigour that shrivelled the curiosity of the inquirer ; then he went to his room, and spent a wretched night, pacing to and fro through half the hours of darkness, and the other half huddled on the bed, now wide awake, now sleeping uneasily, dogged by nightmare and awaking to formless fears more gruelling than his evil dreams.

In the morning he went down to the Sûreté with his inquiry for news. He was received by a subordinate, who, after consulting with his superior, announced that as yet there was no information about the missing lady. The statement was coupled with an assurance that the moment any news was available monsieur would be informed at his hotel. There was nothing to be done, and he went out into the street again, a man beset by apprehension. His original purpose was quite forgotten. The thought of Warborough never so much as crossed his mind. He wandered up and down the streets, staring into the faces of the bizarre crowd as it drifted by him ; hoping against hope that he might surprise that of Steinmann and so perhaps get a line on Cornelia.

He passed through strange shadowy places, where the hot sunlight flickered in a chequered way through pergolas of woven grasses and trellised vines, down narrow alleys where the houses rose blindly on either side like cliffs, through bazaars where he jostled shoulders with half the races of Africa and most of those of Southern Europe, by Koranic schools whence came the voices of the children of the Faithful in monotonous repetition of the learning of Islam, past places where was the sound of mills turned by water grinding the corn for bread.

Now he was in a wide street, that a few yards further on became a path narrow almost as that which leads to Paradise, where he was crushed against the wall by a string of the small Moorish donkeys which are the true burden-bearers of the land. He noted dully the tiny shops, craftsmen at work, veiled women intent on marketing, Berbers from the untamed Atlas, negroes from the South, a motley host of diverse faces, but nowhere the face that he sought ; and presently, without intent came to the Bab Guissa and passed through. A little dizzy with fatigue, with his back to the high red walls, sick at heart he stared forth on the olive groves on the slopes of the hills and on the road running north, following what in distant time was the bed of the sea before the Mediterranean found a new way through the great Pillars to the Atlantic.

There was much traffic in and out of the gate, and he watched it dully, apathetically, with the indifference of a man absorbed in other things. But presently there came a pair who quickened his interest a little—two men, one tall, the other of moderate height. They were dressed in dirty white djellabas, their bare feet thrust into loose, heelless babooches of yellow leather ; and between them they led a seemingly recalcitrant donkey, lightly laden, whilst the shorter of the two shouted angrily to a crowd of children that blocked their way :

" Balek !   Balek ! "

The children mocked them, but scattered apart, one
boy however falling under the hoofs of the donkey, whence
he was snatched screaming by the taller of the two men,
who set him on his feet, and stayed his howling with a
coin.    There was nothing unusual in the incident unless
it was the giving of the money ; but for the moment it
fixed Mr. Standish's interest on the pair ; and as he
watched them he noted that as they marched forward
they glanced continually backward towards the gate.

" They are afraid that someone will follow them," he
thought, and himself gave some attention to the backward
way.

Nothing of interest befell.   No one, it seemed, was pur-
suing the pair hot-foot from the city, and in a little while
both donkey and drivers were lost to sight, merged in
the stream of traffic to and from the gate.

After a time, spent fruitlessly in aimless thought, he
made his way back to the hotel, and there found a message
awaiting him from the official whom he had interviewed
on the previous night—a message which took him hot-
foot to the sender.

" You have news, monsieur.   You have found madame ? "
he burst out as he was shown into the official's presence.

The official waved him to a chair, and waited until the
door closed behind the black servant, then he said quietly :

" One should be discreet, monsieur.   It is well not to
talk before servants, if one does not want his business to be
whispered on all the housetops of Fez.   But there is news
for monsieur, a very little news, and it is not good.   There
is reason to believe that madame may have left the city."

" When ? " asked Mr. Standish hoarsely.

" This morning when the gates were opened.   I can
say little more than that.   The information is meagre,
but the suspicion arising from it is, I think, warranted.
Indeed, the man whom you met here last night is so sure
that he has left Fez on the track of madame."

" But who has she gone with ?   How was she taken ? "

" If the information is correct, she went with the household of a Moorish notable—a veiled stranger among veiled women, an easy but efficient disguise in this land, monsieur."

" But the notable ?   Who was he ?   Give me his name ! I'll follow the rascal to Timbuktu if need be."

The official hummed and hawed a little, then spoke slowly :

" I am afraid I cannot oblige you, monsieur. Just now things are inflammable here.  A little incident might start a conflagration—and we cannot afford that.  The man in whose household madame is journeying has influence, and he is suspected not only of being disloyal to the Administration, but of being hand and glove with that Steinmann, who, if your suspicions are right, induced madame to leave her hotel.  But at the moment we cannot act with the high hand.  These are critical days—beyond what is known outside the Administration——"

" So you will sacrifice a helpless woman ! " jerked in the other roughly.

" Monsieur, you are unjust.  I have not said we shall sacrifice madame.  I am saying we must not at this moment pour oil on a smouldering fire, and you must leave us to secure madame's return in our own way. . . . You comprehend ? "

" Comprehend ? . . . Hell ! am——"

The rest of Mr. Standish's utterance was too lurid to be chronicled.  As with most men not customarily given to profanity, in the background of his mind was a reservoir of unparliamentary words which now broke through the barriers of politeness, and poured themselves upon the unfortunate official in a roaring spate.  Red in the face, and spluttering with rage, the official rose from his chair.

" Monsieur, you pass the bounds.  I must ask you to remove yourself, or I will have you thrown out."

He touched a bell as he spoke, and as the black orderly

hurried in, began to give directions.  Garfield Standish recognized that it was time to go, and still muttering maledictions, he found his way to the street.  There his heat of mind died down a little, and as he walked along indifferent to the hurrying tide of life and the panorama of the street, he began to consider what he had heard.  It was on review, little enough.  Cornelia had left Fez as a Moorish woman ; and the teller-of-tales had gone in pursuit—a pursuit which he himself was tacitly forbidden to follow.  That angered him a great deal.

" If I only knew—where . . . I'd show them ! " he muttered in jerks, then stopped so suddenly in the crowded street that a fat negress walking behind cannoned against him rather heavily.

He scarcely noticed the bump.  He was staring in front of him, seeing nothing of the variegated crowd, but with his mind's eye watching two men passing from the Bab Guissa along the Taza road, with a lightly ladened donkey between them.  One of those two men was tall, as tall as the teller-of-tales, the other might be the old man who had beaten the square tambourine.  The revelation did not stop there.  As in a transformation picture on a cinema-screen the little scene outside the northern gate which his mind had recalled gave place to another, and again he saw two men standing together on the quay at Oran— both in uniform.  Except for their respective height there apparently was nothing in common with the pair who had marched that morning from the city, but in his mind was an unreasoning, overwhelming conviction that they were the same men.

" By the living Jingo ! . . . Yes ! " He thought to himself.  " Warborough, and Grandpère Jacques—for a thousand dollars.  And they went North—on the Taza road !  That means Cornelia is being taken that way. . . . And I am not to butt in."  He laughed scornfully.  " I'll show that fool in the office back there——"

He began to hurry forward.  Conviction grew in him

as he marched.  By the time he reached the hotel he
would have pledged his soul that he was right ; and without
questioning his intuition or the wisdom of following its
indication, plunged into a very welter of preparation ;
and two hours later, with a Moorish guide and a couple
of pack animals, mounted on a strong mule, he rode from
the shadow of the Bab Guissa, past the little fort named
after the heroic Chardonnet, out to the northern road,
and afar off caught the gleam of great Atlas, silver and
blue, like some height of dreamland.  But for the beauty
of the latter nor for the vivid life of the highway had he
any eye.  Before him as he rode, in vision, there moved
two men in dirty white djellabas leading a donkey between
them, and beyond them, a slow-travelling caravan, made
up of a Moorish household, among the veiled women of
which jogged Cornelia Maxwell.  His own mules were
good, and they were lightly laden.  He had lost hours,
but his pace would even the handicap.

" By to-night," he muttered with conviction, " at the
first camping place ! "

And as he rode on in that assurance, in a riot of fancy
he saw Cornelia's dark eyes flash with tenderness as they
welcomed her deliverer.


## CHAPTER XIII

### MARRAKESH THE RED

AT the sight of the mirthful old hag standing with her
younger companion, barring the way to the curtained entrance, Cornelia Maxwell suffered a new surge of
fear.  The thin cackling laughter chilled her like an icy
wind, and for a second or two she stood quite still, dumb,
apprehensive of unknown things.  Then bracing herself
she advanced from the balcony into the chamber, carrying
herself with a brave air, and using the French tongue
demanded that they should show her the way to the street.

Whether the pair understood her words or not she had no means of knowing ; but the only answer she received was a new burst of shrill laughter from the crone, who turning said something to her companion, moving her in turn to laughter.

The old woman stared at her appraisingly, and Cornelia returned the stare with interest, marking the glint of cruelty in the keen old eyes, and the mirthful scorn in those of the younger woman. Their attitude frightened her, and from demands she passed to pleading, offering them the jewels she wore for help to escape from that evil house. They might not comprehend her words ; but it was clear they divined her desire ; and certain that the jewels in her hand thrust out imploringly, attracted the older woman ; for her eyes blazed with a sudden covetous light, and on the wrinkled face came an expression of utter cupidity.

Cornelia's supplications became more vehement. If only she could move the crone, she might yet escape from the gulf which yawned before her ; and once in the street —— A new burst of laughter quenched the flicker of hope within her ; and the old woman shook her head decisively, and made a curt reply in Moghrebbin, of which Cornelia understood not a word. Then the woman approached her and by signs indicated that she was to disrobe. She refused indignantly and turned away ; but even as she did so the younger woman leaped forward and sinuous arms gripped her from behind, holding her firmly. She struggled desperately, crying out in the extremity of her fear ; and the hag-like old woman slipped in front of her, and stretching a skinny hand, threatened her eyes with claw-like fingers.

That menacing gesture sapped her impulsive resistance. In a flash she remembered the blind beggars of every city in Morocco, and divined that all things were possible to such women as these, who, as Steinmann had hinted, mutilated both living and dead enemies in ways horrible and unmentionable. The gesture might be no more than an empty threat, but the bare possibility of the horror it suggested was sufficient to scare her, not to compliance, but to an apprehensive passivity, in which, shrilling laughter, the pair tore her clothing from her until she stood almost stark. Then the younger passed from the chamber, leaving her alone with the hag, who amused herself by pinching her white flesh, pawing her significantly and indulging in a silent but inexpressibly ribald pantomime which made her sick with fear and loathing. For a second or two she thought of trying to overcome the elderly witch, and make her way from the house ; but the thought of her stark condition and of the dark, strange streets through which she must pass, if she won free, stayed her hand.

Helplessly she stood there waiting for what was to follow, then somewhere outside the chamber a man's laugh sounded, giving keener edge to her terror. The old witch with her loathly gestures was horrible, but that man whose dark eyes had flashed wonder and admiration was the cold reality. A sound of flapping babooches followed the laughter. The man, she thought, was approaching the chamber. In another moment——

Distraught by sheer terror, she remembered the balcony and the deeps below. There, after all, lay the one way of escape. In a frenzy of despair she flung towards the hangings, reached them and was tearing them aside when the old woman, moving with surprising agility, gripped her and held her back. For a time betwixt fear and despair she reverted to the primitive, fought as a woman of the Stone Age might have done, shrilling inarticulate cries and struggling insanely to break the hag's hold. Then through the mists of frenzy she saw the person whose steps she had heard enter the room—the younger woman, with an armful of clothing.

In her reaction from the extremity of fear she collapsed to the floor, then passively suffered them to clothe her

as they themselves were clothed in the dark draperies of
Moorish women ; and still too shaken to struggle more
was conducted to a divan, where, crouched upon silken
cushions, she waited, alert with fear, hopeless ; with the
two women watching her like hawks, one between her
and the door, the other barring the way to the balcony
and the deeps that offered dark release.

The hours passed with heavy feet. Time, it seemed,
stood still ; but at last with the lamp smoking and fluttering to extinction, a faint, colourless light crept between
the balcony-hangings, and the utter stillness of the city
was broken by the muezzin's cry, echoing sonorously from
minaret to minaret :

" *La ilah ill-ilhau !* "

The morning call to prayer ! The night of terror was
over, daybreak was at hand, bringing with it the unknown,
new perils perhaps, horrors inconceivable to be escaped
only by death. She shuddered at the contemplation ;
and almost immediately was called to endure new harsh-
ness. Scarcely had the muezzin's calls ceased to echo,
when she was forcibly gagged, veiled after the fashion of
Moorish women, and taken to the courtyard. There she
was cunningly bound to a mule, and among a number of
veiled women of Mohammed's household, as like them in
outward appearance as a pea is like another, unable to
cry out or to make even a sign to attract attention to her
parlous condition under the eyes of the French guard at
the gate, marched with a small caravan from the city to
a destination that she knew not.

Five miles from the city the gag was removed and her
hands freed, her captors, it appeared, having now no fear
of any appeal to passers-by. That very release deepened
her despair ; none upon this sun-baked road, it seemed,
would trouble to regard her appeal. Once or twice her
mind reverted to Garfield Standish. Steinmann had
declared that he had last seen him lying senseless on the
cobbles, and that it was likely that he was stripped and

dead ; in which case there was for her no help anywhere.
She shivered as, looking ahead, she saw the tall form of
Si Mohammed Amaati riding a fine barb, and from time
to time casting a backward glance in her direction.

Where was the Moor taking her ?  And to what fate ?
What would she find at the end of this forced journey—
Steinmann again ?  It was possible, she thought.  From
what the man had said, he must have fled from Fez under
cover of darkness ;  was he awaiting her somewhere down
this road, which shimmered in the heat, or among those
wild hills ahead lifting snowy peaks to the burnished sky ?
She almost prayed that he was.  Now in the face of a fate
that confronted her, she would gladly yield to his black-
mailing demand.  The opportunity, however, was not
afforded.  The day passed without any sign of the German,
and when the camp was pitched he was still missing.

It was the same on the next day, and in the days that
followed it ;  and in the accumulating hopelessness she
lost account of time.  The days came and went, and at
first in the apathy into which she sank she scarcely marked
their coming or their going.  Only once did she have a
quickening thought, and that was when she remembered
the man, following whom on the bitter trail of vengeance,
had brought her to this dreadful pass.  If Warborough
had indeed been the tale-teller of the Bab Guissa, he must
almost certainly have marked her entry into the city ;
and if his interest had been in Steinmann, as by the
latter's own avowal it was, then it was just possible that
their trails might yet converge ;  and deliverance come to
her by the hand that had slain her husband.  If it should
happen, her actress's sense told her it would be a strange
drama, presenting new problems ;  but none to equal that
which confronted her now.  But such drama was of the
theatre, remote from the possibilities of life ;  and, if
Steinmann had not come this way, utterly unlikely.
Furthermore, knowing that she sought to be the avenger
of blood and aware of his own guilt, even should their

ways cross, there was but one chance in a thousand that he would lift a finger to save her.

The passage of days, however, combined with the ever-changing panorama of the world through which she rode, presently broke through her apathy, and things began to force themselves upon her interest. Each mile of the journey brought something new. Now a caravan of camels ambled by, the drivers goading the beasts cruelly, and shouting in a frenzy of excitement:

" Arr zit !　Arr zit ! "

Then towards the slopes of Atlas a gleam of blue water with the sun upon it broke on her vision—a lake of turquoise dreaming under the fiery sky, promising refreshment and coolness—but which whilst she watched it vanished into thin air, the unsubstantial, incredible, mysterious mirage.　The road ran through a sun-scorched land, withered and parched and dead.　It throbbed in the heat and glare, the hot dust of it rose in a cloud, whilst the mountains still wore their dazzling, cool caps of snow. Sometimes from patches of palm the white walls and towers of desert towns lifted to view ; but they entered none of them ; though occasionally, as she noted, when the camp was pitched almost in the shadow of their walls, strangers of his own race came furtively in the darkness to talk to Si Mohammed, often remaining far into the night, in excited discussion of things to which she had no clue.

Twice it happened that an eagle-eyed man of the desert, with rifle slung behind the shoulder, mounted on a superb dromedary, joined their cavalcade, rode for an hour by Si Mohammed's side, then moved off, gathering speed, until dromedary and rider were to her watching eyes but a little cloud of dust on the brown plain.

All this she marked with increasing interest ; but in the background of her mind was one consuming thought. Each yard of the way took her further from the hope of deliverance ; each mile, slowly accomplished, was like a new zone set between her and hope.　From the sun she was able to judge the direction, and knew that the caravan was moving almost due south, and presently she began to conjecture its destination. It was moving towards the great desert, where in some oasis, prisoned by leagues on leagues of sand, she would be utterly lost beyond all reach of deliverance; unless Steinmann came to collect his black dues. What would happen to her in that case? Since leaving Fez, Si Mohammed had not once spoken to her; but she had several times surprised his dark eyes staring at her with an intensity that shrivelled her soul.

She recalled an account she had read somewhere of a Christian traveller, who, venturing in disguise the pilgrimage to Mecca, there had met one who had once been an English lady, now a withered old woman, who had been abducted and taken into her captor's harem, and who, lost to hope and life, had forgotten all but a few words of her mother tongue. Was that to be her own fate—somewhere in the blistering sands, less accessible than Mecca itself?

Shudderingly she faced the question, appalled at the possibility, then unexpectedly her mind was switched from melancholy foreboding by the sound of an excited voice, shouting exultantly:

" Marrakesh Al-Hamra."

She looked round quickly, and ahead, shimmering in the glare, saw a vast stretch of palms, a wide, dark green splash in the brown waste; from the very midst of which a great minaret of rose-tinted stone lifted itself high in the air, its golden balls flashing in the burning light. The palms stretched for miles, and behind them, far away still, there loomed hazily, as in a dream-picture, the lofty, jagged mountains of Great Atlas, shadowy and mysterious, a great background for the tall, square minaret which challenged the eyes more than the mountains.

There was a buzz among the women about her, who excitedly repeated the name the man had shouted:

" Marrakesh Al-Hamra ! "

Marrakesh the Red.  Dimly she recalled the name of
the Great Saharan city, once more powerful than Fez
itself, and still a place of vast importance ; where con-
verged the fierce tides of the desert life ; which of old
had sent its armies to conquer Spain ; had gathered spoil
from far Timbuktu, and which even yet might furnish
the fanatical zealots to turn back the tide of civilization.
A city of ancient violence, a place pregnant with fiery
possibility still ; but to Cornelia, as she stared at its chaste
minaret, a city of hope, for she remembered suddenly
that there would be a French garrison in its walls.  She
had but to bide her time, wait until some soldier passed
by, or cry out to the officer in charge of the gate, and she
would be free of Si Mohammed Amaati and Steinmann
and all their works.

She shook with excitement at the thought, and yearning
as a wife to her own hearthstone, watched the palms grow
clearer, and saw the line of the great seven-mile wall
emerge.  Then suddenly her hope was dashed to the dust.
At a word from its master, whilst still two miles from the
city, the caravan halted.  Was it not to enter, after all ?
Was it to pass by or to camp only at a discreet distance
from its wall ?

A moment later the reason for the sudden halt was
made clear to her.  At a word from Si Mohammed the
two women who had been her gaolers slipped from their
mules, and moved towards her.  The old woman produced from her voluminous robe the gag which had been
used on leaving Fez, whilst the other carried the bands
with which her arms had been bound to her side.  Understanding came to her in a flash.  They were to enter
Marrakesh, but she was to enter as she had left Fez, dumb
and helpless.

" No !  No !  You shall not ! " she cried out in anguish
at this rude dashing of her hopes, struggling violently as
they proceeded to perform their task ; but other women
came to help their friends ; and soon she was tied to the

mule, gagged, with the veil dropped over her face, and to all appearances one with the Moorish women about her.

Half-crazed by her despair, despite the gag, she made a moaning sound. It was a prayer though none could have guessed it.

" God help me !  God deliver me ! "

That was the shape it had in her mind, and it was a true prayer, born as the sincerest prayers are in agony of mind. But the fiery heavens above, it seemed, were of brass.

" Forward ! " cried Si Mohammed with the peremptoriness of the masterful.

The march was resumed.  With eyes brimming with despairing tears she saw Red Marrakesh grow clear among its thousands of palms.  The road dipped through a jungle of Barbary cacti and feathery bamboo ;  then quite suddenly, as it seemed, her mule was ambling under one of the two hundred towers of the sun-baked wall.  One of the ten gates of the city lifted itself in a Moorish arch, through which as in a fine frame the rose-tinted minaret gleamed like a picture of dream.  A trio of grinning legionaires watched the cavalcade pass through.  Cornelia Maxwell turned towards them with eyes despairingly imploring.  The veil hid her dumb appeal ;  and with arms bound to her sides she struggled vainly, swaying this way and that, trying to throw herself from the mule, and so win the soldiers' attention.  One of them marked her antics, and made a ribald jest to his fellows who broke into coarse laughter ;  and to that sound, which mocked her despair, she passed to the thronged streets of the city and to the great square of the Djemaa-El-Enaa—the Meeting Place of the Dead ;  so vivid and so noisy with the clamorous living of all the turbulent clans whose homes fringe the great desert or lie in its sandy heart.

## CHAPTER XIV

### A FORGOTTEN GATE

FOUR hours after the caravan of Mohammed Amaati had passed through the gate, two travellers leading a tired donkey arrived at the Bab El Khemis—the northern gate of Marrakesh. Without delay they entered the city, following a winding lane of a street protected from the sun by a meagre thatch of dried palm-branches, supported by flimsy poles. Presently they reached a building, the blind front of which was broken by a single doorway opening into the courtyard of one of the thousand filthy caravanserais the city boasted. It was a noisome place. Asses and mules and camels were roughly stabled all around, the stench was terrific, the babel of tongues beyond imagination.

" A little hell, monsieur," said the shorter of the pair, who was Grandpère Jacques.

" Or the forecourt of one," laughed Warborough. " It at least calls for fire to consume it."

" How long do we remain ? " asked Grandpère, holding his nose.

" Until we have done our job, Jacques. The best place to hide a stone is a quarry, and for a brace of vagabonds like we are this place is the quarry. Also there are many places as like it as a row of beans are like each other. Unless we have been followed from the gate——"

" We have not. I watched the rear closely, monsieur."

" Then to find us, a man would have to comb through every seria in Marrakesh—a week's task, and even then he might fail." He waved a hand. " Here we fit in ; and he would not see the stones for the rock."

Grandpère Jacques chuckled. " Stones in a quarry, hey, monsieur. Likelier thieves among bandits. Here are no honest men."

" Only ourselves," laughed Captain Warborough, and without delay proceeded to make himself at home. The

proprietor of the caravanserai provided meals of a sort
—sausages with an ancient smell, mutton cooked in rancid
argan oil, and the thin maize gruel on which half Morocco
sups. A bowl of the latter and a couple of prickly Barbary figs by way of dessert sufficed Warborough ; then
leaving the donkey in charge of a negro who swore to
abide by it until the stars should fall, the pair passed
from the courtyard, separately, Grandpère Jacques saun-
tering with the careless air of any other idler a few yards
behind his officer. He appeared indifferent to everything
about him, but was in fact alert as a hawk, with an eye
for every passer-by and with an occasional glance round
for any man who might be shadowing them behind.

Presently they passed through the massive and formidable doorway of the Mellah—the Jewish quarter. The
place spawned humanity, and thrusting a way through
a swarm of women and children, Warborough turned into
a lane that was as unclean as it was narrow ; and as he
did so, he lifted a hand, which brought Grandpère Jacques
to a sudden halt at the corner, attracted as it seemed by
a fruit stall, presided over by an enormous Jewess. There
he loitered, twisting himself a cigarette, and whilst apparently bored to extinction, watched the street with eyes
that missed nothing. Warborough himself followed the
winding lane, and half-way down it came to a door, on
which, after a swift glance to right and left, he knocked.

The door opened with surprising promptness. He gave
a name to the obviously Jewish girl who acted as portress,
passed within, and with the door closed and bolted behind
him, followed the girl into the courtyard round which
the house was built and up the stairs into a chamber
which looked down into the yard itself. The chamber
was of Moorish design, but the furniture was European
of a rich but flamboyant style which accorded ill with
the room itself ; and in the manner of one much at home,
Warborough selected a chair, and searching the folds of
his begrimed djellaba, produced and lit a cigarette. He

had taken no more than a couple of whiffs when an old Jew of patriarchal appearance shuffled into the chamber —bearded like a prophet, clothed simply in the black gaberdine and the spotted black and white neckerchief which in the days of his power the Mussulman imposed upon the hated Jew. As he saw Warborough his old face lit up, and the soldier rose swiftly to his feet, for this simple-looking old man was not merely the richest man in all Marrakesh, but also a great gentleman.

"So you are come, my friend," said the old man in Arabic.

"As you see, Ischoua," replied the other in the same tongue.

"For five days I have expected you."

"There was need for delay," laughed Warborough. "One does not over-ride the hounds nor yet the fox."

The Jew waved him back to his chair, seated himself, and then spoke abruptly :

"Mohammed Amaati entered the city to-day.  He had his women with him."

"That I know.  Where does he lodge ? "

"At the house of his friend Abdullah Hammou."

"Good.  And the other one—the German ?  He is here also ? "

A worried look came on Ischoua's face.

"It may be.  I cannot say, my friend.  I have not found him or heard any word of him, which disturbs me. He is secret—that one !  But this very night Mohammed goes to the house of Ben Moussa where the others will also gather."

"So soon ! " Warborough whistled softly.  "Then Steinmann is here.  Mohammed Amaati would not move without him. . . . And the time ?  You have that, Ischoua ? "

The Jew nodded.  "Midnight when all but the evil sleep."

"It is a good hour to do a secret thing."  Warborough

smiled as he spoke. " With every gate shut, none can leave Marrakesh. . . . And if that pair we know of are taken——"

" The others will flee like jackals."

" That is my thought. But Steinmann is the most important. It is through him the rifles come."

The old man nodded. " And rifles persuade more than gold or words. With them in their hands these desert ones are wolves."

For a moment or two Warborough did not speak, then he asked a question :

" And the house of Ben Moussa ? "

" It is in the narrow street by the mosque of Sidi-bel-Abbès, by the quarter where live the blind beggars and the lepers."

" And how shall I know it, my friend ? "

" It has a great door patterned strangely with copper nails. There is no other such door in the street, and a man could be sure of it on the darkest night by the touch of his fingers."

" Then to-night, I shall find it." Again for a time the soldier was silent, lost in thought ; then he spoke praisefully : " You have done well, Ischoua."

The patriarch showed no gratification at the praise, but lifted a deprecating hand.

" I serve my people," he answered quietly. " If Mohammed Amaati has his way, and the men of the desert and those of Marrakesh play jackal to that lion El-Krim, when they have treacherously destroyed the garrison, it is in the Mellah the massacre will begin—always in the Mellah. So it was in my father's time, and he was hunted through the streets by the tigerish women, and slowly hacked to death with small knives. . . . To the Amaati and his friends the men of my race are dogs and worse."

" But there will be no massacre this time, Ischoua," said Jeff Warborough as he rose from his chair. " I go to make sure of that."

Ischoua accompanied him to the courtyard, and at the doorway Warborough spoke a last word:

"To-morrow I shall send the news."

"God grant that it may be good," said the Jew piously, and as he opened the door he looked up and down the narrow street, then nodded, and as his guest slipped out, quickly closed the door.

The street appeared empty, and Warborough walked quickly towards the turn of it. There, more from habit than for any precautionary purpose, he looked back and surprised a man's head protruding from a doorway a few yards from the house which he had just left. The head was swiftly withdrawn, and that action to Warborough was significant.

"A spy," he muttered to himself.

He hurried forward, reached the corner where Grand-père Jacques still lounged indolently alert, and spoke swiftly in French:

"If one comes running, stop him, Grandpère."

Grandpère Jacques grinned, and as his officer plunged into the weltering tide of humanity in the broader street, he himself slid towards the corner. He was no more than in time. A man in Moorish garb, running like a hare, cannoned into him, recoiled sharply, almost stumbling; and before he could recover the legionary's foot shot upwards in a terrible kick of the Paris Apache's. The still stumbling man shot backwards a full yard and then crashed senseless to the ground. Jacques flashed one look at him.

"A good kick! You will follow no more for a while, my too-curious friend."

Then, leaving the man lying there, he walked non-chalantly away, making his way to the stinking caravan-serai to report the fact to his master.

. . . A full hour before midnight Jeff Warborough and his legionary leading their donkey made their way together to the Sidi-bel-Abbès mosque. There in the shadow of the mosque they left the donkey tethered and crept to the alley of a street where the house of Ben Moussa was situated. The alley was black as pitch, but Warborough found the door and made sure of it, by the touch of his hands as Ischoua had declared a man might do in the dark. That done, he explored the street beyond and discovered that it was a mere cul-de-sac ending against the wall of a house that had no door into the alley.

"So much the better," he explained to Jacques. "There is but one way to watch."

They disposed themselves in a strategic doorway across the alley and, crouching there, waited. A profound silence fell upon the quarter, and the darkness seemed to grow more intense. Presently the old legionary asked a question :

"But, monsieur, in this blackness how shall we know the two we seek from the others ? "

"By their steps ! " answered Warborough. "Mohammed Amaati has a slight limp due to a bullet in the leg when he and his kind raised the dust in Fez. We must listen carefully."

"And the other one ? "

"Did you ever know a European who did not shuffle in babooshes, Jacques ? "

"Only one, my captain, and he is known also to you."

Warborough laughed silently at the compliment, and whispered back :

"The German is clumsy. In this stillness we shall hear his shuffles a mile away."

They waited in silence for some time, then Grandpère Jacques touched his companion.

"One comes," he whispered.

"Two," corrected Warborough.

The steps in the alley became clearer. Through the darkness stirred a ghost-like blur of white, and then voices speaking in low-toned Arabic.

"Not our men," Warborough whispered, and crouched closer in his hiding-place.

The two men halted at the door opposite, knocked and were admitted. Scarcely had they disappeared when Jacques whispered : " There are others coming, my captain. They carry a light to guide their steps in this gut of darkness."

It was true. At the entrance to the alley there was the yellow glow of a lantern and behind it the gleam of a white linen garment. Warborough swore softly.

" The devil ! I never thought one might bring a lantern. If we are seen——"

" They are three to two, monsieur. If the two plums we are to pluck be of them——"

" We must take the risk. The lantern will tell us if it is so. And we must use our little silencers swiftly. You comprehend ? Amaati and the German must not enter that house to-night."

" Have no fear, monsieur. At the word I shall strike as swift as the lightning."

They waited breathlessly. Warborough tensed himself for the spring, and gripped the loaded stick he carried. If the two for whom they waited were of that trio with the lantern, action would have to be very swift indeed to get them before they could cry out or knock on the door opposite. The bobbing lantern drew nearer. The figures of the three men became clearly outlined in its light ; but their faces were in shadow, and he was not sure until the man carrying the lantern lifted it to examine a door a few yards up the alley. Then he drew a breath of relief. The faces that he had glimpsed were not those of the men for whom he waited, and now he was assured that Jacques and himself would have at the most two men to encounter.

The three men resumed their way, stopped outside the patterned door and examined it with the aid of the lantern. Then the man who carried the light gave a grunt of satisfaction, rapped on the door and a minute and a half later passed the threshold. Profound silence fell on the alley once more. Some minutes passed, then through the inky night came a faint sound of steps from the far end of the alley. The steps grew clearer.

" One who knows his way," commented Grandpère Jacques. " He walks with confidence in this pit of darkness."

Warborough strained his ears. The man coming down the alley walked quickly, but one foot trod less firmly than the other.

" Mohammed Amaati," he whispered. " Get ready, Jacques ! "

The surprise was perfect. The man who moved so surely in the Cimmerian darkness was not anticipating any attack, and as Jacques launched himself upon him, he went down like a ninepin, striking his head upon the cobbles, and before he could cry out the legionary's hand at his throat choked his mouth open, and Warborough slipped in a gag. Then before he could recover from the shock of his fall they proceeded to bind him expeditiously and expertly, working by touch. The task was almost completed and Jacques chuckled mirthfully.

" One plum from the tree, my captain. The other——"

A beam of light cut the darkness of the alley like a sword. It came from behind them, and in the glare Warborough visioned his companion's face, with jaw dropped in amazement that was almost comic. He glanced swiftly round and was almost blinded by the glare of an electric torch shining full into his eyes. The holder of the torch was invisible, but not for a moment did Warborough doubt the man's identity, and as the torch was extinguished he lifted himself upright and leaped in the direction of the place where the man had stood. He found emptiness, and at the risk of being felled by an unseen person he stood still, listening. The faint plunk of padded shoes reached him receding down the alley, and with a thought that Steinmann after all had worn not babooshes but rubber-shoes enabling him to move silently, he whispered a sharp direction to Jacques,

and raced down the alley, on the trail of the fleeing man.
He reached the end of the alley, where the mosque loomed
in the darkness, and there for a second paused to listen.
Faint sounds came up the wider street.  Steinmann it
seemed had gone that way, and slipping off his shoes he
raced after him.  The street was a winding one, and he
could see nothing, and at the point where it debouched
into a market-place, he gave up the chase.  Half a dozen
alley-ways offered themselves to the fugitive, and to take
one at random would be mere folly.  Besides there were
Grandpère Jacques and his prisoner to think of.  He began
to return, and in the shadow of the mosque met his friend
with the Moor thrown over his shoulder like a sack.

" What luck, my captain ? " asked the legionary, grunting with his burden.

" None !  I lost the German in the darkness."

" But we have plucked this plum—a right heavy one."

" And the other can be taken openly in daylight.  The
arrest of a Roum will stir no fanaticism."

" And the gates are closed.  The man is in a trap.
Also we have prevented the meeting of the rebels.  I
should like to see the faces of those five as they wait."

" They will not wait long.  When neither this bird
of ours nor the German appear they will grow alarmed,
and in the morning every man of them will flee at the
opening of the gates."

Jacques laughed.  " To your tents, O Israel, *hein*. . . .
Here is that she-ass of ours who will carry the plum we
have plucked."

They bound Mohammed Amaati on the donkey's back,
and began to move from the quarter.  Grandpère Jacques
chuckled to himself.

" That Allemand—he will not know we were but two,
or he might return and raise the devil.  He will think
that maybe there was a raid.  A whole platoon maybe,
and he will still be running like a sheep, thinking those
others also have been gathered by the authorities."

" They are unimportant without Mohammed here, who, like Steinmann, is El-Krim's agent. . . . And we do not raise the dust by taking him so ; for he is a stranger in Marrakesh. None will miss him save his friend Abdullah and those who wait back there, and they will be silent as the grave."

Grandpère Jacques cogitated for a moment, then asked a question :

" That is why we did not pluck him in Fez where he is known ? "

" Yes ! To have done it there openly might have kindled a fire hard to extinguish."

" And now there is not even a puff of smoke ! " Jacques chuckled mirthfully, then grew suddenly sober. " And the lady whom he lifted from her lover ? What of her, my captain ? "

" Our next business, and an easy one. Abdullah will be scared when the demand for her return is made and will hurry to wash his hands of a perilous thing. There will be no difficulty."

They came to a great, barred, timber-gate that separated one quarter of the city from another. Grandpère Jacques kicked the slumbering negro who was gate-keeper into wakefulness ; and for a moment the man's big eyes rolled in wonder at the donkey's burden. Warborough laughed meaningly.

" A sinner who has ignored the Prophet's command and drunk infidel wine, and being overtaken by the folly of the fool we take him to his home."

He chinked a couple of francs in his palm. The gate-keeper grinned understanding, and turned to the great wooden bar. The gate creaked and screeched vociferously as if in pain, wakening a beggar sleeping on the further side, who immediately broke into the mendicants' cry :

" Allah ! Allah ! Allah ! "

Warborough thrust a coin into his hand to silence him, and they passed on, following tortuous ways to

M

another gate, and by other winding lanes ; and at last passed a door into a court where a massive pile lifted itself against the clear-burning stars.  A moment later out of the shadows of the building came a challenging voice :

" *Halte là !* "

A bayonet reflected the gleam of a star, and the sentry moved forward.  Warborough answered him tersely, and they were permitted to proceed, and five minutes later a much dishevelled Mohammed Amaati blinking in the lamplight was standing in a wide chamber, before a desk at which was seated a French officer, who looked at the prisoner with steady appraising eyes, then turned to Warborough.

" One only ? " he asked crisply.

" The German avoided the net.  But he will not go to the house of Ben Moussa—and without him and this one, the others are sheep who will scatter at the opening of the gates."

" But we must have Steinmann, *mon ami*.  He is the chief agent in the South—a dangerous man."

" He is somewhere in the city.  Maybe Mohammed Amaati knows his whereabouts.  In any case a close scrutiny at the gates in the morning will deliver him to our hands.  I will wager his feet are burning to be quit of Marrakesh as quickly as possible."

The officer nodded.  " That is true ; and this one is next in importance for us.  Maybe he can be induced to talk.  I will question him presently.  When he knows the game is up, his tongue will loosen.  In the meantime there is the lady of whom you told me.  Have you found her ? "

" She is at the house of Abdullah Hammou with this man's women.  I will fetch her now, if I may have a sergeant's squad.  It will give a colour of authority, and Abdullah by this will be in a very blue funk—and not disposed to resist."

The officer nodded.  " I know Abdullah Hammou.  He values his skin."

He touched a bell, gave a sharp command to the orderly who answered it, and whilst Warborough waited for his squad the officer talked.

" I will give orders for the scrutiny at the gates. We must get the German, but those others go free for the moment. We know them and that is sufficient. When you get madame, what will you do with her ? "

" Send her to Mogador under escort."

" And afterwards, my friend ? "

" Go North again. There is a man up there to be scotched, as Mohammed here has been scotched to-night."

The officer nodded.

" Perilous work ! But if you can check the trouble, France will not forget ; and the Maréchal's gratitude is worth much to a soldier."

Warborough smiled, then through the night-stillness sounded the tramp of booted feet, and a harsh voice crying an order : " *Halte !* "

" Your guard, *mon ami*. Off with you—to dry Madame Maxwell's tears."

So dismissed, Warborough went forth, and with Grand-père Jacques and the guard he had asked for, took his way to the house of Abdullah Hammou. Their arrival almost synchronized with that of a man who was rapping on the door, and who, trying to flee, was forced against the wall. The opening of the door and the light that streamed forth revealed the man's identity. It was Abdullah himself—shivering with fright and the anticipation of conscious guilt. Jeff Warborough wasted no time.

" Abdullah Hammou," he said, " I have come for the Roum woman who came with Mohammed Amaati's women. Give your servant word to bring her forth."

Relief showed in the Moor's face. He spoke hurriedly in a shaking voice to the big negro slave. Warborough kept his ears open, and started at the negro's reply.

" The Roum woman is gone ! " said Abdullah in a stricken voice. " She was taken away to-night."

So much Warborough had already gathered from the slave's answer, and it was not difficult to divine who had taken Cornelia away ; but he insisted on exact information.

"With whom went she ? "

He got the name and other information.

"The man came and took her forth in haste. It is not known where."

"And do you not know where Steinmann is ? "

"No, by the Prophet's beard, I swear it. The man is secret as a bird in the night."

Warborough believed him. Between the negro and his master there could have been no collusion to mislead him ; and he guessed that Steinmann on the run had snatched at Cornelia as a man snatches at a fortune he is in danger of losing—a desperate action that might well prove the man's undoing. He nodded, gave the Moor a sharp warning to watch his steps, then permitted him to enter his own door, and gave the order to return to his guard. As they marched down the street, Grandpère Jacques spoke once, consolingly :

"At dawn, at the gates we shall take the Allemand and madame. He cannot escape to-night, for the gates would not open even for an Archangel."

That also was the opinion of the officer at the Cabinet Politique et Militaire, to whom Warborough reported.

"What matter, my friend ? A few hours more of captivity are nothing. At daybreak we shall take Steinmann and madame at one of the ten gates. Already the order has been given to watch clearly, and an officer has gone to each gate. Go ! sleep until the hour of the morning prayer, then you and I will make the round of the gates together until we find the one which the German renegade has failed to pass. I will send further word about the lady, who it appears is like to be as the old man of the sea upon the fellow's back."

There was nothing else to be done, and in the morning

Warborough, wearing the uniform of the Legion, made the round of the ten gates of Marrakesh with his friend. At each gate they drew a blank, and at the tenth the friend spoke cheerfully :

" We are over-early. The German keeps his den still, but before the day is spent——"

He laughed significantly and together they returned to the Residency, Warborough with uneasy forebodings shadowing his former confidence—forebodings that as it chanced were justified. As they entered the official's room a secretary approached him with a report—and an explanation. Warborough's friend listened carefully, read what was written, then broke out in chagrin :

" *Diable !* "

" What is it ? " asked Warborough, fearing the worst.

" How many gates do you say there are in Marrakesh, my friend ? "

" Ten ! "

" So I thought, and we toured them all. But we forgot there was another."

" Another ? "

" Yes, *mon ami*. Marrakesh uses ten gates, but there is an eleventh which was made for a special purpose——"

" By Allah ! " cried Warborough in sharp remembrance. " The postern gate of the Mamounia ! "

" Yes ! The little postern gate of the Mamounia. It was broken open in the night for someone to leave the city, secretly."

For a moment Warborough stood there dumb, visioning the gate in the wall outside the gardens of the old palace built by Sultan Mohammed ben Abdullah for his son Mamoun. In the vicissitudes of time the palace was now a hospital ; but once it was a residence assigned to European ambassadors visiting the old Moroccan capital, and there had come an English envoy, whose heart failed him so that he fell dead in his dining-room in the palace of Mamounia. The fierce intolerance of Islam forbade the infidel's body being carried through the streets of holy Marrakesh, so a new door was cut through the great wall on which the gardens of the palace adjoined, and through that door the dead envoy went home to English earth. Warborough knew the story. He had seen the gate shut ; but now in vision he saw it open, and in imagination heard it creaking on its rusted hinges as it swung in the dawn wind. Then he drew a sharp breath.

"Yes," he said, more to himself than to his friend. "Yes. He knows Marrakesh well. He went that way —by the eleventh gate."

"And Madame Cornelia with him—I would wager a thousand francs upon it. . . . You will not want that escort to Mogador to-day. No ! Nor yet to-morrow, unless you have great luck, *mon ami*."

And as Jeff Warborough thought of the ways a fugitive might take—westward across the sun-scorched *Bled*, east towards the fastnesses of Grand Atlas, or South to Anti-Atlas and beyond to the great desert, again the fear of the worst gripped his heart and set a chill upon his spirit.

## CHAPTER XV

### THE RESCUE

IT was three days later when Warborough stumbled on the clue which gave him knowledge of the fugitive Steinmann's direction. In the intervening time he had searched high and low for news, interviewed separately Ben Moussa at whose house the German was to have presented himself, and questioned dozens of copers with mules and camels to sell, in the hope that from them he might learn of animals sold to one who might be Steinmann. Everywhere he had drawn a blank, and in despair, following a merely vagrant fancy, he had strolled through the gardens of the Mamounia to look at the door through which the German had fled. It was still unrepaired and he passed through to the plain beyond, and stood for a little while staring thoughtfully about him.

A small gipsy-like encampment some distance away caught his eyes, and he moved towards it idly, wondering who could have his home there, outside the walls with the city so close to hand. He found an old man, a native craftsman, busy carving a little box to be offered in the Thursday market. As Warborough greeted him he looked up, responded morosely, and continued his task, no doubt resenting the curiosity which brought the Roum to stare at him as if he were some strange beast. His visitor did not resent his surly attitude, but seeking an opening asked a question.

" You live here outside the walls, my friend ? "

" I do not love the city, and here the lodging place is free," answered the old man.

" And you are not afraid of being robbed ? " asked Warborough carelessly, but with a sudden gleam in his eyes as he marked a quantity of trampled ordure, and a stake or two where plainly four-footed beasts had been hobbled.

" Thieves do not rob the poor," was the curt reply.

" But your mules ?  Are you not afraid they will be stolen ? "

The old man started a little at the question, then answered sharply :

" I am a poor man without even an ass to bear my burdens.  Mules are for the rich."

Warborough nodded.  " True ! "  Then curbing the excitement which was mounting within him, he continued : " But you have had mules in your camp ? "

" They were not mine," replied the other shortly.

" No," answered Warborough, then drew a bow at a venture.  " The mules belonged to the Roum, who three nights ago came here with a veiled woman, and rode away hot-foot in the darkness."

The old Moor's bearded chin sagged a little.  His

bleared eyes shot a half-scared glance at his visitor, and he was plainly much out of countenance, so much that he found no words to deny Warborough's statement. The soldier continued, guessing at the facts.

" The Roum left his mules in your care, for which he paid you well, knowing that he might need them in haste at an hour when they could not pass the gates. He found that need, and in the night came to you through the little door in the wall there by the Mamounia. He was in great haste to be gone. Is it not so ? "

The sagging jaw tightened suddenly, and the sullen look came back to the Moor's face.

" Who are you to ask these things ? " he demanded.

Warborough smiled cheerfully. " I am from the Residency. It is my duty to know all about the Roum who left his mules with you, and broke through the little gate. So if you are wise you will keep nothing back."

" Was the Roum a thief, then ? " asked the old man, whose mind it seemed knew no other crime.

" More than a thief. He stole the woman who was with him."

" Then he rides under the curse of Allah ! He who steals gold is a thief, but he who robs a man of his wife is guilty of the seven-fold sin. I will tell. It is true that the Roum paid me to watch his mules for two nights. Also it is true that he came with the woman in the night, though I knew not that he came from the city until in the dawn I saw the broken gate. His haste was great, and I might have known his errand was an evil one. He went that way across the *Bled*, and before his going he inquired how far was the ride to the wells at Tameslout, and again how many hours beyond to the flowing water of Oued Nfis. Then he went off in the night, the woman riding by his side. That is all that I can tell."

" It is sufficient," answered Warborough, and giving largess, took his way exultantly to the Residency, where he explained the situation to his friend.

" To the Oasis of Tameslout and then to the river
Oued.   The river comes down the long valley that splits
the Great Atlas like a sword.   It is for the mountains he
is making."

" And he does not know that country, apparently."

" No.   As like as not he will wander wide.   I shall
gather him like a straying mule."

The officer laughed.   " And the lady will be like hobbles
to his feet—a check upon his going.   He will not be able
to travel fast.   My friend, you will indeed gather him,
though he has three days' start."

" I shall go at once before the gates are closed.   An
hour's preparation will be sufficient.   I shall take Jacques
with me.   He is a great man in a tight corner."

" In what character will you go ? "

" As a Berber of the Atlas.   I have to travel fast—
and armed.   No other character will serve up in the hills
where they would rob a travelling merchant and roast
a pedlar for his cheap wares."

" You will want two good horses, then——"

" With native accoutrements and saddles—which last
Jacques will curse.   We shall be of the dissidents, anxious
for service with the insurgent forces of the North.   The
type will be popular in the hills just now, and Grandpère
and I have played the parts before in the Bou Idji
country."

The other laughed.   " You have a wonderful repertory,
Warborough, and go vivid ways.   I could find it in my
heart to envy you who do these mad things whilst I stew
at a desk.   But bring in that cursed stirrer-up of strife
and I shall be consoled."

" If I have to lift him out of El-Krim's own palace, he
shall come," laughed Warborough, and went his way.

Two hours later, at the moment when the gates were
closing, the pair slipped from the city, mounted on stallion
barbs such as the hillmen used, clothed in every detail as
Berbers of the hills, but carrying modern rifles instead of

ornamented jezails. None followed them out, as War-borough was careful to note, and with the quick dusk falling they rode into the silent *Bled*—the great barren plain outside the city, their barbs' noses towards Tames-lout and the valley of the Oued Nfis and beyond to the ragged masses of Great Atlas.

. . . A whole week later in a mud-house set in a huddled village under the looming hills, Warborough learned that not only was he on the track of the man he sought, but was almost on his heels. The calipha of the village and most of the men were absent on some raiding expedition as it seemed, and it was from a withered, paralysed old man that he got the news he sought.

" The Roum and the woman lay here two nights ago, and departed at the hour of the morning prayer."

" They were alone ? "

" No ! They had with them one to guide them through the hills—a brigand and the son of a brigand if there is truth in a man's face."

" And they went up the valley ? "

" No ! They followed the track up the hillside which the salt-carriers use, and they were in haste."

" As we are," answered Warborough, and giving largess pushed on, taking the track that climbed the mountain side. The road was steep and narrow, a track on the face of the rock. The vegetation was thin and dwarfed, with the grotesque look of age of the trees and shrubs grown in the rock gardens of China and Japan. Clumps of little firs lifted tiny spires, cabbage-palms and junipers grew from baked crevices that in the rainy season gathered water, and occasionally the exotic argan trees loaded with olive-like nuts shaded the goat-track which moved now up, now down, as the contour of the hillside dictated. Once they met a caravan of laden pack-asses, and had to squeeze their horses against the rock whilst the caravan crept by ; and further up at a sharp turn in the track, where the cliff was sheer dropping seven hundred feet to its base, they encountered a brace of camels, whose drivers, crying fiercely, beat the heads of their ungainly beasts against the rough cliff in order to make the stubborn creatures yield the few inches of room to allow the sure-footed barbs' precarious passage.

At the crest of the track they came to a nameless height, barren beyond belief, heaped with great boulders, which lay in an extraordinary confusion ; and from that point, through the glasses which he carried carefully concealed under his caftan, Warborough surveyed the way ahead.

The prospect offered a jumble of mountains, of grey hillsides flecked here and there with green, of blue ridges thrust like shovel-headed spears into the sky. The mule-track, as he noted carefully, wound along precipices sheer as a wall, across pebbly slopes where a slip would be as dangerous as a slip on the edge of an abyss, or turned dizzily round great boulders which had planted themselves as if to shoulder wayfarers from the track to the deeps below. He traced it to a point where it disappeared round a great bluff, picked it up again further on and a little beyond saw a mountain village perched steeply on a slope. He pointed it out to Grandpère Jacques.

" Perhaps there——" he began.

" They are further on, my captain. And we cannot camp here without being frozen in the night. There will be a wind when the sun goes down."

They rode forward, and in the dusk halted in a little wood of stunted pines to reconnoitre.

" One does not put his head in the lion's mouth," said Jacques. " We take the rifles."

Twenty minutes later they crouched at the edge of an unwalled village, which for the moment was, as it seemed, deserted. But whilst they lay watching, a crazy door opened and a woman carrying a lamp emerged. By its light Jacques saw two mules, hobbled in the open and still saddled, and whispered sharply :

" There, monsieur. By the large house the mules we seek."

" By Allah——"

" Allah Akbar ! . . . Allah Akbar ! "

The fierce cry of fanatical Islam broke the mountain stillness, and sounds of commotion came from the village, setting the pair guessing.

" There is trouble there. Apparently the man we follow has fallen into a nest of hornets."

" Who may sting him to death for me," answered Warborough. " But we must save the lady, Jacques."

" But how, my captain ? I have counted the huts. There are nine—say a dozen men. A good handful in these hills, monsieur."

" Craft and the night will help us. We will take the chance, Grandpère. Let us go for the horses."

They rode boldly into the village, and as they neared the huts the sound of the barbs' hoofs brought a woman to a door, who seeing them ran shrieking towards a hut larger than the rest, from which hurried a couple of men, one of whom carried a lantern. Warborough gave the greeting of a pious Moslem and asked for a lodging for the night. One of the men, who wore the Médaille Militaire on a tattered tunic proving that he had sometime served France in a Moroccan regiment, answered him ; and after an inquiry or two, and a brief consultation with his fellow, led the pair to a hut built of mud with rough beams, a roof of the same material plastered over sticks and poles—a place almost as primitive as a hut of the Stone Age. Two stall-like rooms opened from a minia- ture courtyard, primitively furnished with a clay-stove, a hand-mill for grinding corn, a tea-kettle, and a few dishes for preparing *kouskous* and gruel. The man in- dicated one of the sheds.

" Here you may rest till morning. Straw for the horses may be purchased at a price."

Warborough tried to drive a bargain for corn, but

failed, and with a grudging air paid the price of straw, then looked through the open gateway at the hobbled mules which were like shadows in the dusk, and shot a question :

" You have other strangers here ? "

" The curse of Allah be on them ! Yes ! A Roum and his woman, who fed their mules on the corn stacked by a marabout's tomb."

Warborough almost whistled. Sacrilege ! His mind made the silent ejaculation and he realized that whatever had happened Steinmann had slipped into a folly ; the consequences of which it would be difficult to evade. The fact was thrust upon him sharply by the man's next words :

" There was another—a man of the land. Who died at the hand of the man who came upon him in the unholy act." Dimly Warborough guessed what had happened. Somewhere in the neighbourhood of the village Steinmann's guide had fed their animals upon corn stacked by the tomb of some saint—corn that was protected by the tomb. The Moor had already paid the price, and it seemed likely that the man who had employed him must pay also.

" Infidel dogs ! " he ejaculated with the fervour of the true believer ; then asked curiously, " The woman is young ? "

" Young enough for a man." The villager laughed. " She will fetch a price in the market where old men buy—enough to pay for the corn and to spare."

" And the Roum ? "

" He will pay the price. The women will work their will, and when they have finished——"

The man left the sentence uncompleted, and Warborough, who had an imagination and had seen the finished work of Berber women on men of the Legion, shivered a little. Then the hillman spoke again :

" I must go back. The Roum is speaking much—but already he is a dead man."

He slipped away in the darkness, leaving them the
lantern, and as he went Jacques chuckled softly.

"The German is in a deep hole. If these barbarians
do not listen——"

"S-s-s-h-h!"

The form of a woman was dimly outlined against the
doorway across the court. Apparently she was watching
them, and Warborough, pretending to busy himself about
his horse, lifted the lantern. By its light he saw that
the woman was veiled, and his heart leaped at the sight,
for Berber women of the Atlas customarily go with un-
covered faces. He looked swiftly round. They had the
courtyard to themselves, and moving towards the woman,
he whispered sharply in English:

"Madame, you look for a friend?"

He saw the woman start violently, then the veil was
thrown back and he had a glimpse of Cornelia Maxwell,
her face of a death-like pallor, dark eyes burning as with
fever.

"Who——" she began in a startled voice, too loud for
Warborough's liking.

"Softly, madame," he whispered in quick warning.
"We must not be heard—or seen. Go back into the
shadow of the room, and I will talk. . . . Listen carefully."

"But who are——"

"Go back!" he almost hissed, as a step sounded on
the stones outside the courtyard.

Apparently the woman caught the step also, for she
slipped back into the shadows, and Warborough, again
busy with the barb, saw a Berber woman halt by the
door of the tiny courtyard, stare curiously for a moment,
and then pass on. He waited for a little while, then
spoke whisperingly into the darkness:

"Madame!"

"Ah!" The interjection came quick as a pistol-shot.
"I have remembered; I know your voice. You are——"

" Madame, that is a small thing. Your danger is great.
The man who brought you here is likely to be slain——"

" I could pray God he might be ! "

" And for you there is peril also."

" I am not afraid of death ! "

" Death ! That would be a great mercy. The peril
is that you may be sold in some secret market to go to
a Moorish harem. Already that is being discussed."

" God help me ! "

The ejaculation reached Warborough in a whisper, and
its tremulous fervency shook him a little.

" Madame," he said. " Already your prayer is
answered. My friend and I were sent to deliver you."

" You ? " she whispered strangely. " You ? "

" Myself—and Grandpère Jacques."

" But . . . but——"

He made a guess at the objection she would have
urged ; and as it chanced guessed wrongly.

" The men of this place are busy discussing the fate of
that scoundrel Steinmann. We can slip away—now if
you have courage."

" Courage ! to live. I have that."

" Then if you will prepare ! When I give the word.
. . . There are risks on this mountain road, but——"

" They are nothing to those I shall flee from."

" Then—if you will be ready. Be alert. Do not sleep.
When the moon comes over the hills and we can see our
way, we will slip from this place. In the meantime eat
what food may have been given."

" That will not take long."

" You have nothing ? No matter ! Jacques is a cook
among a thousand. In a little while I will set food at
your door. Now go back into the shadows."

He himself turned away and gave instructions to the
old legionary, who busied himself with the preparation of
a meal as if peril were a thousand miles away. Warborough smiled and commented on his phlegm.

"What would you, *mon capitaine*? Courage lies in a well-filled stomach. Your hero is never an empty man."

Warborough himself listened with strained ears to the sounds which came from the large hut where the villagers were assembled. At first there was a clamour of voices, then one voice speaking in a droning way which presently quickened to fervency, and was broken by shouts of fanatical zeal.

"Allah Akbar! Allah! Allah!"

The fanatical shouts had in them no note of fierce malevolence, rather they had a tone of zealous approval; and at last, with an uneasy sense that things were not going quite to schedule, he moved out of the little court-yard, and standing in the shadow of the wall, listened carefully to the voice droning through the night. After a time he knew that it was Steinmann's. The man was talking fluently, explaining the position in the North, and moving the fanatical tribesmen out of their animosity to himself. The speech broke off, for a time only a low murmur of voices reached him, then came a shout:

"Allah be praised!"

From the tone of the words, he guessed that Steinmann, hard beset as he had been, had saved his life by eloquence. In a little time he would perhaps come forth to seek Cornelia, knowing nothing of the presence of Grandpère Jacques and himself. But when he heard of the arrival of two strangers in the village he would be curious, perhaps suspicious; and if he penetrated their disguise, he would denounce them to these fanatical hillmen. There was, it seemed, little time to lose. If he were to save Cornelia, the thing must be done at once. He looked round. There was a glow in the violet sky, a faint silvery radiance on one of the high peaks. The moon was rising. In ten minutes it would lift itself above the hills. By then they must be on the move. He hurried back to Jacques, and gave him instructions to lead the barbs down the trail away from the Marrakesh, since when Steinmann heard of their visit and missed his captive, putting things together, his natural conclusion would be that they had gone that way. The other way, deeper into the hills, had its risks; but they were not so certain as the other. Then he called to Cornelia and bade her follow the legionary and the horses, whilst he himself released one of the mules.

The task he had set himself was not an easy one. The hobbled beasts had the viciousness of their kind. The one he first tried to secure squealed and kicked so violently that the sound brought a woman to the door of one of the huts, forcing him to lie flat upon the ground in imminent danger of having his brains scattered by the kicking mule. The woman stood there for a moment watchful, listening. From the hut where Steinmann talked for his life came a sudden frenzied fanatical shout:

"Allah! Allah! Akbar!"

The German, it seemed, was prevailing. He looked again towards the doorway where the Berber woman had been. She was still there, her figure outlined in the faint radiance of a lamp within. He cursed her in his heart. Any moment the meeting in the other hut might break up, and Steinmann emerge to reassure Cornelia and to discover her flight. Yet he could do nothing until the Beber woman withdrew. He hugged the ground, waiting. Each moment that passed seemed an eternity. Then a child's cry sounded in the night. The woman turned and disappeared from the door; and moving swiftly he tackled his task anew. The mule plunged and squealed again, but exultant shouting from the larger hut drowned the noise it made. He struck the beast savagely with his clenched fist, beating it into quiescence, and then with the moon floating majestically and serenely over the tops of the mountains led the beast down the trail. Rousing voices followed him.

"Allah! Allah!"

He did not pause to learn what had happened. As he

N

dipped out of sight of the village, the sound of voices grew clearer, and he knew that the owners had left the hut.    Within five minutes the flight would be discovered. With the butt of his rifle he drove the mule forward.    The trail dipped downward into shadow, but he plunged on, taking a stupendous risk.    He came to a place where argan trees made the track a place of utter darkness.

" *Mon capitaine ?* "    Jacques' voice hailed him softly.

Back in the village there was a sudden, sharp babel of voices that told its own tale.    He found the place where the legionary and Cornelia awaited him.    Without a word he caught the woman in his arms and swung her on to the mule's back.    Then he snapped a command.

" Forward, Jacques.    Forward, madame ! "

He watched them go, the legionary leading, and then mounting his own barb he followed ; in his ears the sound of growing tumult coming from the huts behind him.

## CHAPTER XVI

### A PERILOUS PASSAGE

LONG after, to Warborough's ears out of the darkness ahead there came a sound of stumbling, then Grandpère Jacques' voice ejaculated sharply :

" *Diable !* "

" What is it, Jacques ? "

" The goat-track has lost itself in the wood.    We can do nothing, my captain, till the dawn."

Warborough looked round and saw—nothing.    For an hour or more the moon had been lost over the high hills, and now its light was completely gone.    In the darkness sounded a faint trickle of water.    There was no other sound, the night, with the cessation of the noise made by their mounts' hoofs, having grown desperately still, most suddenly.

" Then we must wait for the dawn.    It cannot be long

delayed. Tether your horse to the tree, Grandpère, also madame's mule."

As he spoke Warborough slid from his barb, found a tree by touch, and fastened his beast to it ; then groped his way to the mule.

" Madame," he said to its rider, " we rest a while."

His hands found her, lifted her, and swung her to the ground. He felt her sagging, and caught a whispered cry :

" Oh, I . . . cannot . . . stand."

" There is no need that you should," he said, and holding her firmly slid to the ground, his back against a tree. " Rest," he said tersely. " Sleep if you can. The time will be brief enough."

Cornelia made a little impulsive movement as if to release herself, but he spoke sharply :

" No ! You will find the ground damp. You may take a fever. Lie still."

He held her firmly and after another mute attempt to free herself, the woman ceased her silent protest and lay still ; and after an interval her supineness and regular breathing told him that she slept. The scrape of a match sounded in the stillness, as Jacques lit a cigarette. Its little flame threw a dim radiance in which Warborough for a brief moment saw Cornelia's face, pale, but, in the unconsciousness of sleep, very peaceful and serene. The beauty of it moved him deeply, the rise and fall of her breasts against his heart quickened his blood, and her helplessness unsealed deeper springs than mere pity. He saw her for the briefest moment of time before Jacques threw the match away, but again he was conscious of the surge of emotion and exhilaration that he had known when he had walked with her in the moonlight on the packet from Marseilles.

Then he smiled a little grimly. He knew what had brought her to this turbulent land, and found something humorously ironical in the fact that now she should be sleeping in his arms, there, in the dark wood under the

shadows of Atlas.   She believed, not without reason, that
he was the slayer of her husband, and she had come
seeking him to drag him to justice, and now she was
utterly dependent upon him.   What her relations with
Steinmann might be he was not sure, nor was it clear to
him why the German should have gone to such lengths to
get her in his keeping ; but there were things that he
could tell her when the moment came—things that would
induce her to see things from a new point of view.

He found the thought a little consoling as he sat there
in the darkness listening to her breathing ; then by some
trick of association he remembered Garfield Standish
twiddling his thumbs, as he thought, helplessly in Fez,
and smiled again.   Standish would have the shock of his
life could he be transported on some magic carpet and see
him sitting in this dark wood of the Atlas with Cornelia
in his arms.   He remembered the four occasions he had
seen him—by the church at Carston Magna, in Greek
Street, on the quay at Oran, and in the office at Fez.   At
the last meeting Standish had not recognized him, but, as
he reflected, he realized how the other three occasions
would seem to warrant the suspicions the man entertained,
and indeed give them the force of conviction.   He himself had not been discreet in either his words or actions,
but how was he to know that meddling fool would hit so
near the truth and follow him to Morocco ?   Well, there
was no helping that now, what was past was not to be
recalled ; but he could explain to this woman in his arms,
sleeping from utter weariness, and he would compel her
to believe.

So reflecting, he waited for the dawn, alert, watchful,
conscious that Grandpère Jacques was deep in slumber.
The darkness perceptibly lightened, the light grew
broader ; it became possible to see the trees of the wood
and the tethered animals.   Jacques woke, yawned and
stretched himself to wakefulness, then stood up and
looked round.

" *Bon jour,* monsieur. It is the devil of a cold morning."

" It will be warmer presently."

" If we remain in this valley, yes—a very oven.—You have not slept——"

Cornelia Maxwell stirred suddenly. Her eyes opened, looking directly into Warborough's own. He saw a light of wonder grow in them, a light that changed swiftly to something not so attractive. Her face flamed scarlet, and in that moment was to him disturbingly beautiful; then the blood receded, an austere look came on her face, and rising abruptly she waited till he also rose to his feet, which he did stiffly and awkwardly, for he was cramped by the weight he had borne through the night, and aware also of a soreness in his bones due to the dampness of the earth against which he had warned her.

" *Bon jour,* madame," he said with forced cheerfulness. " You have slept well, I hope."

" I slept in your arms, through the night ? " she asked abruptly.

" Through the night," he answered with a smile.

" Then I shall walk in shame till I die," she said sharply, and with a swift movement drew down the Moslem veil to hide her face.

" But, madame——" began Warborough in vehement protest, only to be interrupted by Grandpère Jacques.

" Hark, monsieur ! "

The note of alarm in the legionary's words checked Warborough's vehemence. He looked swiftly at his subordinate.

" What——"

" I hear hoofs. Horses or mules, my captain," whispered Grandpère quickly.

Warborough stood tensely, listening. Faintly through the wood came the sound of iron-shod hoofs on rock.

" Yes," he whispered back. " There are several passing over there. A caravan of salt-carriers maybe."

" Or maybe those who search for us."

" True, we must make sure. Remain here with madame. I will reconnoitre."

In a moment he was lost in the trees, and Jacques looked at Cornelia.

" A brave one that, madame," he whispered praisefully. " There is nothing in the world can daunt him, not even the she-devils of these hills, who will do worse than flay us if we are taken."

The actress made no reply, gave not so much as a hint that she had heard. Veiled and remote, she stood there still as a masked image, listening to the sounds which came through the great stillness of the valley. Occasionally voices mingled with the ring of hoofs on the rock. Once it seemed from the sound a beast stumbled, and was roundly cursed by its rider. She waited, a little breathlessly, though Grandpère Jacques did not know it, for the issue of this unexpected thing. Minutes dragged by slowly. The sound of hoofs and of voices receded, died away altogether, then silently as a wraith Warborough emerged from the trees. His eyes told Grandpère Jacques that he brought no good news.

" Steinmann," said Warborough quietly, " and five of the villagers—all armed."

" And they seek for us—and madame down that goattrack of theirs ? "

" Unquestionably."

" The way then is to double back and go the way they have not taken, monsieur."

Warborough shook his head. " No, Grandpère. That was the first thought that came to me—— But if they go this way, it is certain that others have taken the road by which we came. Steinmann is no fool, and God knows by what wild tale he has influenced the men in the village. One thing is certain—wherever we strike the track and whichever way we go, forward or backward, we are between two parties, one of which must find us."

Grandpère Jacques whistled softly to himself, and stared through an opening in the trees to the frowning battlements of the hills. Then he spoke quietly in the Moghrebbin tongue :

" There will be other ways, my captain, the ways where the goats go and the Barbary sheep climb. You and I could go these ways as we have done before. If we left the woman——"

" Jacques ! "

The old legionary laughed. " Oh, I know you will not do that. But if madame is to accompany us, she must have a cool head for the heights. . . . When we have breakfasted, I will seek a way, whilst the German chases us along a road we did not go."

" Yes . . . we will eat first, and afterwards——"

" Achieve the impossible, *mon capitaine* ? " laughed Grandpère Jacques.

The breakfast was simple in the extreme, some dates, native cakes washed down with water from the stream, and when it was over Jacques picked up his rifle.

" One shot, monsieur, will mean a dead man somewhere. Many shots—with one at the last after an interval will mean you find your own road. Dead—I do not mind ; but living I will not fall into the hands of the women of these hills. We know them—you and I, *hein !* "

He moved away in the wood, leaving Cornelia and Warborough alone. For a time there was a constrained silence. Remembering what the woman had said about her shame at having slept in his arms, Warborough was too sore to attempt explanation, whilst the actress sat with a brooding look in her eyes, absorbed in thought. But to loiter in that constrained silence was beyond Warborough, and he busied himself by watering the animals, and seeing to girths and saddles ready for the moment when Jacques should return. He was so engaged when Cornelia broke the silence with an abrupt question :

" What is that man Steinmann ? "

" A rascal ! " replied Warborough tersely, and then elaborated. " A German who once served his country in the diplomatic service—on the lower rungs. He needed money, and sold secrets. He was found out and fled to save his neck. He served a term in the Foreign Legion here in Morocco, and is now in service with El-Krim. There are many like him, all dangerous men, but none more unscrupulous. He is the foulest bird in the flock— a sort of political agent, who aspires to become the power behind the throne in the new Sultanate to which El-Krim aspires. He is very avaricious—with the fever for money in his bones."

" Yes," said Cornelia more to herself than to him. " He seeks money."

" From you ? " asked Warborough sharply.

" From me," answered Cornelia, and fell silent again, apparently lost in thought.

Warborough refrained from breaking on her reflections, and presently she spoke again :

" He—Steinmann—knew my husband."

" There is abundant proof of that, I should say," replied Warborough with a thought of certain documents in the archives at Fez.

" You also knew Simon Maxwell ? "

The question was sharp as a pistol-shot and there was a note of accusation in it. Warborough suppressed a smile. Cornelia, it seemed, was coming to grips at last.

" I—er—met him a few times, but only once under the name he adopted when——"

" The last occasion was on the night he was foully slain ? " Again the question had an accusing note, and Warborough for his own purposes decided to gain a little time.

" I wonder why you say that, madame."

There was a flash of contempt in Cornelia's dark eyes, and it was like a sting in her tone as she answered him.

" Because it is not to be questioned. You came to Carston Magna in an aeroplane——"

" That fool Standish told you that." He laughed a little harshly, and added, " Believe me on that occasion my intentions were wholly benevolent."

" Benevolent !—You came to kill a man secretly in the night, and you talk——"

" You think I killed Simon Maxwell ? That also is that fool Standish's idea, I suppose ? "

" Not his only. You do not deny that you were at Farholme that night ? "

" At any rate I have not yet admitted that I——"

" There is no need you should," she said with whispered vehemence. " I have the proofs."

" Proofs ? " echoed Warborough.

" Yes ! In my portmanteau at Fez there is a railway-ticket—unused. It bears the name of the junction where a man who had suffered an accident—or so he claimed— left a little pool of blood on the platform where he stood waiting for the train. The date on it is September 30th of this year—the date of my marriage and of my husband's death. You dropped it on the steamer coming from Marseilles——"

" And you—er—picked it up ? "

" As you say. There are other things. You had suffered an accident whilst in England. You owned as much to account for your lameness. That man who caught the last train at the junction limped a little——"

" You said he had suffered an accident——"

" There was a sword in Simon Maxwell's hand when they found him. It was blood-stained at the point. Before he died he had wounded the man who slew him so foully with the poignard in the throat. That was the accident the man who caught the train had suffered."

Warborough smiled imperturbably.

" That sounds like the theory of friend Standish, but as evidence it is not conclusive."

Cornelia made an impatient gesture.

" By itself, no. But there is another thing. In the pocket of the man who was found dead in the dove-tower——"

" Caillé ? "

" Yes, Caillé. In his pocket was a telegram. It was in French. It announced briefly the hour of my wedding —which, as I thought, was known to none. It was addressed to Caillé at an address in Greek Street, Soho ——"

She broke off, her dark eyes searching his face intently for any sign of guilt that might be there. She found only intense interest, and in the pause he jerked a word impatiently :

" Yes ? "

" You knew the hour."

" Because I came to Carston Magna you argue that I had sight of that telegram——"

" Wait ! " interrupted Cornelia. " On that night when you dropped that unclipped railway-ticket—I suppose you paid the fare somewhere on the line to blind any pursuit—you dropped something else——"

Warborough suddenly remembered, and laughed oddly.

" A love letter—you said. I recall it. You read it——"

" At your own expressed wish," she said quickly.

" And you threw it overboard—finding it an old hotel bill." He laughed again.

" An hotel bill or something like it," she answered swiftly. " It was that. It was the account for a luncheon that someone ate—you, I presume—on the day I was married to Simon Maxwell."

" A man must eat ! " he responded lightly.

" That luncheon was eaten at the address in Greek Street where that telegram found Caillé——"

" An odd coincidence ! " commented Warborough, still in the same light tone.

" Where later Mr. Standish found you——"

" No ! You are wrong there. It was I who found him sprawling senseless on the pavement, having suffered a knock-out blow."

" From one of your friends," she said tensely—" a man who came there to meet a woman who, from Mr. Standish's description, had deputized for my maid."

" You count her among my friends also ? " he asked, still with the irresponsible lightness he affected. His apparent carelessness stung her.

" What matter ? " she asked, with sudden passion. " Already you have convicted yourself by the things of which I have spoken—unless—unless you have an explanation. . . . Tell me, if you dare, why did you come to Carston Magna in such haste that day ? "

" I believe the estimable Standish has already suggested the reason," he retorted cheerfully. " I think I will not contradict him."

" You admit it ? You came to stop my marriage ? Why ? "

" Because——" he began impetuously,—and checked as sharply. " No. I will not tell you that. There is no need—now that Maxwell is dead."

" A subterfuge ! " she cried tensely. " Or a mere evasion to hide what would convict you utterly."

Warborough answered her only indirectly. " Madame," he said quietly, " there is one thing I would have you ask yourself. You have been in great peril—greater than you know, I think. You have been in the clutches of one whom you know is a blackguard. Last night when I saw you standing at the door of that hut, you were a most unhappy woman——"

" Do you think I am happier now ? " cried Cornelia quiveringly.

" That is not the point. To the place where you were, for the moment in peril increased a hundredfold, came two men. They might have refused to concern them-

selves about your parlous situation. They could easily
have continued their journey—unmolested. Instead they
snatched you from the peril in which you stood at some
risk to themselves. One of them, if what is in your mind
were true, would have benefited himself by leaving you
——"

There was a sudden change in Cornelia's face. Her eyes
lost their hostility and were flooded with troubled light.

" Oh, I know," she whispered. " Do you think I did
not ask myself many times last night why *you* should help
me. As we rode in the dark, that question was like a
hammer in my brain, beating, beating till I thought my
head must burst. . . . I cannot understand. If you
were to explain why you came in such haste to Carston
Magna——"

" No ! " he said abruptly. " I shall never do that now.
The need for such explanation, as I said, is over."

" And you will not explain why you came back that
night——"

Warborough lifted a warning hand, then caught up his
rifle.

" Madame," he whispered swiftly, " the moment is not
propitious. Someone comes. It may be Jacques—or
another. Hide behind the rock there, quick."

His urgency moved her to obedience. She slipped
behind the rock he indicated, whilst he himself dropped
on one knee and concealed by scrubby growth, waited
with his rifle pointed in the direction from which came the
sound he had heard. Cornelia watched him with troubled
eyes, doubts of the conviction she had entertained assail-
ing her, and then dying before her suspicions. She had
scarcely a thought for the man coming through the wood,
for whom he waited rifle in hand. Was he guilty or
innocent ? One thing—that which he had indicated—
came with overwhelming force. She was here, snatched
from the hands of Steinmann, by him, when he might
have left her to her fate to his own advantage——

Warborough moved suddenly, straightened himself and gave a laugh of relief.

"Grandpère Jacques! Madame, you may leave your hiding-place."

Grandpère came forward smilingly.

"There is a path, my captain. A drunken spider might have made it, but sheep and goats use it. It goes up the hill there, and turns into a dry stream. Beyond that who shall say? But it is the one way that we can leave this valley without taking the caravan road where these others seek us."

"Then we will go that way, Jacques. We will start at once. Madame, if you are ready."

They started without delay. The track merited the legionary's description, meandering this way and that in the craziest way, but leading to the dry bed of a stream full of loose stones and blocked by immense boulders. When they reached it Jacques marched ahead, driving the barbs, whilst Warborough led Cornelia's mule. As the sun mounted the heat became terrific, the dry stream-bed like a thrice-heated oven. But they could not leave it. The slopes on either side were precipitous, strewn with rocks perched precariously, with here and there stunted evergreen shrubs. To have ventured on them would have meant a swift glissade to death, so they sweated, then baked in the rocky stream-bed; Jacques cursing the barbs forward, Warborough now dragging the burdened mule, now beating it mercilessly when it halted stubbornly in some difficult place.

Broad noon arrived. The heat was unbearable, but there was nothing for it but to keep on. Cornelia sagged on the mule; Warborough, toiling like Hercules, was near the end of his strength, and Jacques had ceased to curse, when ahead a huge, water-worn rock blocked the way.

"Here ends this gut!" said Jacques, staring at the rocky face. "When the water flows it comes over there —but how the goats go up, God knows."

They found a track, a thin line, winding among strange jagged rocks, banded with streaks of yellow sulphur, proving their volcanic origin. The track brought them to the head of the rock, and to an abrupt slope up which, after a rest, they climbed to find themselves in the bed of a great dead crater, piled everywhere with rocks and heaped cones of volcanic sediment and spotted with dwarf argan trees. Upon all lay a bluish dust which rose in clouds as they marched, troubling eyes and throat, and creating an intolerable thirst.

" A slag heap of Hell," coughed Jacques, and led the way across.

Cairns of stones plainly made by human hands lifted themselves in the blue-green plain, moving the legionary's curiosity.

" What fools piled these, monsieur ? "

" Men who have passed this way, who feared the djinn which guards the place. Each stone stands for a prayer."

" A devil's den, surely ! Though devil I see none."

The spider's track led straight across the crater to a precipitous slope, strewn with titanic wreckage of porous slag ; but in the valley below there was the green of laurels and cacti, and nearer scraggy olives and struggling evergreens. Jacques considered the distant valley.

" There will be water there."

" And man if I mistake not," added Warborough. " But we must take the chance."

With the white hawks wheeling about them, they moved on. The day wore to late afternoon and still the green valley with its promise of water mocked them ; whilst the path wandered in and out, among giant boulders, skirted dizzily the edge of precipices, or meandered across slopes of detritus, which, set in movement by their passage, sent avalanches of stone crashing towards the valley, making a sound like machine-gun fire long after they had passed the peril. On one of these stone-slopes disaster befell. Jacques was driving the sure-footed barbs before him, whilst Warborough led Cornelia's mule. The former had reached the firmer ground and the others were three parts of the way across when there was a rattle of stone higher up. Jacques shouted a warning!

" Hurry, my captain."

A stone shot by Warborough's ears with such force that it might have come from a catapult. A second stone hit the mule sharply on its nose, causing it to squeal and plunge. The loose stones under its hoofs slid downwards, and the beast slid with them. Warborough tugged at the reins, but felt himself slipping, and knew his helplessness.

" Slip off!" he cried to Cornelia. " Throw yourself flat."

Cornelia hesitated to obey. The mule plunged more wildly and slid further from the track. Behind them up the hill was a perfect fusillade of rattling stone set in motion by the movement lower down. Warborough caught the sound and knew that the whole stone-slide was in motion, moving down the hill, and peril was imminent. The mule was still sliding, and he himself was sliding with it. Once his weight was removed the beast must be swept downward. He yelled to make himself heard above the rattle of stones :

" For God's sake, get off."

This time she obeyed him ; and as she slipped from the saddle, and losing her footing was thrown prone on to the moving stone-river, Warborough let the mule go, and, flinging himself down, gripped the woman.

" Cover your head with your arms," he bawled in her ear. There was no need for the warning. Loose stones were shooting by them, any one of which would smash a man's skull as easy as an egg-shell. Cornelia heard him and obeyed, lying face down in the stone-river.

" Dig your toes down!" he shouted again, and himself strove mightily to check their gathering pace. It was a hopeless effort. All the stones were on the move, sliding downwards with increasing momentum. To stand

up would be impossible, to lie there might mean death.
Recognizing the inevitable, he put an arm round his companion.  If they were to die, they would die together.
He lifted his head, and saw Grandpère Jacques gesticula-
ting wildly, and, as he guessed, shouting.  He heard
nothing of the words, but looked round.  The mule was
below them, wedged against a jutting rock worn smooth
with the constant passage of rubble, and the stones were
piling against it.  Beyond he saw the rubble shooting
into the void, as water plunges over a fall.  What depth
there was below, he could not guess ; but if they slid over,
whether the fall was deep or not, the falling stones would
batter them to pulp and bury them.  The mule was their
only chance, and he watched it as a man watches his
one possible salvation.  They slid nearer, and then with
a superhuman effort, he got his feet against its quivering
back, and ceasing to slide, was anchored in that stream
of death, with Cornelia in his arms.

## CHAPTER XVII

### TRYING HOURS

WITH one arm about Cornelia, and within an ace of
death, Jeff Warborough waited breathlessly for
the issue of their misadventure.  A stone larger than the
rest caught the mule's head—a terrific blow—and the poor
beast ceased to quiver.  Another went by Warborough's
ear with a vicious sound, a third struck him on the brow,
splitting it open as cleanly as a knife might have done,
almost knocking him senseless, and leaving him very sick
and dizzy.  He heard Cornelia give a sharp cry of pain
and felt her relax under his arm.  That she had been
struck he guessed, and thought that she had been knocked
senseless ; but for the moment he could do nothing, and
waited for what seemed an age, lying prone, quite without
hope.

Then gradually the movement of the stones ceased, and presently all were at rest, and through the deathly stillness which followed the noise made by the stone-slide, came Grandpère Jacques' voice, imploring, full of apprehension :

"My captain ! "

Warborough lifted his head cautiously, but was scarcely able to see for the red mist of blood from his wound.

"*Grâce à Dieu !*" cried Jacques fervently, and began to give directions. "I have made a rope of the reins and the stirrup-leathers. Be alert to watch when I throw. Look not back. The fall is a sheer one to Hell. If the stones quicken to life again——"

The rest was left to Warborough's imagination, and he cried out softly that he understood—softly, because it seemed to him that a word loudly spoken, a mere breath almost, might set that terrible stone-river flowing anew. Cornelia stirred sharply at his side ; and whilst relieved to find that she was conscious, the movement filled him with apprehension.

"For God's sake, lie still ! " he whispered tensely.

He heard a swish and clutched the improvised rope as it fell close to his hand. Cautiously he set to work, buckling the loop-like arrangement that Jacques had devised about Cornelia, then he whispered instructions to her ; and bracing himself against the mule gave Jacques the word :

"Now ! "

There was a faint rattle of loose stones set in motion as Jacques set his weight on the rope. Warborough held his breath. If the movement of the stones became general, there was no hope. The pressure of them would be too great for either the rope or for the man's strength. But the rubble was for the moment static, and presently a triumphant grunt from Jacques told him that the woman was safe. A minute later the rope swished again, and he grasped it with heartfelt thankfulness, and buckled it

o

about him.   Then knowing that his own weight would be
more than Jacques could manage unaided, he stretched
himself frog-wise and inch by inch began to worm himself
across the rubble.   Once or twice there was an ominous
movement of the stones, causing him to flatten himself
and lay still as a hare in its form ; then, as the movement
ceased, he began his crawl afresh.   When but a yard and
a half separated him from solid earth, he saw the legionary's face twist in sudden apprehension, and heard the
rattle begin anew higher up the slide.

"Quick, *mon capitaine*.   Oh, quick !   The stones begin
their devil's march."

He wasted no time, for there was none to waste.   With
a great effort he lifted himself up, and with the stones
already in movement under his feet, leaped for safety,
Grandpère Jacques helping with a sharp jerk of the rope.
The jerk and the leap carried him clear of the stone-
slide.   He fell sprawling on the farther side, struck
his head against a stone, and lapsed into unconsciousness.

When he came to himself he felt very sick, the mountain
world seemed to be whirling about him in a sort of mad
Dervish dance, there was a mist before his eyes ; but
through the whirl and the mist he was conscious of one
figure kneeling by his side, and of Cornelia's face full of
concern.   Then he heard her cry out in a voice expressing
relief from intolerable fear :

"He lives !   Oh, thank God, Jacques, he lives."

Grandpère Jacques laughed gruffly.   " A crack on the
head only.   Nothing, madame, if the brains are not scattered."

He waited.   The mountains ceased to gyrate, the mist
lifted, and he saw Cornelia's dark eyes bright with tears.
Then her hands became busy, as she bound his head with
the veil torn from her Moorish head-dress ; and he smiled
a little as he thought that what in the morning she had
used to hide herself from him was now gone for ever.

After a few minutes he was able to sit up, and then she spoke :

" How shall I ever thank you, my friend ? But for you——" She glanced towards the depths to which the stones were still flowing, and shuddered.

" All in the day's work," he said lightly.

" And the work is not yet done, monsieur, though the day declines. We cannot sit here through the night, and the mule is lost."

Warborough, knowing the bitter need for haste, made a shift to rise, and stood swaying with Cornelia supporting him.

" I cannot walk, Jacques——"

" Walk ! " Jacques, already busy buckling bridles on the barbs, looked round. " There are two horses still—one for madame and the other for you. To me, who have marched with the Legion, the descent to the valley will be nothing."

And it was so that they resumed their flight, with Jacques leading Cornelia's horse, and Warborough riding on behind, a sick, shaken man, clinging to the saddle only by an effort. The track improved, swung round towards the valley, and two hours later, with the dusk of night creeping down the hillside, Jacques gave an excited shout :

" Goats, monsieur, and a herd ! We approach a house or village."

There was no response to his cry and he looked sharply round. The barb was following its companion, but its rider, still in the saddle, sagged across its neck, like a dead man. Grandpère Jacques hurried back, and lifted the sagging rider. The eyes were half-open, the face deadly pale, and there was no response to his question.

" *Mon capitaine*, you are sick, in pain ? "

Cornelia slipped from her barb and ran towards the pair.

" Oh," she whispered tragically, " he is dead ? "

" No ! not dead ! . . . It is the concussion—or a

fever ! Dolt that I am, I might have guessed, I who have
seen a man who had suffered a crack on the head march
to his cot, and there lie down and die without a word.
Madame, you must cherish him, whilst I talk to the herd
down there. If we have luck, all may yet be well ; if not,
it is the end for all of us, for I cannot leave monsieur, even
to save you."

" I would not allow you," answered Cornelia sharply.

" Good ! . . . That is what I should expect of madame.
Now I talk to the herder of goats."

He went down the hillside through the dusk, leaving
the woman alone with the man who had twice saved her.
She knelt by his side, and touching his cheek found it
cold. She marked the feeble respiration, and grasping
his wrist noted the slow pulse. She had no doubt that
Grandpère Jacques was right, and in a stress of apprehension prayed fervently :

" God . . . God . . . give me his life."

Presently Jacques returned, with him the goatherd—
the latter a tall Berber of fierce aspect, who stared at
Cornelia in wonder. She noted a medal pinned to his
ragged djellaba and knew before Jacques spoke that here
was an ex-soldier of France's colonial levies.

" Madame, we have the luck. There is but one house—
a mere shed, but this man is the owner, and he has served
France, and is of loyal heart. We shall save monsieur,
yet."

The house to which they took the unconscious man
merited Jacques' description. It was the poorest kind of
place, not unlike that in which they had been lodged in
the village across the hills—a place built of mud and timber
with a courtyard in which the goats were made secure
for the night. But there was a cot of sorts, and on this
they laid Warborough ; and Jacques, like all men of his
service something of a doctor, heated stones in the fire,
and set them at the patient's feet, covering him with
dressed goatskins by way of blankets.

Then they watched for any revival, which as it chanced was long in coming. The coma continued, and far into the night whilst their host slept, Jacques and Cornelia watched, consumed with anxiety, and at times talked in whispers.

" You have known Captain Warborough long, Grand-père Jacques ? " asked Cornelia, moved by curiosity.

" Ten—no !—nine years, madame. He is of the bravest. Many times have we been together in strange places in this land and in the desert on secret work. There is none to equal him there."

" And you think he can do no wrong ? "

" I would pledge my life on it."

" But if I told you he had killed a man by foul means ——"

" Madame, I should vow the man deserved it ! That the deed was one of justice."

It seemed that there was no half-heartedness in the legionary's faith in his officer, and Cornelia refrained from pressing the matter ; but presently she asked another question :

" You have been long in the Legion, Grandpère Jacques, you must have known many men ? Did you by any chance ever meet one Alex Steffanson, who was a sergeant in the first regiment of the Legion ? "

Jacques answered that question much as he had answered it on a former occasion.

" That black devil ! Whom Caillé and Steinmann killed in his fine house in England."

" He was my husband, Jacques," said Cornelia quietly. The words calmly spoken might have been a bursting shell from the way the legionary jumped. He stared at her incredulously, then he broke out :

" Impossible ! It cannot be ! "

" Why ? " she demanded sharply.

" Madame is too young, for—for——"

" For what ? " she asked, watching him closely as he broke off in some embarrassment.

" To have been that black scoundrel's wife. The other one, now——"

Again he checked himself sharply, as if conscious that he skirted an indiscretion ; but the woman was not to be denied.

" The other one ? " she asked in a whisper so hard that Jacques shuddered. " What do you mean ? That there was another woman ? "

Jacques saw that the gate of evasion was closed to him. Madame was not to be turned aside, and he answered tersely :

" *Oui !* His wife ! "

" His wife ? "

Cornelia's voice had a ring of steel. Her dark eyes were like glowing coals, her beautiful face was drawn and tense.

" These eleven years. She had a legionaries' café at Sidi-bel-Abbès, and Steffanson used to wash the cups and the glasses, and help to maintain order. Then he married her—and later left her. She is still at bel-Abbès, a woman much the worse for wear, and grown enormous. If Steffanson married again——"

Cornelia was not interested in the argument. The news she had heard had been a tremendous shock to her ; but not for a moment did she question the truth of it. Grandpère Jacques was too matter-of-fact to be romancing, and his voice had a ring of truth. She crouched there on the saddle that served her for seat, her mind in a whirl, but seeking to fasten on essential things. Suddenly she snapped an inquiry :

" Did he know of that . . . that marriage ? "

" The captain ? I do not know. It is possible. He was at that time one of us—a soldier with a sou a day. He laughed to see Steffanson wash the cups. . . . *Oui !* He may have known. It was no secret and there were many who envied Steffanson his luck ; for a man does not pay his wife for the red wine and the tobacco."

Cornelia sat quite still, a far-away look in her eyes, whilst Grandpère Jacques wondered what was in her mind. As a matter of fact she was thinking how Warborough had flown to Carston Magna to stop her wedding with Simon Maxwell, and after a little time she nodded her head.

"Yes! he must have known," she whispered—more to herself than to Jacques. "That was why he came, and here is what he would not tell me last night—because the need was past. . . ." Then another thought clashed on the heels of the one that she had spoken. "But how could he know?"

Grandpère Jacques had no clue to the second thought and quite naturally confused it with the first.

"But, madame, I have explained. All the regiment knew, and——"

"I was not thinking of that!" interrupted Cornelia. "It is another thing that is in my mind. Did you know that he flew to Simon—that is to Alex Steffanson's house in England to prevent his false marriage with me?"

"*Tiens!* no! But that is like my captain."

"But how did he know the marriage was to be—and the place and the time?" she asked, thinking of the telegram which Standish had found in Caillé's pocket.

Grandpère Jacques shook his head.

"How should I know? He is a great one to find out secrets and to keep them—as many in this land know."

Cornelia pondered. She had no clue to the truth, and Jacques could not help her; and her mind harked back to the thing she knew now beyond all question.

"That was it," she whispered. "To save me—whom he did not know—from shame. And for that reason he killed Simon."

A sudden light came in her eyes. Her face grew extraordinarily tender. Her heart burned with gratitude to the man who had done so much to save her. That he had killed a man seemed a small thing now; almost a commendable thing, since it was for her sake the deed had been wrought, and she was overwhelmed as she thought how she had treated him no later than the morning which now seemed ages away. Suddenly she broke out passionately:

"Grandpère, he must not die! We must save him, we must, you and I. If he should die before I can tell him certain things, I must wear sackcloth or go to a convent and pray for him till I also die."

Grandpère Jacques smiled and permitted himself a compliment.

"A convent! Only the ugly and those whom love has passed by go there. Madame is too beautiful to join those—the dead in life! . . . But have no fear. We shall snatch him from death's skinny hand. When the shock has passed, he will be his own man again." He spoke hopefully, but as he stared through the open doorway to the courtyard where the goats were bleating in the darkness, a shadowed look came on his face. "If only that devil Steinmann does not come!"

"You think he may?" asked Cornelia quickly.

"It is possible. By this he must know we did not take the caravan way up or down the valley——"

"He may think we are ahead!"

"No, Madame," answered Grandpère, shaking his head. "He will know that we are not. He could not march for half a day along that track without meeting someone—salt-carriers from the mines, a camel-driver with dates, or maybe a Jewish pedlar. And one of them would tell him that we had not passed. . . . Knowing that he will return, he will search, maybe he will find the path we found. And in that case——"

"But they may not find us. The way was very tortuous."

"They will see the mule, madame, with which the

ravens will be busy. They may think we are lost, but the Allemand comes of a breed which is thorough. He will search the valley to make sure. He will see this solitary house and then——" He shrugged his shoulders. " Our hope lay in keeping ahead of the pursuit ; but here we are chained by the leg like a parrot to its perch."

Cornelia shared his apprehensions. There was not merely herself as lure for Steinmann, but these two men who worked to defeat his nefarious activities. Here in the stony heart of the Atlas he could work his will unchecked ; and she guessed sufficiently the work on which the pair were engaged to know that if they disappeared completely their disappearance would be docketed in some office and accepted as the more or less expected. And if they went, she herself—— She shivered, leaving the thought unfinished ; but as she watched the sick man through the hours of darkness, the shadow of Steinmann loomed ever more formidable and threatening, for in the remote hills a ruthless man might work his will with none to say him nay.

In the course of the next day a change came in the patient's condition. The coma passed, but on its heels came the restlessness and delirium of fever, caused, as she guessed, by some inflammation. The herd had gone with his goats to their pasturage, and Grandpère Jacques, on the plea of taking the air, had accompanied him, taking his rifle with him. The plea, as she knew, was the merest excuse. The legionary had gone to keep watch on the spidery track across the hills, that he might have early information of the German's coming if that should happen.

Seated on a goatskin by the sick Warborough, she did for him what little was possible, laying cooling cloths upon his head, giving him water on occasion, and listening to the babble of delirious words that occasionally broke from him. The most of it was unintelligible, or referred to events in his boyish life, but now and again came words, the meaning of which she was able to guess at. Once he laughed deliriously.

" On their knees . . . to the living woman."

She caught the words and knew that in the heats of fever he was living again the moments of their first meeting. She flushed a little as she had not flushed at the first hearing of the words ; then crouched there with a very thoughtful look in her eyes. For a time the man lay silent. She hoped that the fever was abating, that he was sleeping, but almost on the heels of the hope came a torrent of broken words that wrecked the hope. Then, quite suddenly, came an utterance which startled her, and tautened all her senses.

" So, Sergeant Steffanson, we meet again."

There followed a laugh that made her shiver. She knew that in the mimic life of fever he was confronting Simon Maxwell in that great room at Farholme ; and she burned with eagerness to know what had befallen that night. That she stood on the brink of the revelation was clear and she waited, her ears straining. The next words came in a hoarse whisper :

" You remember ? . . . We found him . . . two days later . . . those women . . . mutilated him, shockingly. He was crazed with horror at what had overtaken him. . . . Mercifully he died. He was but a boy . . . my friend, and you, you infernal Judas, were the cause——"

The words broke off. The silence of the little hovel was almost unendurable to the waiting woman. Outside in the courtyard a tethered goat that had been left behind with a very young kid bleated plaintively, and somewhere not far away a raven croaked. Cornelia waited tensely, watching the lips of the sick man moving in soundless words, then after an interval came a sudden sharp cry of anger.

" Keep away from that desk, swine ! . . . You shall have your chance, but not that way. . . . Your chance, but I shall kill . . . for that boy's sake, and to save. . . . If I told her of that woman at Sidi-bel-Abbès——"

Again the words trickled to silence, and she was left burning with impatience to learn what had followed on that night of tragedy. But she was not to learn immediately. When Warborough's delirium recommenced it took another twist, and in his fevered brain he lived anew some episode of his desert life remote from that which she burned to know, leaving her conjecturing about the circumstances of Simon Maxwell's death. On one thing her mind fastened. Warborough had known what Grandpère Jacques knew about the wife living in the soldiers' café at Sidi-bel-Abbès. Unquestionably she had been in his mind when he had fronted the master of Farholme, but there had been a second motive for his attack. That boy! who was he? What had befallen that Simon Maxwell should be charged with treachery that had led to the boy's undoing?

She sat there asking herself first this question and then that. Warborough's delirious babblings died away, and again an oppressive silence reigned in the hovel, and when it was broken by the mother-goat's plaintive bleating that tried her nerves even more than the silence. She was about to rise and go to the door, when the sick man made a convulsive movement, throwing his arms wide, the hand working as if to clutch something. To soothe him she stretched her own hand and the sick man's closed about it and held it. She made no attempt to withdraw it, but sat quite still, rejoicing when he fell quiet once more.

Outside she caught a sound of footsteps. Jacques returning, she thought to herself, and did not turn her head. The footsteps reached the doorway, halted, then came a sudden sharp laugh which chilled her to the marrow:

" A very pretty tableau. The sick man and the devoted——"

She swung round to see Steinmann standing in the doorway—with a look of evil mirth on his scarred face.

## CHAPTER XVIII

### A TURNING OF TABLES

SLOWLY Cornelia released her hand from the sick man's grasp, then rose to her feet, and shaking with fear though she was, she faced the German bravely. He stood there smiling his evil smile, and behind him she caught sight of four Berbers, all armed. She had a feeling that the situation was hopeless, that for Warborough the end had come, and for her the way of escape was closed ; but fought back her despair whilst she waited for him to speak again.

" A long chase," he said after a little time, " but not to be regretted, since it gives me not merely the pretty bird who flew, but the tiger whom I sought."

He moved into the hut, and thrusting by her looked down at the sick man. There was black hatred in his eyes, a look of cold fury on his face.

" Fool ! " he muttered. " And helpless as a blind kitten ! Well, one kills the kitten and does not spare the sick tiger."

His hand thrust itself into the folds of the djellaba that he wore and reappeared holding a pistol. To Cornelia his intention was clear, and moved by almost crazy apprehension she flung herself upon him, crying hysterically :

" No ! No ! You shall not."

Steinmann flung her from him roughly, and looked at her a little wonderingly.

" Why this concern ? You sought to bring the man to justice for the murder of your husband——"

" Simon Maxwell was not my husband——"

" *Der liebe Gott !* You know that ? That fool there told you ? "

" No. He spared me the knowledge. I learned the truth elsewhere."

" You learned about that fat Frau at Sidi-bel-Abbès

and he did not tell you ? Then it must have been the other, that cursed Jacques. . . . Where is he ? "

At the question Cornelia's heart gave a little bound. Steinmann and his jackals had not seen Grandpère ; and possibly the latter was waiting his opportunity. The thought braced her a little.

" I do not know," she answered quietly.

Steinmann laughed. " No matter. I have the master and the servant is not important. He can be found later. Also I have you——"

" But not the money you demand," interrupted Cornelia significantly.

" True ! " The man laughed harshly. " But to have the cow is to have the milk. You will pay, madame——"

" For what ? "

The German was exasperated by the coolness of the question.

" *Tausand teufels !* " he roared. " You ask that ? . . . For yourself, who else ? "

" But if I will not redeem myself with Simon Maxwell's money——"

" If you will not," Steinmann laughed brutally. " You forget you are worth a price in this land. Our mutual friend Mohammed Amaati would pay quite a large sum— and there are others to whom you would be desirable. There are men whom I might bribe with so fair an offering —men who at present are on the fence, who watch and wait to see how the cat jumps. You . . ." he laughed again. " You might prove an inducement. It would not be the first time a woman has altered the history of an empire, and these men have the fancies of connoisseurs. . . . In the market you might fetch a thousand pounds, or better still five hundred rifles with men to carry them——"

" You would not be so vile."'

The man laughed at her protest.

" You are mistaken. There is nothing vile about money, nor about the means to power. I am a soldier of fortune

. . . as Maxwell was.   You pay—or I pay myself through
you.   It is very simple."

" And——"

She did not finish the question.   Her eyes went to
Warborough, and Steinmann understood.   His face
darkened.

" That one !   He shall roast.   Not all Simon Maxwell's
money shall save him.   You do not understand.   He has
thwarted me not once but a dozen times.   But for him
the Administration would now be fighting for its life in
Fez—as it fought when the Moors rose against the Protectorate in the hour of proclamation, and as it fought
during the war in a dozen places.   El-Krim would pay
his weight in gold for him, and—*Gott im Himmel !*—he
shall !   I thought to shoot him ; but sick as he is now,
he would not know.   The other is the better way.   When
the sickness is past, he will know me, and I shall laugh in
his face—and——"   He broke off with a burst of harsh
laughter—then completed his thought.   " I shall revenge
Simon Maxwell.   That is a droll thought.   I shall do
what you came to do ; and punish the man who slew——"

" You are sure he did that ? "

Her question was quick as a pistol-shot.   It threw the
man out of his stride.   For a second or two words failed
him whilst he stared at her doubtfully.   Then again his
strident laughter sounded, as he replied :

" As sure as a man can be who saw the thing done."
His words surprised Cornelia.   For a moment she was
silent, then she broke out :

" You are not afraid to own that ? "

" Why should I be ?   I was watching from the shrubs
by the window—with Caillé a corpse in the pleasaunce.
I saw all—heard all that was spoken."

There was a swift change in Cornelia's face, a sudden
glow in the dark eyes.

" Then you can tell me what he said to Maxwell about
me ? "

The German laughed brutally.

"Is that the way the wind blows ? . . . You were not in his mind. You were never mentioned. It is not flattering to your vanity, but——"

"You liar ! I know the truth. He mentioned a boy —a friend of his betrayed to death or worse by Simon Maxwell, and he said that for that boy's sake he would kill him and so save me. He mentioned also that wife at Sidi-bel-Abbès——"

"*Der teufel !* " cried Steinmann in amazement. "You also were listening—watching—— But no ! That cannot have been. You come to Fez to find the man—to punish him. He has told you a twisted tale to turn you aside from vengeance, and you have listened. That is it, hey ? . . . Well, women have soft hearts, and——"

There was a sharp word spoken by one of the men in the doorway, a sound of quick movement, and then the crack of a rifle. One of the Berbers cried out, and fell with a crash in the doorway, whilst the others jumped for cover. Steinmann rapped a quick oath, and shouted a question. A voice outside replied, and the German dropping prone crept to the doorway and looked forth. Cornelia watched him with elation. The shot which had brought the Berber down could only mean that Grandpère Jacques, aware of the hostile visitors, had come into action. She heard Steinmann giving angry orders, then at a sound of movement behind her turned quickly round. The sick man had lifted himself on his elbow. There was a wild look in his eyes. Whether some interval of sanity had been granted whilst Steinmann had been talking she did not know, but it seemed to her that he was aware of the German's presence, and was anxious for her to do something. She bent swiftly towards him, and caught a broken whisper :

"The . . . pistol——"

As the words were spoken he fell back on the goat-skins, his eyes closed, a twisted look of pain on his face.

Cornelia, deeply concerned for him as she was, understood what was in his mind, and wasted no time. The pistol which Warborough had carried had been set in a corner with his rifle and the saddles, and without delay she secured it, and hid it in her dress. Then she looked at Warborough to give the signal that she had understood, but his eyes remained closed, and his lips began to move, as they had moved a little while before, without words. From outside came a sharp exclamation, then the crack of a rifle. One of the Berbers apparently had seen Grandpère and had fired.

Consumed by apprehension she waited, then heard a grunt of disappointment. The man had plainly missed his target. A moment later the phut of a bullet and the almost simultaneous sound of the rifle that had fired it confirmed the fact, and on the heels of the sounds there was a sudden rush of the three Berbers who remained for the shelter that the house afforded. Steinmann addressed them with heat, but to no purpose. Apparently he was urging them to go out and attack, but they clung to the cover of the mud-walls, averse from the risk that waited them outside. The man gnashed his teeth with rage, and rifle in hand himself moved towards the door. Possibly he thought that with his friends in the hut Grandpère would not take the risk of firing. But in that he was mistaken. Scarcely had he reached the doorway when a bullet crashed into the rough beam over his head, and he backed swiftly indoors.

" *Gott !* " he muttered, as he crouched in the shadow, staring across the courtyard into the sunlight, and again, " *Gott !* "

That he was in a quandary Cornelia knew. With little knowledge of warfare, the position was quite clear to her. From some cover where he lay hidden, Grandpère Jacques, who must have observed the arrival of the pursuit, commanded the hut with his rifle, so that none could enter or leave it without becoming his target ; and until they could locate him, he held the lives of those within in the hollow of his hand. The position was almost devastatingly simple ; and Cornelia could have laughed aloud.

To Steinmann it must have been equally clear, for he crouched not far from the doorway, a black look on his face, muttering curses to himself. Some time elapsed without anything further happening, then the German left his place by the doorway, and began to pace about in the manner of a man revolving some knotty problem. Cornelia smiled to herself and stared past the men crouched against the walls of the hut to the opposite hillside. There was a scrub of olives there, and somewhere in the grey-green screen Grandpère Jacques crouched, master of the situation. If only he could keep it up——

Her thought got no further. Steinmann, pacing like a wolf in its cage, in the very act of passing, gripped one of her arms, and twisted it behind her with such force as to make her cry out with pain. The German held it in such a way that she could not turn, and he laughed harshly in her ear.

" Forward," he said. " Let us see if your friend out there is a respecter of persons."

He jerked the arm he held, impelling her towards the door. When she reached it he grasped the rifle which he had rested close by and laughed again.

" A classic way of the old wars. To shoot me, that devil out there must aim past you, and he will not dare."

He thrust her forward into the open courtyard, and then dropped on one knee.

" Kneel ! " he said harshly, and sharply twisting the arm compelled her to do his bidding.

He rested something on her shoulder, and in sudden panic she realized that it was the rifle, the barrel of which projected well beyond her face. She heard the man chuckle behind her.

" Here is a problem for friend Jacques ! When he moves or fires, I shall get him. Keep quite still, or the

P

consequences may be ugly. I should not like to blow away that pretty ear."

Cornelia shivered and with apprehensive eyes stared at the scrub. Grandpère Jacques might be a marksman, but he could not possibly fire on such a target. If he did——

She heard the German addressing the man in the hut, without knowing what he said. Deliberately, she looked round. One of the Berbers, it seemed, was exposing himself to draw Jacques' fire, and so induce him to betray his whereabouts. But the legionary was for the moment not to be tempted. No shot broke the stillness, and the scrub might have been utterly deserted. Steinmann whispered an oath expressive of chagrin.

" Curse the fellow. He is as cunning as a hunting cat."

Five long minutes passed. From the hut there came delirious words which wrung Cornelia's heart. The strain of the position she was in with the mental tension tried her sorely, and she felt her head reeling. In a little time, as she was sure, she would faint unless relief came. Steinmann himself appeared to be feeling the strain of waiting. Another whispered oath came from him, then for Cornelia the relief came in a totally unexpected fashion.

" Phut ! "

She caught the sound, and the German's cry wrenched from him by pain, mingled with the report of the rifle. Steinmann's own weapon slipped from her shoulder and fell with a clatter to the ground, whilst the owner leaping to his feet ran for the hovel. Cornelia stood upright and looked round. Away to the right she saw a faint plume of smoke, and realized that Grandpère had utilized those moments of tense waiting to move round to the flank. Now, no doubt, he was hurrying to change his ground again, and put himself beyond reach of any blind retaliation. As she herself turned to the hut she could have laughed with exultation. The legionary, as it seemed, was in full command of the situation.

Within she found Steinmann, mouthing black oaths, whilst one of the Berbers bound an arm smashed at the elbow by the rifle bullet that had found it. The three natives, as she noted, were betraying signs of apprehension, and she had no doubt that before long they would be the prey of panic.

When the rough bandaging was finished, Steinmann spoke to the three men at length. Cornelia could not understand a single word of his speech, but from the fervour of his tones and the vehemence of his questions, she divined that he was urging them to go out and attack the sharpshooter. His eloquence, however, was wasted. With a man, who was an expert with a rifle, safely hidden in cover which he could change at will, to advance across the open would have been utter folly, as the three men knew. They pointed to Steinmann's arm, to their own stricken comrade and plainly refused to budge.

The German turned away. There was a look of blazing rage in his eyes as they met Cornelia's, and saw in them the exultation she could not suppress, and his rage voiced itself in speech.

" You think that fool out there has us in a trap ! That we cannot move. But when dusk falls I will show you. We will hunt him as these men hunt a wild goat. And when we get him he shall pray us to kill him. *Mein Gott !* but he shall twist like a smake in the fire."

Another hour passed and the stalemate continued. Whenever one of the men ventured to show himself a a shot from the hill drove him hurriedly back to cover, then came a change which threatened to rob Jacques of the advantage he had gained and sustained. The day grew swiftly overcast. There was the flame of lightning and the crash of thunder, followed by a torrential downpour and a steaming mist rose from the baked ground. Steinmann shouted exultantly and there was a change in the attitude of the tribesmen. The mist and the rain were a veil hiding their movements from anyone half a score of yards away, and as they moved towards the door it was clear to Cornelia that they were going forth to stalk Jacques. Steinmann confirmed the conviction.

" Now we shall get that swine. In the open he will be no match for three men born in these hills. Presently you will see him brought in like a trussed chicken."

Cornelia made no reply. Steinmann, it seemed, was to remain behind ; possibly to keep a watch on her ; though where she could flee to alone, in the wild hills of the Atlas, did not appear. She moved towards the door to watch the going of the three Berbers, realizing that once they were out of the courtyard and in the scrub the chances of Jacques escaping them were very small. She saw them fading in the watery veil, and waited for any shot from Jacques. None came or she did not hear it in the downpour. She heard Steinmann chuckle behind her.

" The rain blinds him. In an hour——"

There were sounds of sudden commotion in the courtyard beyond the range of her vision, a noise of blows, wild yells, a single shot, and one of the men who had just left the hovel came into view running, two men at his heels, one of whom, as she recognized, was the goatherd. She caught the German's voice behind her, raised in consternation.

" *Mein Gott*——"

She did not know quite what was happening ; but that help of some kind had unexpectedly arrived she was sure. Steinmann, as it seemed, was equally convinced.

" Stand aside," he growled in her ear.

That he meant to escape she guessed, and turned to front him. His face was working with mingled fear and rage, and he was struggling to reach something with his uninjured hand and arm—his pistol, she guessed, and on the second remembered her own. He was still fumbling left-handedly at a right-hand pocket, cursing softly, when she produced the weapon, and standing just outside the doorway, in the drenching rain, fronted him. For a second his jaw dropped and he stood there the most amazed man in all the Atlas. Then his cold eyes blazed.

" Stand aside, you harlot——" he growled in ferocious menace.

But Cornelia did not yield. Through the downpour she caught the sound of the legionary's laughing voice, and she cried desperately :

" Grandpère ! Grand——"

Risking the pistol in her hand, Steinmann leaped and struck ferociously. The pistol was discharged as Cornelia fell, but the bullet went wide. The German with the way clear before him began to run, but even as he did so, Grandpere Jacques' voice sounded again :

" No, my good citizen——"

A clubbed rifle felled the German like an ox in the abattoir-yard, and he lay prone and still, whilst the legionary helped Cornelia to her feet.

" A near shave, but we have that black limb of Satan now. I trust you are not hurt, madame. Poof ! How wet the rain is ! Excuse me, I must find rope to bind that rascal."

A quarter of an hour later, with Steinmann safely bound in a corner, and the sunlight gleaming on the wet olives across the valley, Cornelia heard the story of Jacques' exploit.

" When I went forth with Omar there—our host—it was not to herd goats, madame comprehends. It was in my mind that Allemand would find our way across the hills and follow, and whilst Omar watched his flock, I for my part watched the steep hillside, and talked to our friend of what must be done, if Steinmann there should come. I learned from him that up the valley there is a village, the men of which are loyal to France, and always at daggers with the men across the hills, who are bandits —stealers of goats and women, madame understands ? That is what the heart might have wished for, nothing better, for the loyal ones would come to our help, if word were sent, and when after a time we saw the German and the others toiling across that devil's track we followed yesterday, I made my depositions as a soldier should. First I sent Omar to bring the men of the village against raiding bandits who were coming to steal his goats, and then I myself took cover, where I could command this poor dwelling.

"There was a risk in that, as I knew. If this Steinmann here was hasty, he might shoot my captain out-of-hand ; but there was you, madame, to prevent that, and there was also the German's lust for revenge. He would be in no hurry to slay a man who would not know that he was to be slain. Steinmann, I thought, would desire to play with Captain Warborough as the cat plays with the mouse, for long the merest touch of the claws, the playful pat, and then the killing stroke. . . . The Allemand would not hurry. No ! He would desire to chew the cud of revenge. . . . Also there was another reason why I should wait. If whilst these men were on the hillside I fired a shot I might kill one, but the rest would be warned ; they would bolt to cover, and whilst I stalked one as one stalks the mountain sheep, the others might close on me. But if they entered this house, with but one entrance and a narrow gateway into the court, one man with a rifle could command the doorway, so that none could come forth save at the peril of his life from a flying bullet.

"So I reasoned. Once in the hut here they were in the bottle which I would cork—with my rifle. So I took my risk, as every man must at some time, sure that I could hold the bandits here until Omar and his tribesmen arrived. . . . And madame knows how the strategy has worked."

"It was good strategy, Jacques."

Grandpère Jacques laughed.

"The wine is proved in the drinking ! But there were two moments when I thought the vintage had gone sour. The first was when the German used madame as a shield. He is a marksman. When he was in the Legion he was

the best rifleman in his company. If he but saw a whiff
of smoke among the olives, or if a leaf stirred in his sight,
a bullet would be there to find me. But whilst he watched
the front, I crept like a snake to the flank and I took a
risk, madame, when I fired. If he had moved backward
in that second——"

"But he did not move, Grandpère, till your bullet
found him."

"*Grâce à Dieu!* No. But the risk of hurting madame
was there. I might have killed him then ; but I knew
the man has secrets that Monsieur Warborough must
learn from him, so I fired to disable."

"A good shot, Grandpère ! "

"The second bad moment was when the storm broke.
The mist and the rain were a better screen than my olive-
trees, and when it began I said, here is the water that will
wash away my hopes ; for I guessed that Steinmann
would send his fellows forth under cover of it, and was
in despair. But Omar the herd and his villagers arrived
before I expected them, and, as madame knows, we met
the enemy in the gate——"

Jacques broke off with a laugh, and Cornelia spoke
with heartfelt gratitude.

"Grandpère, you are a brave man and a wise one——"

"Poof ! " he said with a merry laugh. "An old soldier
of the Legion worth one sou per day."

Cornelia looked at Steinmann. "What will you do
with him ? "

"Cherish him as a mother does her first-born, until my
captain can pass judgment. No doubt I shall have to
fight these tribesmen to save him alive from their women.
But were it not that he is a locked safe with secrets—
they could have him to work their will."

A little groan broke from the German, and Grandpère
turned to him.

"You hear, Steinmann, *hein*? . . . It will be well to
reflect what you will do when the moment comes. . . .

You know what a Berber woman's knife can do, and only a willing tongue can save you from that. Reflect well, whilst the chance is yours ; for time flies swiftly, and the hours of grace are few for the wicked."

On his goatskin couch Jeff Warborough stirred uneasily, drawing the eyes of his friends. A feverish babble broke from his lips, and both Cornelia and Jacques moved towards him. Then in the midst of the delirious flow, he suddenly flung himself into a sitting posture, with wild eyes fixed on the mud-wall as one who sees visions, then he whispered in horror :

" My God ! Straight through the throat."

The intelligible words broke off abruptly, and the speaker sank back heavily again, babbling meaningless things. Cornelia turned to put a cooling cloth on the burning brow, and when he lay still and silent once more, she looked at the legionary.

" You heard that, Grandpère ? "

" *Oui*, madame ! Through the throat—a killing stroke always. Doubtless my captain is thinking of some man of the desert whom once he killed. There are moments when the thought takes us all that way."

" It was no man of the desert of whom he thought, Grandpère Jacques. It was of Alex Steffanson."

" That *cochon* ! *Mordieu* ! What matters the killing of such—a viper in the grass ? Through the throat." Jacques laughed. " It is well to make sure."

" Yes," said Cornelia, with an odd note in her voice. " It is well to make sure."


## CHAPTER XIX

### A CONFESSION

THE hours of grace for the wicked, as Jacques averred, might be few, but for Cornelia the hours of vigil were long. It was a whole eight days after, when looking into Jeff Warborough's eyes, clear of fever at last, she knew that her watch was over and that he would live. She saw his gaze rove round the primitive hovel, a little wonderingly, and then came back to herself.

" You ? " he said in a weak voice.

" In the flesh still," she said, with forced lightness. " As, thank Heaven, you are also."

" I have been ill—long ? "

" Ten days—that for the length of them might have been ten eternities."

" And you have watched, nursed me ? "

" A woman's privilege, and a service of gratitude. It was in saving me you were hurt."

For a little time he did not speak. His brows creased in an effort of remembrance. Then as memory served him he whispered :

" The stone-slide . . . It was after. I was hurt——"

" To the death, I was afraid ! But thank God I was mistaken."

" Thank God ! . . . But I thought——"

" I know now what you would not tell me," she said steadily. " I know why you came to Carston Magna on my wedding-day—to save me from the shame of a bigamous marriage."

" Ah ! I have been delirious."

" Yes ! But it was not from you I learned it. Grandpère Jacques revealed the truth innocently enough ; and I had confirmation of it."

Warborough did not ask the source of the confirmation. The ghost of a smile came in his sunken eyes, and he said in a whisper :

" Then now I am discharged from the court without a stain on my character."

" Even if you had killed Simon Maxwell——"

" I didn't," he said simply. " Though I meant to. It was another man that slew him."

" Who ? " she asked quickly. " You saw him ? "

"No! But I knew, and one day I shall make him own the truth when I catch him."

Cornelia had an inspiration.

"Ah!" she cried suddenly. "Now I know. It was Steinmann. He was there that night." She gave a little hard laugh. "But you will not have to catch him, for he is already caught."

"Caught! Steinmann? He is here? . . . A prisoner?"

"Safe as a bird in a cage, and Grandpère Jacques watches him more assiduously than a mother her firstborn. There is need for that, for he is in some peril from the men who helped to take him, and whose coming saved us."

"By Jove," he whispered. "That is great news. . . . I must see Jacques at once."

Cornelia frowned. "I don't think you ought to. Excitement cannot be good for you."

"But I must. It is important."

"Oh well—for a few minutes if you must. But you must listen and not talk, and after you have talked and eaten you must sleep again."

He laughed a little weakly. "Any order you like to give after! But first I must see Jacques."

Cornelia nodded and passed from the room, and presently another step sounded.

"*Bon jour, mon capitaine.* It makes a fine day to behold you well again."

The legionary stood at attention, but Warborough waved a hand.

"Sit down in the saddle there, Grandpère, where I can see you, and tell me all there is to tell. . . . The order is that I must not talk!"

"Madame!" ejaculated Jacques. "But she is a treasure among women. Day and night she has watched you with the solicitude of one who loves——"

"Jacques!"

" It is the truth, my captain. I have seen her—when she has not known I was watching—and her eyes were an open book. But as I was saying she has watched night and day, and the rest of the time she has helped to guard Steinmann, who lies trussed like a chicken for the oven. Even now she sits with the pistol—and if necessary would shoot as she shot once before to prevent his going."

" Tell me, Jacques! Everything."

Jacques told, graphically enough, and at the end pointed the moral. " But for madame, you comprehend ? *mon capitaine*, Steinmann must have broken clear, and in the rain and mist we should not have found him ; and again but for madame's devotion I should not have been telling the story, for you would not have been here to listen."

" And but for you, Jacques, none of us would have been——"

" Poof ! That is nothing ! All in the day's work, monsieur. With madame it was different. . . . But there are other things of import to be spoken of. There is that pig, Steinmann. Omar's friends desire to have him, to make an end of him, you comprehend ? He was in league with those bandits from across the hills who came to steal Omar's goats——" Jacques broke off and laughed. " A pleasant fiction that, my captain, which the goatherd devised, and it served, almost too well. I am worn to a shadow keeping Steinmann alive." He laughed again. " Those men so desire him——"

" They must not have him, Jacques."

" *Dieu !* Do I not know that ? I have made it clear to the beggars that the matter lies with you. . . . Nevertheless they will steal him if they can."

" Then I must see them——"

" Presently, monsieur. There is time yet," said Jacques hurriedly. " We shall have to make the rascal speak, and then——"

" It will be difficult——"

Grandpère Jacques laughed a little oddly.

" There are ways," he said enigmatically. " If we take this man to Fez, he will be set against a wall and shot —is not that so ? "

" Of course—though he might purchase his life by betraying all that he knows ! "

" True ! But there are things the man fears more than death by the swift bullet. Always, when those goatherds come he is deadly afraid. He grovels and prays that I will not let them take him. . . . If the threat were made, earnestly, he would I think unbosom himself —oh yes, to the last word and letter."

Jeff Warborough laughed suddenly.

" I want the unbosoming to happen. . . . But the other things—Jacques, decent men draw the line at that."

" At the reality, *oui* ! I would shoot the poor devil myself rather than let him face the tender mercies of those tribesmen. . . . But a threat, monsieur. That is nothing, yet it might serve."

" Yes ! If it were properly staged."

" Have no fear, my captain. It shall be staged to make Steinmann's soul shake, and shiver his tongue to speech. I will see to that. And now I go—or madame will wither me with a look."

He went, and deliberately began to prepare Steinmann for the ordeal before him.

" The captain is in two minds, friend Steinmann. I have talked with him. The way to Fez is long, and the chances of the mountain roads are many. If you were to break free, he would be blamed, you comprehend ? But if he carried back to the Maréchal the news that you were certainly dead——"

" *Gott !* You mean he will shoot me in cold blood."

Jacques shook his head. " He would not so soil his hands—with the blood of a pig. But there is another

way. Something he urges is due to those herders of
goats——"

" *Himmel !* Not that ! " cried Steinmann starkly. " I
would not deliver a dog to them."

" A dog, *mon ami*, is to be cherished, a creature that
keeps faith. But you, now, but you——"

He left it there, and moving away laughed silently
to himself.

" Oho ! the leaven will work," he whispered to himself.
" In the end there will be no secrets untold."

Following a deliberate purpose, he refrained from speech
with the prisoner as far as was possible, contented to let
the leaven of fear he had planted in the German's mind
do its work, but watching slyly the other's increasing
apprehension. Then a few days later, when Warborough
was on his feet again, divining the time was ripe, he
dropped another hint.

" Those goatherds come to-night, Steinmann, and the
captain talks with them. No doubt between them they
will settle your hash."

" *Der liebe Gott !* But he cannot mean to . . . to——"

" Who shall say. Monsieur is of those who keeps his
counsel and gives his order."

" But there are things that I could tell him——"
Jacques rejoiced to hear it, but laughed in contempt.
" Tell them to the women of these goatherds. Perhaps
they will hold their sharp little knives whilst they listen.
Who knows ? "

" He cannot mean to see me carved like a dead sheep,"
spluttered the wretched Steinmann.

Jacques stared thoughtfully at the hills.

" Like a dead sheep. Have no fear. These women do
not wait till one is dead. Surely that is known to you, my
friend ? I have seen a man or two on whom they have
wrought their infernal artistry whilst they lived and——"

He shrugged his shoulders, and Steinmann, who had
seen the same things, grovelled.

" For the dear Gott's sake, bring Captain Warborough to me."

" I will tell him of your desire," said Jacques carelessly, "but I much fear he will not come.   He is a hard one that, when the mood is on him, and it is possible he will remember what you would have done to him.   Yes!   It is possible."

Chuckling to himself, he took his way to Warborough.

" The leaven works, monsieur.   There is nothing the pig will not tell when the hour comes.   I must talk to Omar the herdsman.   There must be much noise made when those other goatherds come to-night—that nothing may be wanting."

And that night there was noise enough to satisfy even Grandpère Jacques' artistic soul—yells, mingled with menaces and demands of blood-curdling nature, all so loudly made that the German lying in the darkness could not choose but hear.   The din continued for some time, then to the miserable room came Jacques with a lantern.

" You hear," he said curtly.   " They have come for you, Steinmann.   You go to monsieur, and afterwards ——"

" Afterwards ?   What ? "

" Allah knows !   Those pious ones love not infidels who join with bandits to steal their goats."

" But——"

" March, my friend.   Would you have the hillmen fetch you ? "

He prodded the German forward, past the tribesmen who hailed him with ferocious yells, on to the room where Warborough and Cornelia awaited him.   As he saw the former seated on a saddle set on a bundle of goatskins, he flung himself on his knees, and cried out imploringly, promising all that was hoped and more.   Warborough listened, making no move until the man's bleatings became mere whimperings, and those in turn faded into silence, then he spoke.

" You ask a difficult thing. Those men outside are imperative in their demands, and I will not make a promise that I cannot hope to keep."

" But, Herr Warborough, you can try. They will be persuaded if rewards are promised. I have money in Fez——"

" You would ransom yourself——"

" From those devils—yes! A thousand times ! "

" But the money ? "

" It is with a Jew in the Ghetto there—Moses Corcos, who——"

" I know the man. A fool to his race, who pawns its very safety for gain."

" I could write an order—now," Steinmann babbled on, fearfully. " The money could be brought here——"

Warborough nodded. " That is possible," he owned. " A number of the villagers are to go with me as guard, being old soldiers of a Moroccan regiment. But I should have to go bond——"

" You would lose nothing—nothing ! " cried the German.

" I might persuade them," said Warborough doubtfully, " on those terms, but that would ransom you only from them, not from me."

" It would spare me a dog's death ! "

" But there might be a firing party for you at Fez."

" I am not afraid of a bullet—that is a clean death, but the other——" He broke off shudderingly. " The thought of it makes my soul crawl."

Warborough nodded, then said slowly : " It is possible that you might ransom your life from France also, if you paid the full price and told all you know about the underground activities in which you have been engaged. I do not promise. That lies with the Maréchal. He might think that Devil's Island would meet your case——"

The German, plucking hope, laughed hysterically.

" Devil's Island.   One escapes from there sometimes, but no man escapes from the grave.   It is a bargain !   I know you.   Your word will be kept.   I will tell all and you will use your influence with the Maréchal.   If I am not mistaken, you will know that I tell the truth—for already you know much."

" Very well.   It is a bargain.   I will save you at the worst for Devil's Island.   But there must be no reservations on your part."

" There shall be none, I swear."

" Very well, we will begin.   Jacques, my little book."

The book was brought, and Steinmann began his story of the underground intrigue—the issue which in the months immediately following the recital threatened the whole stability of the French Adminstration.   There were lists of names, the locality of secret rifle dumps, the names of agents supplying arms from Europe, of Europeans, mostly Germans, in El-Krim's service ;   of disaffected tribes, records of secret preparations, and of men, waverers, yet to be bought over—all the usual concomitants of a widespread secret conspiracy against an overlordship ;   and when the last question had been answered, Steinmann drew breath.

" That is about all."

" Not quite all," said Warborough crisply.

The German frowned in an effort of remembrance, then he shook his head.

" I can think of nothing more."

" But I can."   The soldier laughed a little hardly. " There is one thing more.   You will now tell Madame Cornelia about the Three Black Dots—and why you killed Alex Steffanson, whom she knew as Simon Maxwell."

" God ! " cried the German.   " You know ? "

" No !   But I guessed.   You were the man who threw the knife that struck him in the throat."

Steinmann's face went a sickly white, he mumbled

something that was not clear, and Warborough spoke harshly.

"Answer, man. You threw the knife?"

"But not at Steffanson," mumbled the German. "Only the fool would kill the goose that lays the golden eggs, and Steffanson was so golden a goose——"

A light of understanding flashed in Warborough's eyes, and he broke into sudden laughter.

"The knife was not for Steffanson. Then who was it for?"

Steinmann shuffled his feet uncomfortably, and Warborough laughed again.

"It was for me, hey? . . . I never guessed that. You surprise me, Steinmann, but I bear no grudge. Tell your story. Madame burns to hear it, and I myself am curious. Why did you seek out Steffanson that night with Caillé?"

"To make him pay," answered Steinmann with a sudden snarl. "He had been in the Legion with us, you know that as you know many other things. We were as brothers——"

"A trinity of evil! *Oui!*" broke in Grandpère Jacques.

"We worked together in all things, in an equal partnership. There was an affair at El-Sar at the edge of the Riff country during the war——"

"Ah! That business when the garrison of the little fort was sold to the Riffs, and paid for with German money."

"It was Steffanson who sold it—for a large sum. Germany paid well to foment trouble and keep French troops in Morocco."

"And the man whom the world knew so well as Simon Maxwell had the Judas money? Yes, I learned that afterwards."

"But he did not share. I was in hospital at Marseilles, and Caillé was at Verdun when the thing happened. We did not meet until the end of the war, when Steffanson

Q

was already discharged, and was on the point of sailing for America. He boasted of the sum he had received, but, *der teufel*, he would not share. And we could not move to make him."

"No! He sure had you with a leg up."

"Caillé would have killed him then and gone to the guillotine whistling, but I counselled waiting. Our time in the Legion was soon to expire, and then we should be free to follow and make him disgorge. . . . As it chanced we lost him—for years! The trouble in Spanish Morocco was growing, and there was room for us there, and after we left the Legion Caillé and I first served with the Spaniards, and then went over to El-Krim——"

"True mercenaries!" laughed Warborough. "The Moor pays well—and you were both men of culture whom he could use for something better than cannon-fodder. Go on."

"One day, five months ago, we were in Tangier together waiting for a consignment of—er—pianofortes——"

"Machine-guns! Yes, continue——"

"In a restaurant Caillé picked up an English paper, and staring him in the face was a picture of Steffanson—under a new name——"

"Simon Maxwell—yes."

"There was an article there. The Romance of a Millionaire. We read it with pleasure. It was mostly lies, but it did not lie about the man's wealth, and it told us that now he was domiciled in England. Further there was a statement that the romance was shortly to be rounded off by a marriage with a famous cinema actress ——"

"I contradicted that at the time," broke in Cornelia.

"We did not see the contradiction ; but we saw something very clearly, and that was that if Steffanson, or Maxwell as he chose to be known, did marry we had him in a pair of nut-crackers—for there was the fat café-proprietress at Sidi-bel-Abbès, whom he had married legally. If she still lived and had not been divorced, then Steffanson was a cow to be milked—one whose milk was cream."

" Blackmailed ! "

" The same thing, but we thought of it as getting our own, for the partnership which we had shared had been a tight one, and Steffanson had cheated us. We laid our plans accordingly. I took a risk and went to Sidi-bel-Abbès to make sure about the café-keeper. She cursed Steffanson root and branch, but she was still his wife, and anxious to learn his whereabouts that she might proceed for maintenance. That knowledge was sufficient for us. We had but to wait until Steffanson married madame here—and he must be wax in our hands. Caillé, who was less engaged than I was and was often in England, made careful inquiries, and to get information embarked upon an affair with a friend of madame's maid——"

" The woman Henriette ! "

" That was her name. Our luck was in. Madame's regular maid fell ill, and Henriette became her deputy. She knew from what she had overheard that the marriage was in immediate contemplation, and we arranged to be in London and wait for the news. Caillé lodged at a place in Greek Street."

" And you in a small private hotel over a shop in Southampton Row," broke in Warborough.

" The devil, you knew that ? " cried Steinmann in surprise.

" I was watching you. A certain Continental manufacturer, who sold machine-guns surreptitiously, was there also. He ventured to make his return via Paris—where he is making a longer stay than he expected whilst his business languishes."

" That is interesting," commented Steinmann. " You hold so many threads, Captain Warborough."

" Enough to make ropes for half a dozen necks," laughed Warborough. " Pray continue."

" One day, Henriette sent a telegram to Caillé at his lodging place in Greek Street announcing that the ceremony we waited for was due that day ; and an hour afterwards I learned the news——"

" I also," chuckled Warborough. " At the same time and from the same lips, only I did not know it was of Steffanson you spoke. I thought only of Maxwell."

Steinmann's face had a look of comic wonder. " You —you were there ? "

" I was the Russian gentleman, ' bearded like the pard,' who could not understand his account which you were kind enough to explain to him. Madame here also knows of that account——" He flashed a laughing glance at Cornelia. " She mistook it for a love-letter."

" For a——"

" Never mind. Continue ! Or these goatherds may grow impatient."

" To us that telegram was good news. It meant that Steffanson was lighting the fire before which we could roast him brown. We did not wish to save him from a crime——"

" Or madame here from a wrong."

" Our concern was with the man."

" And mine with the lady." He turned to Cornelia. " I went down to Croydon and chartered an airplane. I had no luck. We had engine trouble on the way—a slight thing but enough to delay, and I arrived too late——"

" But you came," said Cornelia softly.

" I could do no more at the moment. I had to keep an eye on this man and Caillé, and I returned to Town and oddly enough I did not know at that time that Simon Maxwell and Steffanson were one and the same, for they had used the name under which he was naturalized. When I got back to Town I found they had gone and would not return that night. But I knew their destination and I followed. It was a moonlight night when I arrived at Farholme—but Steinmann tells the tale. Proceed, man ! "

" We caught an early train, went down to Steffanson's home, and posted a card with a symbol that he would know making an appointment at the dove-tower, of which we had heard from Henriette. We were sure that he would come to us, but to give him confidence, we arranged that only Caillé should be visible, whilst I watched from the bushes. He came to time, and when I saw his face in the moonlight I knew the man was in a black temper. He greeted Caillé harshly and asked his business like a man impatient to be gone. Caillé did not use the velvet glove. He was heavy-handed always, and at the time he was very sure of his ground. He went straight to the point—and the point pricked Steffanson sorely. I knew that. In the moonlight, I saw his eyes. They were raging, and Caillé might have been warned. But he was not, and the other's voice was hoarse and shaking as he asked : ' How much ? '

" Caillé named the sum we had agreed, and Steffanson laughed like a madman.

" ' You think you will get away with this, Caillé, and that I shall play the part of milk-cow to a rogue ? For what do you take me ? By God——"

" The next I heard was the crack of a pistol. Caillé cried out as he fell, and lay on the turf dead as a stone. I knew that ; and when Steffanson looked round, I feared for my life, for a knife which was the only weapon I carried is a poor thing against a pistol. But Steffanson was not looking for me. He did not know that I was there in the bushes close at hand ; and he was but making sure that none had heard the shot——"

" I heard both the shot and Caillé's death scream," commented Warborough.

" You were there at the dove-tower ? " asked the German in amazement.

" No. Passing through the gates. Continue ! "

" Steffanson waited a very little time, then he picked up Caillé as he might have picked up a sack, threw him over his shoulder, and carried him to the dove-tower, passing inside. He was there but a very little time, and when he reappeared he stood in the doorway for a space, staring about him and listening, whilst I watched. Then he went off across the park.

" I was in no hurry to follow. I crouched there, thinking out things. Steffanson, having killed Caillé, was doubly in my hands. There was no price that I could not ask for my silence now, but I knew that I must be careful where I asked it. A letter would be safer, I thought ; but I must know everything ; and as Steffanson would not leave the dead Caillé in the dove-tower for one of his servants to find, it was in my mind that he would return in the dead of night to dispose of him ; and I must know how. I determined to watch for his reappearance, and after a little time, since that tower with the dead man in it made me shiver, I crept towards that great house, to keep my vigil there. I saw lights there, and crept across the lawn on my belly like a snake, till I reached some bushes, and then through the stillness of the night I caught a sound of men talking and after a little time a rasp of steel against steel. I knew the sound well, but it astonished me there, and lifting my head above the bushes I looked straight into a great room, where two men fought with swords, fought as men fight for dear life. One of them was Steffanson, and the other . . . the other . . . Herr Warborough——"

" Was I ? I am not ashamed of it. Get on."

" Recovering from my amazement, I crept nearer the window—one of those which are like a door, and which stood open to the night. The men within never saw me. They fought silently, and though on Steffanson's point there was a gleam of red in the light I knew that he had no chance ; that you, Captain, were the better swordsman. The other knew it also. The knowledge was written on his face, and there was the fear of death in his eyes. When I saw that a sudden fear came to me. One cannot squeeze a dead man for money; and if Steffanson were killed the fortune for which I hoped died with him. I must take a hand, save him from the man who would slay him. . . . But how? I remembered my knife. I could throw it like any juggler; and I marked the place where it should stick—below the right shoulder blade—a disabling stroke for a swordsman.

" I waited. The opportunity came presently. Your back was towards me, well in the light—an easy target. I lifted myself knife in hand and threw. But in that moment Steffanson made a fierce lunge and you leaped aside, Captain Warborough——"

" And saw the knife take him in the throat," said Warborough grimly.

" I knew then that I had lost my fortune, and I did not wait. There was death in the air, and to hang is an unpleasant way to die. I fled recklessly, anxious only to be gone from the place, and that is all I know, except that on the morrow when I met Henriette in Greek Street, I had a great scare from a man who offered me news of Caillé, and whom I knocked senseless in the street—the man who was with madame when she came to Fez, searching for the slayer of the man whom she married. I am that man; but it was, as I have explained, an accident; for one, as I said, would not kill the Golden Goose. I swear that, madame, by all things holy. You will have mercy? "

" There is nothing holy to you, Judas," said Grandpère Jacques, and spat in great contempt.

Cornelia did not speak to Steinmann. She gave him a single withering glance, then she turned to Warborough with a soft light shining in her eyes.

" Tell me what happened? " she said simply. " Why did you fight? "

## CHAPTER XX

### HAVEN

"BECAUSE Simon Maxwell was Alex Steffanson, the man who sold the little fort at El-Sar to the Riffs for a large sum. I did not know his identity, as I have explained, when I went down to Carston Magna. It was in my mind to save a lady, whose silent acting had greatly moved me, from bitter wrong ; and when I returned on the heels of this rascal and his fellow, after hearing the shot I made straight for the house. There were lights overhead, and a broad light in a room downstairs, where through the open window I saw a man pacing to and fro in some agitation, as it appeared. I hadn't a doubt that he was Simon Maxwell, and from the shot and scream I had an inkling that something tragical had happened. But I thought of you, and I went straight to the open window, meaning to tax him with the wickedness of his marriage and remind him of the *propriétaire* of the café at Sidi-bel-Abbès, of whom I had heard Caillé and this man speak without a thought of Steffanson.

"His back was towards me as I slipped into the room, but when in his pacing he turned and saw me there, he stopped like a man who had suffered a mortal blow. Then he recognized me, and relief came on his face.

"'Captain Warborough, is it not ? ' he asked gruffly.

"In the second when he turned I had been puzzled by his likeness to someone whom I had known. In the years of prosperity he had thickened, and his face had altered with rich living, and the removal from desert heats. But his question brought recognition, and I cried out :

"'Steffanson—by God ! '

"'Yes,' he said in a puzzled way. 'To what do I owe——'

" ' I've come to kill you, villain,' I said, and told him why. . . . You have heard how he sold the fort at El-Sar. There was one there who was my friend, little more than a boy, and that fort was his first command. When it was taken through treachery he was taken with it. . . . I will not tell you what was done to him—but they gave him to the women, who are fiendish with infidels. When we found him he was mad with the horror that had befallen him, and he died by God's mercy, the day after. But I swore then that if ever I found who had been the traitor I would kill him as one kills a snake. Long after, when I was on special service, I got the story from a Riff who took me for other than what I was, and I learned that Sergeant Steffanson was the man, but he had left the Legion then—with an honourable discharge if you please, and I could not get track of him. Imagine my emotion when I found him fronting me in that great room at Farholme, a prosperous man, but a villain still. . . . I forgot Steinmann and Caillé completely ; but I remembered Lieutenant Armand and my oath, and I remembered you—waiting for that Judas somewhere in that great house. I felt that I should kill him, but I resolved that it should not be murder, that it should be an act of justice. So I gave him a chance. He would have played foul, I know. I saw him moving towards a desk and guessed that he had a weapon there, but I drove him from it with my own pistol. Through an open door, I saw swords in the hall on an ornamental stand, and I proposed we should fight with them. He agreed, eagerly, for he was a swordsman——"

" One of the finest," broke in Steinmann. " That was known of him through the Legion."

" I stood over him whilst the swords were secured, and we began to fight. He touched me in the shoulder once, but I knew that I should kill him, as I should have done but for that knife——"

" I am glad it was not you," said Cornelia simply. " It

would have been a hard thing to explain to Inspector Gaddy."

"When Maxwell crashed to the floor, I looked round, but saw no one. Then I drew the knife free, and knew that Armand was avenged though not by my hand. Whose hand I guessed the following day when I read how Caillé had been found in the dove-tower. I knew that to linger there was madness, so throwing down the knife, and leaving the sword, I slipped from the room into the moonlight night, and fled across the park to the road where I had the accident of which I told you ——"

"The story of which I did not believe, though now I am ashamed of my disbelief. But for you——"

There was a clamour of voices without, and Steinmann's face became suddenly apprehensive.

"It is the goatherds, my captain. What ransom do we offer for a dog's life?"

Warborough named a sum. "You can pay that?" he asked Steinmann. "Very well, presently you shall write me an order on Moses Corcos the Jew at Fez. If it is not honoured, I shall know what to do. Also you will sign a statement of what occurred at Farholme that night, which will be witnessed by madame and Jacques—in order that the English police may have an explanation. You agree? . . . Right! Jacques, tell those herdsmen the redemption price will be paid, when they have seen us safe to Fez."

"Very well, my captain. If we let the dog buy his life, we must. But *Grâce à Dieu*, he will be well muzzled at the Isle du Diable in Guiana."

Jacques took his way, and presently returned to take Steinmann back to his quarters, and once in the court-yard, whispered a ferocious warning.

"You escaped the guillotine, it seems, my friend, but if you misbehave be assured there is a bullet here which has your name upon it. . . . You comprehend? Good!

Now we will bind the legs together, for it is hard to run with one leg. . . . So! You will now have leisure to reflect how hard is the way of transgressors, and since a man's sins when they come home are difficult to be borne, I would advise that you forget them all, lest you dream of Hell. *Bon soir*, Judas."

Grandpère Jacques left the prisoner to his meditations and turned towards the room where he had left his officer and Cornelia. But he did not enter, for through the stillness he caught the lady's voice quivering with emotion ; and having in his time listened at many doorways gathering information for official purposes and being without scruples in regard to eavesdropping, he halted in the darkness to listen at this one.

" How could I be so mistaken ? I am ashamed to think that I . . . that I——"

Captain Warborough's voice broke in gay with laughter.

" It was most natural to fall into that mistake—with that fool Standish to help you. I wonder where he is ? "

" Searching for me—somewhere."

" And for me ! " Warborough laughed again. " I have an odd fancy that he hoped to win your favour by presenting you with my head on a charger. Is it not so ? "

" Possibly ! I was crazy against you."

" And now, Cornelia ? "

" I owe my life and more," said the woman softly.

" We're quits there," Warborough answered cheerfully, " and from that point start level." Then the voice took a new note. " Do you know, Cornelia, when I saw you on the screen two years ago I thought you were the most beautiful woman in the world."

" On the screen ? " was the half-laughing interrogation. " Poof ! as Grandpère Jacques would say. That is nothing. Any woman can be made beautiful there. It is here, in the heart of the Atlas, in my dishevelment, that truth appears."

" And here in the Atlas as you are I know my thought was true.  Cornelia, I do not want to take advantage of the situation, but . . . but——"

" I do not see . . . why not . . ." said Cornelia softly.

Then Grandpère Jacques slid back into the darkness and stumbling over the goats in the courtyard, reached the entrance just as the owner emerged from the night.

" Omar the goatherd, you will stay here and talk with me awhile," he said cheerfully.

" But wherefore ? " asked the goatherd.  " The night is cold and dark ;  and within——"

" Within I might be tempted to strain ears to catch a lady's confession, which is not done, oh son of the Faithful !  So we will sit here on the wall and listen to the bleating of your goats, which in the night is very plaintive."

" Plaintive !  I do not know the word, my friend ;  but it is sure that the cry of many kids is profitable, but since it is your wish we will stay and talk of the trouble that is coming in the land, which, who can tell, will maybe turn a goatherd into a soldier once more."

And Jacques having twisted a cigarette they sat upon the wall and talked.

\*       \*       \*       \*       \*

Weeks later, in the afternoon of a burning day, a way-worn and much travel-stained cavalcade presented itself at the gates of the Residency at Fez.   The sentry looked once at the goatherd—Berbers, who accompanied four others, one of whom was a veiled woman, and another of whom wore a dejected air, and sat his mule, chin on his breast, whilst his eyes shot furtive glances to and fro.

" Halte ! " said the soldier, misliking the appearance of the party.  " Your business ? "

One of the party gave a name that surprised the sentry, who calling a comrade, sent him within to make inquiries, and with bayonet ready for action waited ready for hostile action. There were rumours of trouble everywhere and orders were very strict. Grandpère Jacques chaffed him in the argot of the Legion, and the man grinned cheerfully ; but did not alter the position of his challenging bayonet, until his messenger returned ; then the little cavalcade passed the gate, and whilst Jacques entertained the goat-herds in the courtyard, Warborough with Steinmann and Cornelia entered the building and presently passed into a spacious office. An official seated at a desk rose swiftly to greet them.

"Warborough, *mon ami* ! I feared you dead."

"Not yet, Monsieur Gerard," laughed Warborough. "And Jacques is without."

The official's eyes went to the veiled woman a little questioningly and Warborough made the introduction.

"May I present to you, Madame Cornelia——"

The official jumped at the sound of the name.

"*Le diable !*" he ejaculated impolitely.

"No ! my fiancée, Monsieur Gerard."

Cornelia laughed musically at the correction, and Monsieur Gerard explained.

"There is a mad American who every day asks for a lady of that name who disappeared from Fez many weeks ago. He wears our lives out with his entreaties and threats of what will happen if we do not find the lady— I have forbidden him the entrée."

"You can send him word that the lady is found, that she is well and shortly to be married," laughed Warborough. "He will then worry you no more."

The official himself laughed. "Almost at once the news shall be sent, but I doubt if he will find it so good as it seems." Then he turned to the third of the party. "And this gentleman ? You have not introduced ——"

"Steinmann."

"*Mon Dieu !* You got him ? "

"You have the evidence of your eyes, monsieur. It

will be well to put him under guard until we have discussed his future."

" Blithely ! " cried the official, and summoning a guard gave orders for the prisoner to be led away.    As he went Steinmann spoke but once.

" You made a promise——"

" Which I shall keep.    Have no fear."

" What did you promise that villain ? " asked Monsieur Gerard as the door closed behind the German.

" Life on Devil's Island.    Nothing more !    The promise was the price of much information that could not have been obtained elsewhere, and as it was made on the honour of a soldier it must be kept."

" The information is valuable ? "

" Very."

" But it will not prevent the war, *mon cher* Warborough. France acts with Spain at last, and El-Krim is to be hammered into submission.    If he is not, we lose all Morocco.    Your regiment is already moving to the front."

" Phew, phew ! "

Jeff Warborough whistled softly, then looked at Cornelia.    " Here's a complication, my dear.    I cannot run away from battle.    I should be branded for ever."

" I should not think to ask it of any man," said Cornelia with a woman's pride.

" No !    No !    I know that, my dear," answered Jeff Warborough with conviction, and then smiled well content.

*       *       *       *       *

It was fifteen months later when Cornelia received her friend Lady Langford, née Standish, at her house in Kensington.    There was an open telegram on the table, two time-tables and a sheaf of crumpled papers scrawled all over with figures.    Enid Langford saw them both, and then noting her friend's shining eyes jumped to a conclusion.

" At last ? "

" Yes.    Congratulate me, Enid !    He is coming home

—for good, having lost an arm. The telegram came yesterday, and—" she broke into gay laughter as she indicated the crumpled sheets—" I have spent hours calculating the hour of his return. But I have no head for figures——"

A horn hooted in the leafy square and with a swift premonition of the truth Enid Langford moved quickly to the window. A taxi was slowing down, the driver scrutinizing the numbers of the houses as he passed them. She could not see who was the passenger, but had no doubt whatever. The taxi pulled in and she spoke swiftly :

" Cornelia, there is a taxi—it is coming here. . . . I will go."

She departed without ceremony, fairly fleeing down the steps, and buried herself in her own car just as the taxi drew up behind.

" Where, my lady ? "

" Nowhere, yet. Wait ! "

From the window behind the car she peeped forth cautiously. Two men got out of the taxi, the first old and grizzled, who held the door for the second, a tall lean-faced man, with piercing dark eyes, with one empty sleeve pinned to his coat, and with a tiny scarlet ribbon in his button-hole.

" I knew it ! " she whispered, and laughed to herself. She watched Jeff Warborough quickly mount the steps, and disappear in the house.

Still she watched. The grizzled one twisted himself a cigarette, and inspected the street. Presently he began to whistle, and Lady Langford caught the air and hummed it to herself.

" *Tiens voila du boudin ! Voila du boudin ! Voila du boudin !*
*Pour les Alsaciens, les Suisses et les Lorrains*——"

She broke off, and leaving her car slipped behind the *siffleur.*

" *Bon jour!* Grandpère Jacques ! "

Grandpère Jacques turned swiftly. He had seen the lady but twice, once on the quay at Oran and once six months ago when she had visited Tetuan with Cornelia ; but having a memory for faces, he knew her instantly, and drew himself up stiffly in a salute.

" *Bon jour*, milady ! " Then a twinkle came in his puckered eyes, as he jerked his head towards the house. " We leave the desert for Paradise."

Lady Langford laughed, and Jacques suddenly grew serious.

" But it will not be all fruits of sweetness. No ! I, who am old, know. He will miss the Legion, the marching drums, the bugles that sound the reveille over burning ramparts—

> ' Rat tat tat ta, Rat tat tat ta,
> Rat tat tat ta ta ta ta——'

" I hear them now, and that one will hear them sounding through his dreams, surely."

" But not so loudly as to break the dream, I hope, Grandpère," said Enid Langford with a smile.

Then Grandpère Jacques shrugged his shoulders and laughed. " Why no, milady, even a soldier must find haven at last in a woman's arms."